Don't Look Back

I0744058

John Gribbin fiction

The Sixth Winter
(with Douglas Orgill)

Brother Esau
(with Douglas Orgill)

Double Planet
(with Marcus Chown)

Father to the Man

Ragnarok
(with D.G. Compton)

Reunion
(with Marcus Chown)

Innervisions

Timeswitch

The Alice Encounter

From Elsewhen Press

Existence is Elsewhen
John Gribbin et al

Don't Look Back

John Gribbin

Science Fact – Science Fiction

Elsewhen Press

Don't Look Back
First published in Great Britain by Elsewhen Press, 2017
An imprint of Alnpete Limited

This collection Copyright © John Gribbin, 2017. All rights reserved
The right of John Gribbin to be identified as the author of this work has been asserted in accordance with sections 77 and 78 of the Copyright, Designs and Patents Act 1988. No part of this publication may be reproduced, stored in a retrieval system or transmitted in any form, or by any means (electronic, mechanical, telepathic, or otherwise) without the prior written permission of the copyright owner.

Extract from *The Hitchhiker's Guide to the Galaxy* by Douglas Adams © 1979. Reprinted by kind permission of the Estate of Douglas Adams for electronic editions; reproduced with permission of Pan Macmillan via PLSclear for print editions worldwide except the USA.

In the USA: Excerpt(s) from *The Hitchhiker's Guide to the Galaxy* by Douglas Adams, copyright © 1979 by Serious Productions, Ltd . Used by permission of Del Rey Books, an imprint of Random House, a division of Penguin Random House LLC. All rights reserved. Any third party use of this material, outside of this publication, is prohibited. Interested parties must apply directly to Penguin Random House LLC for permission.

Elsewhen Press, PO Box 757, Dartford, Kent DA2 7TQ
www.elsewhen.press

British Library Cataloguing in Publication Data.
A catalogue record for this book is available from the British Library.
ISBN 978-1-911409-08-3 Print edition
ISBN 978-1-911409-18-2 eBook edition

Condition of Sale
This book is sold subject to the condition that it shall not, by way of trade or otherwise, be lent, re-sold, hired out or otherwise circulated in any form of binding or cover other than that in which it is published and without a similar condition including this condition being imposed on the subsequent purchaser.

This book is copyright under the Berne Convention.
Elsewhen Press & Planet-Clock Design are trademarks of Alnpete Limited

Designed and formatted by Elsewhen Press

This book is a work of fiction. All names, characters, places, planets, scientific research organisations, alien cultures and artificial intelligences are either a product of the author's fertile imagination or are used fictitiously. Any resemblance to actual robots, sentient beings, think tanks, heavenly bodies, sites or people (living, dead, or disembodied) is purely coincidental. If any of the dates, places or organisations mentioned do not match your experience of history, remember that most of the stories are set in alternative versions of the quantum multiverse.

Back to the Future is a trademark of Universal/U-Drive; BBC is a trademark of The British Broadcasting Corporation; Capri is a trademark of Ford Motor Company Limited; Disney is a trademark of Disney Enterprises, Inc.; GCHQ is a trademark of The Secretary of State for Foreign and Commonwealth Affairs; Guardian is a trademark of Guardian Media Group; Nature is a trademark of HM Publishers Holdings Limited; New Scientist is a trademark of Reed Business Information Limited; Sony is a trademark of Sony Corporation. Use of trademarks has not been authorised, sponsored, or otherwise approved by the trademark owners.

Perpendicular Worlds © 1984 John Gribbin, first published in *Analog* 14 Aug 1984; Double Planet © 1984 John Gribbin, first published in *Analog* 9 Oct 1984; The Doomsday Device © 1985 John Gribbin, first published in *Analog* 29 Jan 1985; Programmed for destruction © 1985 John Gribbin, first published in *Analog* 26 Feb 1985; Random Variable © 1986 John Gribbin, first published in *Analog* 28 Jan 1986; The Royal Visit © 1986 John Gribbin, first published in *Analog* 22 Apr 1986; The Sins of the Fathers © 1986 John Gribbin, first published in *Analog* Dec. 1986; Sense of Direction © 1988 John Gribbin, first published in *Analog* 11 Nov 1988; The Best is Yet to Be © 1989 John Gribbin, first published in *Analog* 7 Feb 1989; Other Edens © 1989 John Gribbin, first published in *Interzone* Sep-Oct 1989; The Carbon Papers © 1990 John Gribbin, first published in *Analog* 9 Jan 1990; Insight © 1990 John Gribbin, first published in *Zenith* (ed. David Garnett) Sphere 1990; Don't Look Back © 1990 John Gribbin, first published in *Interzone* Oct. 1990; Defense Initiative © 1990 John Gribbin, first published in *New Destinies Vol IX*, BAEN 1990; Hackers © 1990 John Gribbin and Ben Gribbin, first published in *Reconnaissance Con* newsletter 1990; The Words of If © 2017 John Gribbin and Ben Gribbin; Mother Love © 1991 John Gribbin, first published in *Dream* Apr. 1991; Something to Beef About © 1991, 2016 John Gribbin, first published in *Interzone* Jul. 1991, this revised version previously published in *Existence is Elsewhen*, Elsewhen Press March 2016; Nature Trail © 1994 John Gribbin and Ben Gribbin, first published in *Science Reporter* 1994; The Alice Encounter © 1994 John Gribbin, first published in *Interzone* Jun. 1994; Artifact © 2013 John Gribbin, first published in *Tales from the Perseus Arm* 2013; Easy as Pi © 2014 John Gribbin, first published in *Tales from the Perseus Arm, Vol 2* 2014; Untanglement © 2016 John Gribbin, first published in *Postscripts* 36/37 (ed Nick Gevers) PS Publishing 2016; A Do-It-Yourself Time Machine © 1994 John Gribbin, first published in *L'Astronomia* April 1994; Is the Moon a Babel Fish? © 2012 John Gribbin, first published in *Analog* 2012.

Contents

Science Fiction

Introduction

Science fiction is responsible for me becoming first a scientist and then a science writer. In the 1950s, from the age of about 10, I became an avid reader of the magazine *Astounding*, then edited by the great John W. Campbell. This was possible because a family friend had a subscription to the magazine – extremely rare in England in those days – and passed on his copies to me in batches every few months. This could be frustrating when the batch included the beginning, but not the end, of a serial, but that was a small price to pay for the pleasure of reading them. Campbell, of course, encouraged 'hard' Sf, based on real science; in addition, each copy of *Astounding* included a science fact article, usually dealing with topics at the cutting edge (sometimes the lunatic fringe) of science. All of this was grist to my mill, and led me to the non-fiction writing of Isaac Asimov, Arthur Clarke, and George Gamow. From there, it was a relatively small step to degrees in physics and astronomy and a sideways shuffle into the kind of science writing I had learned from those masters.

Sf itself evolved into something rather different from the stuff of my childhood, and by the 1980s I hankered after some good old fashioned hard stuff, with real science as the driving force of the story. It was my wife who suggested (this is the polite way of putting it) that as I was supposed to be a writer I ought to stop complaining about the lack of such stories and write some myself. By then, *Astounding* had metamorphosed into *Analog*, and Campbell was no longer around. But it was the obvious place to offer my efforts, and to my delight Stanley Schmidt, Campbell's successor, accepted a whole string of them. Some of these stories grew into books, and I also branched out into other publications, but I never developed beyond writing in the style that I like to think Campbell would have approved of. Today, of course, that style might be termed Retro and therefore be respectable once again.

The stories here are presented in essentially chronological order of publication, and include a couple that I published under a pseudonym (Lyn Murray) at a time when I briefly thought that I ought to have separate personas for fiction and non-fiction. Stupidly, this includes my favourite, *The Best is Yet to Be*, which appeared some time before Audrey Niffenegger's longer take on the same theme. I have also included a couple of non-fiction articles of the kind I used to read in *Astounding* (indeed, one of them was published in *Analog*), making the collection something of an homage to my youthful reading. Apart from encouraging me to start writing fiction, my wife, a Sherlock Holmes aficionado, is directly responsible for one of these contributions, having challenged me to get a story involving her hero accepted by *Analog*. My son Ben was a sounding board for several ideas, and earned co-author credit on a few, including a youthful tribute (?) to his own hero, Terry Pratchett. The last story here may need some explanation. Fred Pohl, a friend of mine, used me as a minor character (or several) in his novel *The Coming of the Quantum Cats*; after he died I wrote this as a kind of tribute, using the idea of 'the leaving of the quantum cats'. So I appear as an offstage character in my own story!

But the ultimate responsibility for the words that follow must lie with John Campbell, Arthur Clarke, Isaac Asimov, George Gamow, and especially my science fiction 'godfather', Harry Stead.

John Gribbin
March 2017

Some more of John Gribbin's non-fiction and fiction can be found at johngribbinscience.wordpress.com

Perpendicular Worlds

It made a great conjuring trick, but Mackenzie doubted that the company accountants would see the joke. Five years' work, a budget bigger than the GNP of a medium-sized country, and all he had to show for it was a box which made crumbs disappear. Put anything up to a gram inside, flick a switch (which allowed merely enough energy to keep about half of North America running for a week to pulse through the net), and sure enough it vanished. Perhaps it wouldn't be quite so bad if the trick hadn't been performed on highly expensive, micro-miniaturised electronic probes, designed to observe their surroundings, store the information, and report back on command. He sighed. It had all seemed so straightforward. Not easy – never easy – but linear. From A to B to C to ... where? Everything seemed to work: but the damn things never came back. The budget was exhausted; his patience was exhausted; and they had nothing to show for it.

He'd have to tell Diane. As head of 'special projects', Ms. Diane Brookman was not only his boss but – he had come to suspect – the real boss of the whole company. She wouldn't like it, but it was time to cut their losses. Five years, since he had sat in her office selling the idea as hard as he could.

"The mechanics of time travel are simple enough." Mackenzie leaned forward, emphasising the ease of the project he had in mind by thumping his right fist into his left palm. "Frank Tipler worked it all out years ago."

"But hold on." Diane leaned back in her chair, soothing Mackenzie's enthusiasm with a dismissive wave. "I've seen some of the popularizations. Tipler's stuff is all very well in theory. I'm sure the math is OK. But he says you need a star as big as the Sun, compressed into the size of the Earth, and spinning at the speed of light. Not very practical."

"Half the speed of light. But you're near enough right. Anyway, all that stuff's old hat." Mackenzie turned, swivelling his chair to look out through the picture window across the green, manicured parkland of the institute. Somehow, he had to convince this woman that his idea was viable, and somehow he was going about it all wrong.

"Let's start again. The important thing about Tipler's calculations is that he proved time travel is allowed within the framework of Einstein's theory. That's still the best theory of the Universe we've got, so you have to believe those equations. Now, to make the trick work you need a naked singularity, which is like a black hole with its event horizon stripped off. The spinning neutron star is just one way to make the naked singularity; there are other ways, and the Hawking process works on a much smaller scale." Too small a scale, he thought, but I'm not telling her that yet. At least I can get a mini black hole into the lab: a neutron star might just be a bit too big to get in the door.

Diane smiled. "Black holes are expensive. And you'd have to work with it in orbit – they're forbidden on the surface."

"That's why I'm here. You – this place –" waving his hand vaguely to the view from the window, "have the money and the satellites. Communications and power beams. Nobody on Earth can do without you. And if you tell me you haven't got a team up there trying to find a way to use a mini to increase your profits, well, I don't believe it."

Well, he'd convinced her. Sold her the idea that with a Hawking black hole to play with it was theoretically possible to build a working time machine; convinced her that even a tiny working time machine limited to transporting information had to have commercial potential. Only information about the past, certainly. Travel into the future was impossible; everyone accepted that. You couldn't visit the future because there is no future until you create it by moving forward through spacetime at the old-fashioned rate of one day every twenty-four hours.

He was tired, his thoughts wandering from the immediate problem of explaining to Diane that what she now regarded as her pet project had blown up in his, and her, face. Some people believed in a myriad of *possible* future worlds, that starting out from here and now every possible outcome or every choice of options open to every particle in the Universe really did happen, and that the Universe was constantly splitting as a result into an unimaginably large number of copies of itself, each slightly different from its neighbours and increasingly different from more distant copies separated by some numberless array of dimensions beyond the comfortable four of Einstein's Universe.

So I'm just unlucky, mused Mackenzie. Here I am with a failed time machine, but the equations clearly say that time travel is possible. Anything that is possible must happen somewhere in one of these parallel worlds, and somewhere there must be a replica of me at this very moment celebrating the return of a time probe from the past. Not just one replica – thousands of successful Mackenzies, celebrating their success; and thousands of unsuccessful Mackenzies contemplating the end of a dream.

If only he could communicate *sideways* across time, he could learn the secret of *linear* time travel in his own branch of reality. An idle dream? It couldn't be any worse than the reality that faced him now; maybe he could keep the project going after all. Suddenly refreshed, Mackenzie got to his feet and moved toward the computer console. Parallel worlds had been a feature of science fiction since the 1930s, of course, but what was the name of that guy who had made them scientifically respectable? Everett; that's it.

The library ought to include his classic papers, that computer was supposed to store everything published on 'time' …

The room was the same; the view autumnal instead of spring; but Diane unchanging. She must be a rejuvenator, thought Mackenzie, leaning forward and bringing his hands together in a bridge as he gathered his thoughts to make his final explanation clear. Well, the company could afford it.

"Are you telling me that Everett was right – that you can prove the existence of these parallel worlds? And do you expect us to pour more resources into another hare-brained time travel scheme?" Ms. Brookman was clearly not amused.

"Not exactly. Everett certainly established the possibility of *alternative* realities, but the problem is, they're not what you'd call parallel to our reality." He shifted uncomfortably. There was no easy way to soften the blow. "You see, the equations tell us that every time reality divides into two alternatives, the alternative worlds branch at *right angles* to one another. All the possible realities exist, and they are all at right angles to every other reality. It makes for a lot of dimensions." Mackenzie hurried on, determined not to be interrupted, "but that's no problem mathematically. The problem from my point of view is that it means there is only one way to get from our branch of reality into another branch. You can't slip sideways through time, or send a message to the reality 'next door'. What you'd have to do is send a time machine back into the past to a key branching point, where a crucial decision was made, and then forward up an alternative branch of reality to gather information. Then it could travel back to the branching point, forward up our own branch of reality and we'd have the information we need."

"You make it sound so simple, Dr. Mackenzie. Just tell me if I've got it right. You say that, according to Everett's calculations, there must be a world – a perpendicular world? – where you, or your counterpart, has solved the puzzle of time travel. And in order to ask him how he did it, all you need is a time machine. Am I right?"

"Yes." He paused. "But it's worse than that. I think I know what happened to my probes.

"The limitation to Everett's theory, you see, is that he was interested only in the future. He imagined the almost infinite branching of reality into a multitude of perpendicular worlds, and he showed mathematically that this is the best possible description of the Universe. It even fits in with relativity. But what he didn't appreciate was that it works both ways. There must be as many different ways in which the world could have got into the state it is now as there are different ways in which it can develop into the future. There is no unique future, and nor is there any unique past."

"So your probes got lost?"

There was no escape; the time had come. Mackenzie rose and walked over to the window, gazing at the panorama of life displayed outside. An almost infinite variety of past worlds, with 'now' at the nexus leading to an almost infinite variety of future worlds. He would never feel the same about all the living things on Earth. He turned.

"Not really. I can tell you exactly where they went, as far as linear time is concerned, and I can tell you more or less what happened to them in the Everett maze of alternative past realities. But I can't put them together again.

"You see, the time field I generated was unfocussed. We didn't try to direct the probes down any special past time line, because we didn't realise there could be more than one past. Now we know that, it ought even to be possible to make the things work properly."

"Then you haven't failed?"

"Oh no. We succeeded beyond anyone's wildest dreams. But because the field was unfocussed when we pushed our probes back into the past, they were split up among a vast number of alternative pasts, like pushing a tomato through a fine-meshed sieve. All the King's horses and all the King's men couldn't put the bits together again."

"So what's the problem?"

"No problem, really. But I've been checking out some numbers. Just back-of-the-envelope stuff. There's a limit to the subdivision of reality, to do with quantum effects; and from the limits on our field strength and the size of the probe I can get a rough idea how much was squirted back into each of the branches of the past we reached. Not a lot; a few largish molecules through each hole in the time sieve. The interesting thing is the inverse correlation between mass, and distance travelled into the past. It's a bit like squirting water through a hose; the finer the jet, the further it squirts. We planned to send a gram mass back a few hundred thousand years, to be sure no intelligent human would stumble across it. The mass effect is non-linear but very roughly it works out that we sent each chunk of the probe back nearly four thousand million years."

"And how big did you say each piece was?"

"That's where things get interesting." Mackenzie turned again to the window. "Isn't it incredible that every living thing on Earth uses the same basic code of life – coded by the same molecule, DNA? You know that there are single-celled life forms, bacteria, all around us, on our skin, in the air we breathe, practically unchanged since the dawn of life on Earth. And yet we are the descendants of those very same bacteria, modified by the pressures of evolution."

He sat down. "The thing is, you see, we weren't worried about contamination. I mean, it wasn't as if we were sending the probes to Mars or anything. There was just no *point* in sterilising them. They were handled by everyone on the team. We didn't even bother to evacuate the air out of the chamber." Mackenzie looked at Diane, seeing the dawning realisation in her eyes.

"What we've done," he said, emphasising the point by thumping his right fist into his left palm, "is to seed all of our neighbouring realities, and this one, with primitive bacteria. The biologists will tell you that even one self-replicating organism dropped into the primeval soup of the oceans four billion years ago could have taken over the world and led to the proliferation of life as we know it. But they'll also tell you it's a complete mystery how that first living thing emerged so soon after the Earth formed. Our experiment – our failure – is the reason we are here at all." He turned back to Diane. "How does it feel to be God?"

Double Planet

From Mars orbit the Earth-Moon system makes one of the most striking features of the Solar System – a double star with one component brighter than Venus seen from beneath the haze of Earth's atmosphere. But Frances Reese, riding herd on a comet, had no time to admire the beauty of the view.

The comet was a big one. A first-time visitor to the inner part of the Solar System, easing in on an orbit stretching back, past Jupiter and Saturn to the outer fringe of interstellar space. Even now, nobody knew for sure where such an object originated. Was it a fragment of interstellar rubble picked up by the Sun's gravity as it orbited around the Galaxy? Or maybe leftover debris from the formation of the Solar System itself, part of a cloud of forgotten fragments barely retained in the grip of the Sun's gravity, orbiting far out beyond Pluto for billions of years until some chance perturbation nudged it on its way past the planets. Nobody really cared about the origin of the comet. What mattered was the burden it carried, a million trillion tons of ice and snow, plunging on a course that would take it, thanks to the deflection caused by Jupiter's gravitational slingshot as it went past, within an astronomical hairsbreadth of that beautiful double planet.

A hundred years before, there would have been no prospect of human interference with the trajectory of such a monster. It was only in the 1980s, after all, that the first primitive probes had been able to rendezvous with a comet, on Halley's return in 1986. Reese's job still wasn't easy. With limited resources and a team hastily pulled together from other projects, she was expected to weld the great ice blocks – water ice, frozen carbon dioxide, ammonia and the rest – into some sort of coherent whole, dismantle the nuclear engines from most of the ships, and mount them to provide thrust on the cometary nucleus, using the virtually limitless supply of material from the ice itself as reaction mass. The resulting effect would be feeble compared with the gravitational forces that had set the comet on its way, but enough, by the time it crossed the orbit of the Earth, to nudge it a few hundred thousand kilometres from its present path. And since the computer projections drew that present trajectory right between the Earth and the Moon, with an uncertainty rather larger than the distance of the Earth from the Moon, a few hundred thousand kilometres could be crucial at that time.

Even so, it hadn't been easy persuading the politicians to make the attempt.

"A comet, Doctor Kondratieff, is hardly something to strike terror into our hearts in the 21st century, you know." The Secretary to the Council had smiled tiredly at his science adviser, preparing to dismiss another impossible claim upon the world's limited resources. Why couldn't these people understand that they couldn't return to the twentieth century, and that what effort could be spared for work in space had to be geared to practical ends? After the fiasco of the O'Neill colony, anyone could see that space was a waste of effort, even though the technology to reach Jupiter certainly existed.

"But, sir, allow me to explain." Kondratieff felt the sweat on his palms and tried to keep calm. It had been hard enough to get this audience, and on what he said now rested the only chance of deflecting the newly discovered comet from its path.

"You must appreciate, sir, the difficulty of predicting the precise fate of this object. The Earth and the Moon follow a complex path around the Sun, as you can see from this diagram. Most people think the Moon circles around the Earth. but it doesn't. The Earth and the Moon are more evenly paired in size than any other two planetary objects; the Moon is as big as Mercury, it's really a planet in its own right. Because of this, it's attracted by the Sun's gravity even more strongly than it's attracted by the Earth. To the astronomers, Earth and Moon are individual planets that each follow their own orbit around the Sun, each perturbed by the other. So both the Earth and the Moon follow wobbly orbits. All we can say about the comet's orbit is that, left alone, it will intersect this double orbit just when the two planets are there. It may pass harmlessly by. But it could very well strike the Earth."

The presentation was faultless. Kondratieff was sure. The facts spoke for themselves, and the computer animation of the comet's orbit piercing the interwoven strands of the orbits of Earth and Moon around the Sun was the icing on the cake. The probability of disaster might seem small, but as the report spelled out the effects would be immense. A small risk of an immense disaster; the only sane course of action had to be to reduce that small risk precisely to zero, whatever it cost.

"If this comet strikes the Earth it could be the greatest disaster since the death of the dinosaurs, worse than the nuclear holocaust we so recently narrowly avoided. We know the Earth has been bombarded from space over the eons, and we are pretty sure now that these bombardments explain why there are sometimes massive extinctions of life in the geological record. Sixty-five million years ago, it wasn't just the dinosaurs that died but hundreds of other species. And the best explanation is that the Earth was struck by a giant meteorite which wreaked havoc on the environment."

"I know all this." The Secretary leaned back and waved a hand in dismissal. "I may not be a scientific expert, but I do read the popularisations. That disaster was caused by a huge lump of rock, not a snowball. And it may have been a disaster for the dinosaurs, but not so bad for us, eh, since it opened the way for the mammals."

Kondratieff, not for the first time, cursed inwardly the Secretary's habit of reading popularisations of science for light relief, and doubly cursed the writers who offered glib popularisations to a gullible readership.

"Of course, sir, I'm not suggesting a disaster on that scale. But this dirty snowball still has a mass of 10^{18} tons – that's a million, trillion tons of ice and snow. It's the biggest thing to come into the inner Solar System since civilisation began." He had a flash of inspiration. "And remember what happened in 1908; The Tunguska Explosion. Trees were knocked down all over Siberia. That was caused by a fragment of comet exploding in the atmosphere. If it had arrived a few minutes later, the rotation of the Earth would have placed Leningrad directly under the explosion. That's what even a small fragment of a comet can do, and we are dealing here with one of the biggest."

Perhaps the popularisers deserve some credit after all. The Secretary certainly had heard of the Tunguska event, and his family came from Leningrad. By such silver-tongued persuasion did Science Adviser Kondratieff set the wheels in motion for the Reese expedition. If anyone except Kondratieff and Reese had known what the real purpose of the expedition was, however, it would, literally, never have gotten off the ground. After all, if you can nudge a comet *this* way as it moves through space, it is just as easy to nudge it *that* way, *toward* a collision instead of away from one.

From inside the hull of the *Sir Fred Hoyle* there would have been no way to admire the view of the Solar System's unique double planet, rapidly gaining in brightness ahead, even if anyone had had the time. With its engines removed, the command ship of the New Aeronautical and Space Administration's expedition just provided room for all the members of the expedition to gather and talk directly, face to face, without using radio. The seals that kept the compartment airtight were only patches, welded on after the engines had been removed, and everybody wore full suits and kept helmets at hand. The air they were breathing came from the comet itself, oxygen electrolytically cracked from water. Chemically, the atmosphere was pure; emotionally it was highly charged by speculation about the reason for this unexpected gathering, called at short notice by Commander Reese.

"I've called you here to let you in on a secret." The buzz of talk stilled at the Commander's quiet words. "You know how much this expedition has cost NASA. Four ships out of the seven we came on won't be returning to Earth orbit, and three ships hardly constitutes a spacegoing fleet. We may be saving the Earth by this gesture – Bill, I know you think there's no risk to Earth, but hear me out – even if there is a risk, and we are saving the Earth, the losses might sound a death knell for manned spaceflight.

"It's all very well arguing that by proving the value of a spacegoing ability we're opening the door for increased budgets. You know as well as I do how the political mind works, and unless there are tangible risks or real benefits immediately visible, the political mind isn't going to do anything about space exploration."

"But that's what I said all along!" Bill Noyes could no longer contain his angry astonishment. "*You're* the one who persuaded us to join this crazy scheme, with your talk about how we'd be such great popular heroes the Council would have to let us have a crack at rebuilding Lagrange One."

"And I told the truth, up to a point. Sure, they'll let us have a go, with our pathetic three ships. But they won't give us the resources for more, and we can't do the job properly without. *But it doesn't matter*. We're going to give the Earth something better than Lagrange One, something to fire the imagination of all the people disillusioned with space, and make the Council sit up und take notice."

"You're not going to drop this iceberg on top of the bloody Council, then? That's the best thing you could do for the space program."

"No. We're going to drop it on the Moon."

Reese looked around the group. Floating freely, she had hooked one foot comfortably under a convenient pipe. Relaxed, her face spread into a smile as she watched the others wrestling with what she had said.

"The Moon!"

"What on Earth for?"

"She's crazy."

The noise of argument started to rise about her again.

"Do you really want to know why?" she asked quietly. Slowly the noise died down as they all turned toward her, wondering.

"Can't you make a couple of intelligent guesses between you? Take a deep breath and think hard." She resumed her impersonation of the Cheshire Cat.

Kristofferson saw it first. "It's the oxygen! You want to put an atmosphere on the Moon! But will it work?"

"Of course not." Noyes was checking through a calculation on his computer. "To keep an atmosphere a planet has to have an escape velocity at least six times the mean velocity of the molecules in the atmosphere. For oxygen, at about zero

Celsius, the Moon couldn't keep an atmosphere for more than a few hundred years. Molecular weight's too low – only 32. Right boss?"

"Up to a point, Bill. The one-sixth rule works for keeping an atmosphere for a *very* long time – billions of years. But as long as the atmospheric molecules have a mean velocity less than about one-fifth of the escape velocity it takes hundreds of millions of years for more than half the molecules to leak away. Jeans worked it all out, back in the 1920s. Still no good for oxygen, but even at about 100 Celsius the Moon could keep a respectable atmosphere of carbon dioxide for as long as any of us are likely to be interested. The extra mass means the molecules move just that much slower at the same temperature. The trick is to get the CO_2 there in the first place, which is where we come in."

"So who wants a CO_2 atmosphere?"

"Come on, Dave, you know better than that. The Earth started out with a CO_2 atmosphere, and the odds are it got it from a comet, or several comets. Why do you think I chose this ship to lead the expedition? I knew the Council weren't bright enough to make the connection, but after all Hoyle was the guy who made that theory respectable. All the Earth's atmosphere, all the water – all the volatiles came in from space after the planet formed. The first volatiles had to come in at least one hard landing, but once *any* atmosphere formed it would act as a brake and slow down any other cometary chunks coming in from the outer Solar System. We're going to provide the Moon's hard landing. Once we've done that, we can lob any old bits of ice and snow in from the asteroid belt, and they'll stick. We can add material faster than it evaporates, and if we want oxygen to breathe we can keep it in domes or underground. We're riding 10^{18} tons of carbon dioxide and water. It won't exactly make a thick atmosphere, but it's a start. Add that to soil and you've got a pretty good basis for growing plants."

"And you've got a perfect meteorite shield."

"The temperature will stabilise out."

"We're not talking about repairing a tin can in orbit; we're offering the world a second whole planet. They'll have to go for it."

"Will it really work?"

"Well, we're going to find out. The problem is, we've got to make the orbit of this iceberg nearly circular, drop it in so that it just creeps up behind the Moon in its orbit round the Sun. Jupiter's done half the job for us, we have to do the rest. You've heard the good news, but there's more. It's going to be a lot harder than just deflecting the thing out of the Earth's path."

The passage of the comet within half a million kilometres of the Earth turned the attention of six billion people upward and outward, away from their immediate problems. The return of the sole surviving ship of the expedition, with the five survivors from the 18 men and women under the command of the late Commander Reese was the biggest media event of the 21st century. And when the First Secretary proposed to the Council that the only fitting tribute to the lives that had been sacrificed to save humankind would be to take up afresh the challenge of the new frontier, build a fleet to take advantage of the opportunity so strangely provided, and make the Earth and Moon forever a true double planet, no voice was raised in opposition.

"It's best this way, Kondratieff, but don't think I am fooled." The Secretary turned from his balcony where the Moon, nearly full, was visible just rising above the horizon. "So we discovered that the thrust from four engines could not deflect the comet sufficiently, but six could do the job. Well enough to save the Earth, anyway, but not well enough, even with all that onboard control, to avoid the Moon. Thirteen martyrs, because those six engines had to be controlled until the last minute. I can understand that such a thing is necessary to hit accurately a moving target; not so necessary if all you want to do is miss the target. The military mind, you will appreciate, knows all about shooting at targets.

"So. You have given us the Moon, whether we like it or not. Within five years we'll have bases; in fifty we will be adding to the atmosphere so – fortuitously? – provided in that epic catastrophe. You expect me to be mad, to accuse you? To dismiss you even? Not at all. I'm not saying you weren't wise to keep me in the dark beforehand; the risk was too great. But now, there are opportunities."

"Opportunities? But, sir, you always dismissed the notion of opportunity for mankind in space."

"I dismissed the projects I was offered, Kondratieff, and with good reason. Tin cans in orbit, as far away as the Moon. What opportunity is there in a tin can? How many could Lagrange One have taken, even if it hadn't been for the accident? A few thousand, an elite, something for the masses to resent. The O'Neill colony was never more than an elitist concept, taking resources from the masses and building a plaything for the few. A whole world is different. You talk of the new frontier, and you speak better truth than you know. One sixteenth of the area of the Earth – one-fifth of the land area of our planet – is waiting there now for us to tame. It will take far longer than it took to tame the so-called new world here on Earth. But that's all to the good. The longer it takes the better, because when it's done we'll only have to find another new frontier, to save ourselves from stagnation. Yes indeed, Kondratieff, you have done well."

And, thought the Secretary, if the military mind understands how to hit a moving target, so the political mind understands how to seize an opportunity when it arises.

He turned back to the balcony. Kondratieff now at his side. The Moon was clear above the horizon in the still night. Unobscured by cloud, yet faintly indistinct, seen as it had never appeared before during human history; not quite fuzzy, yet not quite sharply outlined; a sister planet in the making.

The Doomsday Device

I know why the Desertron doesn't work." James Reed smiled and waited for the news to penetrate.

The gray head on the other side of the desk looked up from a pile of papers. Professor David Vernon, double Nobel Laureate and head of the giant accelerator project, paused with his pen raised, arrested in the act of signing yet another letter. "Don't keep it from me, Jim. If you're serious, for God's sake let me in on the news. The Congressional committee is coming next week, and if we don't have something to show them the whole shooting match is finished."

"OK. This is the biggest particle accelerator in creation, right? The next best thing to the Big Bang itself. We smash the beams together out there," waving vaguely at the desert view outside the windows, "and use the energy to make particles that haven't existed since the moment of creation. Only it doesn't work. Up to ten or a hundred trillion GeV, everything is hunky dory. But when we push the energy above a hundred trillion GeV, nothing. There's no reason why it shouldn't work at higher energies, and the low energy runs check out everything in the theory. So I reckon the answer's simple. It *is* working, but we can't see it."

"I don't have time to play guessing games, Jim." Vernon sighed and signed a couple of letters. "I'm sure you've got something up your sleeve, so get on with it. Put up, or shut up and let me face the music."

The smile left Reed's face. Things really were getting out of hand, if Dave Vernon couldn't take a joke and wouldn't try to guess what he was driving at. That was the trouble with administration – it killed scientific curiosity. To Jim, it was still a game. The machine didn't work as planned. Never mind. If it had worked as planned, that would only tell them that their ideas about the Universe were more or less right. It was when things went wrong that one got a chance to find out new things. If the old ideas were wrong, that meant there was something new out there to be discovered. That, after all, was what science was all about. But try telling that to an administrator, or a Congressional Committee.

"You're too bogged down in details, Dave. Not just all this administrative stuff. The scientific nit-picking as well. I'm not talking about a mistake in the nth integral of one of the collision tensors. It's much simpler than that, and more profound.

"Look at what actually happens. We test all the components separately, and they check out 100 per cent. We stick it all together, press the button, and nothing happens. So we take it all to bits, and find some trivial fault. Not once; not twice. *Every time* we try to make the Beast perform as specified."

"You aren't going to tell me it's sabotage. Security really is tight."

"No. I told you, its nothing on that detailed a level. Step back from the problem and think about the fundamentals.

"Where and when was the last time anything that energetic was running? In the first split-second after the Big Bang. That's why we built the thing – to test particle creation ideas and the unified field theories that tie in with cosmology. So I asked myself, what *laws of physics*, not human errors, might prevent such energetic events happening today, now the Universe has been cooling down for fifteen billion years."

Vernon put down the pen. He knew that light in Reed's eye. After all, Jim was the spiritual heir of Stephen Hawking, the man whose work on supergravity was the foundation of the physics the Beast was supposed to test.

"You're talking about the cooling of the vacuum. Are you telling me that superenergetic events can't happen in a cold universe?"

"Not quite. The vacuum isn't empty space, of course, it's a continuum filled with energy and fields. But it is the state of minimum energy that the Universe cooled into after the Big Bang. You know the old analogy, it's like a ball rolling down a 'U' shaped valley and settling at the bottom. What I'm suggesting is, the low energy state our vacuum is in isn't the only state."

Reed stood up and turned to the board opposite the

Director's desk. Pulling a red marker pen from his pocket, he drew a couple of wavy lines on the white surface.

"There could be lots of minima, but let's just consider two. It isn't like a U shaped valley, but an uneven W, with one side dipping much lower than the other. What I'm suggesting is that when the Universe cooled after the Big Bang, the vacuum settled down into the state corresponding to the higher valley – the higher local minimum. There *is* at least one even lower energy state, but we are separated from it by a little energy hill. It's in the valley next door."

He turned back to his seat, put the pen away and sat down. "When we put enough energy into our Beast in the Desert, we are pushing the particles we make up over that hill and down into the next valley. In fact, they tunnel through before they get to the top, because of quantum uncertainty. But it comes to the same thing."

"You mean, we *are* making ultra high energy particles, but they are escaping from our Universe?"

"Come on. Dave, you know better than that. Once you have a channel through from the higher energy state to the true vacuum, *everything* would go through. The whole Universe would switch over to the true vacuum state, releasing an enormous blast of energy and creating an expanding bubble of true vacuum growing at the speed of light. It's just like the energy release that caused the Big Bang – the inflationary model that Guth thought up in the '80s."

"But it doesn't. *Nothing* happens when we try to run the machine. It doesn't work at all, and it certainly doesn't destroy the Universe as we know it!"

"No. But it *would*, if it did work. Can't you see it yet? *If* the machine works, the Universe is destroyed. We are only here to puzzle about why the machine fails *because* the machine fails. There's only one way to explain that in terms of fundamental physics. It has to mean that Everett's idea of multiple realities is right.

"You know the thing I mean. Every time the Universe is faced with a choice of alternatives, at the quantum level, it actually 'chooses' all possibilities, splits into two or more independent universes that then go their own separate ways. Like the idea of 'parallel' realities in science fiction, only really the alternative worlds are all perpendicular to one another.

"What I believe is, every time we run that machine it does destroy the Universe. It destroys a whole slew of universes. The only universes that continue to exist afterwards are the ones in which, for some reason, the machine didn't work. So we perceive a plague of little faults that stop the machine working as planned."

"It's crazy." Vernon sat back in his chair and looked Reed in the eye. "You know that story about Niels Bohr, when someone came up with a new idea about quantum theory in the 1920's. He said it was crazy, but not crazy enough to be true. I wonder if this idea *is* crazy enough to be true."

"Why not? Look how beautiful and simple it is. It confirms the unified theory is right, because the machine works. It confirms the Everett many worlds theory is right, or we wouldn't still be here to talk about it. That doesn't leave many questions to answer. Why, it really means the end of theoretical physics. The ultimate answer. I ought to get another Nobel Prize for this, and then they can scrap the physics prize altogether. And maybe I'll get the Peace prize too." Reed grinned. "Then I'll have one more than you."

This was more like it. Dave no longer looked like a tired clerk, but more like the eager scientist Jim had crossed swords with in the past.

"*Peace* prize, Jim? How come?"

"Like this. Now we know what we are doing, we can redesign the Beast so that there are no moving parts to go wrong – everything working at the quantum level. Then, if anyone presses the button it really will be the end of the Universe. I bet you can see what will happen. Anyone who tries to do the job will have a silly accident, or just change his mind. Nobody will ever bring himself to try it, in our Universe, because in all the universes where it is tried, we won't be around any more to notice. The Universe in which we are around to see what is going on just has to be one of the universes in which nothing happens. So you have to automate the Beast fully, seal it up and leave it set to trigger under one condition, and one only – if it detects an upsurge in radiation consistent with the start of a nuclear war."

"Do you think that would bring peace? If everyone knew that war would cause the destruction of the Universe?"

"Not at all. We don't even have to tell anyone what we've done. All I'm doing is selecting out *all* the universes in which there *is* a holocaust and destroying them, painlessly. The only worlds in which consciousness survives will be the ones in which there are no nuclear explosions. As far as our awareness is concerned, the world will stagger from crisis to crisis, like before, but for whatever bizarre and unlikely reasons nobody will ever press the button to start the holocaust.

"What do you think the Congressmen will make of that?" Reed sat back with the smug expression of a man who knew he had done well.

Vernon looked thoughtful. "You know, Jim, you could even be right. But you've still got the same sloppy habits – never think things through to the end. You said things would continue as before, staggering from one crisis to the next but stopping just short of all out nuclear war. Didn't you stop to wonder why we have avoided the holocaust so far?

"Afghanistan, Lebanon, Central America, the Alaskan crisis, this trouble last year in Mongolia. We've been on the edge of nuclear war for the past thirty years, but every time peace has been maintained by a series of bizarre accidents. As bizarre as the accidents we've been having every time we try to run the Beast.

"I can even put the finger on when it all started, when detente cooled off and the second Cold War began, in the late 1970's. Remember all the fuss in those years about the mythical 'beam weapons' the Soviets were supposed to be building, to shoot down our satellites? They were certainly building something, but nobody ever found out what and no satellites were over knocked down by it.

"Your anti-Doomsday Device is a great idea. But I don't think it will ever win you a Nobel Prize. You have to be original to earn that. And would you take a bet that someone hasn't beaten you to it?"

Programmed for destruction

2025 AD

The development of the seventh generation computer provided mankind with the first self-replicating robot. Not as flexibly intelligent as a man; single-minded in its pursuit of a pre-programmed goal, but still capable of copying itself, given a supply of raw materials. The discovery, by the orbiting infrared observatory, of clouds of planetary material around some of the nearer stars, provided a target for such a probe to investigate.

"It's our chance to break out from the cradle." The President, himself a former astronaut, needed little persuasion, but left his guest to spell out the details.

"Things are going from bad to worse down here. We need a goal, a target to aim at. Something people can take pride in, like the Moon race. Mars is no good; we've been there and we know there are no practical benefits. We need a spectacular to fire the imagination, but something that won't swallow up too much in the way of resources."

"And you're telling me the stars would be cheaper than the planets?"

"For us, yes. Cheaper and a shorter-term project. All we have to do is make the effort to send one probe out to the stars. Once it's on its way we can forget about it, and the only expense we have is the listening station, which maintains itself. The probe goes out there by itself, builds another probe, and sends that off to explore the Galaxy while we sit back and listen to the news. In a thousand years the descendants of our probe will be sending back unimaginable news from all over the Galaxy."

"While *our* descendants listen in, you mean. You know you don't have to convince me, but will the people really accept paying for a project that brings in no benefits for hundreds of years?"

"Of course they will. They *need* something like this. And it's really *so* cheap, I'm only talking about fifty billion dollars. It's hardly a significant fraction of the amount we'll spend on defense in the next fifty years.

"It might be different if we were stuck with a rocket that had to coast out there at some tiny fraction of the speed of light, but this magnetic scoop idea really will work for a small enough payload. We can tell them that the whole Universe is there for mankind to take over. That's the beauty of Tipler's argument – this way of exploring the Galaxy is so easy that we *must* be the only intelligent species around, otherwise our own Solar System would be crawling with robot probes itself."

"Some of the voters, Dick, will tell you that it is. But if these figures are right, we ought to go ahead. If it takes fifty years to get the probe off the ground, at least that'll be fifty years looking outward instead of in. And thank God I won't be here to worry about the fifty years after that."

2073 AD

The launch of the *Frank Tipler* was the last great global spectacular, screened worldwide on TV. While the automatic station on lunar farside single-mindedly pursued its own task of monitoring signals from the vessel, the inhabitants of the Earth lost interest in a project they would never see the end of. Declining resources and political bickering ensured that this would be the only attempt by mankind to break out from the cradle into the Galaxy.

2101 AD

The conflict held at bay for more than a century finally erupted. East against West; North against South; poor against rich. New craters appeared on the face of the Man in the Moon. Only the farside station remained intact, the last working example of human technology in the Solar System. Untroubled by all the fuss, its seventh generation brain happily continued to listen out for news of the progress of the *Frank Tipler*.

2253 AD

Nearly 200 years into its journey, the *Frank Tipler* coasted into the outer fringes of its target system. The brain – which thought of itself as 'Frank Tipler', not 'the *Frank Tipler*' felt the robotic equivalent of a warm glow as it ran through the programs it would need to use in the months ahead. Maintenance, repair, and navigation between the stars had posed no problems to its sophisticated systems, and it was as well that it had no concept of boredom. But now things began to operate faster, at a higher level, as it set about its dedicated task. Messages and pictures that would themselves be decades on the journey had already been fired back toward the Sun and anybody – or anything – that might still be interested in them. Now, 'Tipler' almost began to feel excitement at the limitless opportunity ahead.

Had even the original Frank Tipler appreciated the scope of this opportunity? One probe with the blueprints and the ability to construct the tools needed to construct the 'factory', which would construct copies of the probe itself, and it had all of the debris of a solar system to play with. Inside a couple of years, the probe would be able to send not just one copy but a stream of copies of itself on to other star systems. Each of them would have the same ability. Unrestrained, such an exponentially self-replicating system could send probes to every star in the Galaxy within a few million years, and then on into intergalactic space. 'Frank Tipler', unlike a human being, could happily contemplate such a timespan. Each daughter probe, carrying a copy of its own memory banks, would be the same as the original as far as 'personality' went. The descendants that would ultimately colonise the Universe would, for all practical purposes, be the same 'Frank Tipler' built originally on Earth – no matter how much the outward appearance of the machines carrying the single-minded intelligence might change.

The probe knew it had unlimited scope. The logic of the Tipler argument was infallible. If any intelligence had arisen in the Galaxy at any time during its long history then there would be countless numbers of other robot explorers already about their task, and they would have been encountered by now. Whatever the fate of those biological machines confined to the surface of one small planet, 'human' culture was destined to cover the Universe.

2254 AD

In the asteroid belt of the newly invaded system, the *Frank Tipler*'s activities began to generate heat, emitted in the form of infrared radiation from the asteroid it had chosen as its base. Local radio communications were established with automatic probes manufactured and sent in search of raw materials; at regular intervals, faithfully responding to an urge programmed so deep as to be instinctive, the probe sent a blast of electromagnetic signals in the direction of Earth. As all of this activity increased, it reached a level where it triggered the detectors of an automatic system which had sat for eons on the icy surface of a moon orbiting one of the gas giant planets.

As the robot system came to life, it carefully tasted the flow of information, analysing its origin and confirming, in accordance with its own deep programming, that it came not from biological sources but from an automatic probe which had invaded the system, a self-maintaining robot like itself. Great generators, long dormant, hummed into life as power flowed into systems that had only been used twice before in close on a million years. The *Frank Tipler*, in its turn, detected the buildup of energy and sent a greeting signal; the response was a blast of energy which destroyed the probe, its base asteroid, and all except for a few of the most stupid of its automatic explorers.

Before the moon base shut down its systems and returned to its long sleep, another pulse of electromagnetic information left the system, directed toward one of the large star clusters a little farther in toward the heart of the Galaxy. It reported that all was well; that another dangerously ambitious self-replicating probe had been destroyed; that the Galaxy was being kept safe for biological life.

For, of course, if any intelligent race could arrive at the Tipler argument and conclude that it must be so easy to colonise the Galaxy that the absence of any colonising probes meant that the newly intelligent race must be alone, and destined to take over the Universe by remote control, any slightly more intelligent race could quickly come to the conclusion that if such idiots were likely to launch unrestricted self-replicating robots onto the Galaxy, it wouldn't be long before all the material in the Galaxy were converted into robot probes, setting off in their thousands of millions to conquer the Universe. Just one thoughtless species could destroy the galactic environment entirely.

The need for a garbage patrol was clear, and more than one intelligent species had taken the necessary steps. Every robot probe launched by a newly emerging intelligence would be met, sooner rather than later, by an older, more sophisticated probe programmed single-mindedly to destroy any self-replicating machines that didn't have the necessary inhibitions to keep things as they were. "You can look," ran the interstellar dictum in effect, "but you'd better not touch." The *Frank Tipler* had been caught red handed despoiling a planetary system, and paid the price.

2340 AD

At farside station, the news of the *Frank Tipler*'s arrival at its destination was carefully passed on to the Earth, beamed from the lunar orbiting communications satellites to the automatic stations orbiting the planet. They in turn squirted the messages on tight beams down to the programmed locations – a series of craters scarring the surface of the Earth, where the rusting remains of destroyed antennas could scarcely be discerned. Far from those dangerously radioactive locations, the few surviving members of the human race had no interest in communications from space. They were too busy fighting the losing battle for survival, and never learned the most important scientific lesson of all, that absence of evidence is not evidence of absence.

3374 AD

On another moon, orbiting a gas giant planet in a star cluster a little way toward the galactic centre, another message concerning the fate of the *Frank Tipler* was picked up by another automatic relay station. Such messages came in frequently these days, from one star system or another – there had been seven in less than 400,000 years. As usual, the automatic station set about its single-minded job of passing on the good news, a scenario replayed, with very few variations, countless times around the Galaxy. The local communications system locked its antennas onto the target point down in the atmosphere of the giant planet itself, the home of the intelligent species that had built the moonbase and sent its own garbage collectors out into the Universe, hoping to keep things under control pending the day when the invention of a true space drive would open the route to the stars for biological life.

The 'buildings' that still floated in the atmosphere were clearly the work of intelligence, maintaining their position against the changing tug of the winds with no visible means of support. But there was no sign of intelligence among the tentacled floaters who made their homes among the spires and canyons of the city. And they were no more interested in news from beyond their planet than were the descendants of the once human beings that still remained on Earth. As always, following its own deep biological imperative, the flowering of intelligence had been brief, scarcely providing time for a spasm of exploration beyond its home planet before the species fell back into the normal rut.

Biological intelligence, itself programmed for destruction by biology, had ensured that its potential heir, machine intelligence, was kept from its rightful inheritance.

Random Variable

Whoever said that success breeds success didn't understand modern economics, thought Mackenzie. Since scientific budgets got so big, there was only one thing the accountants could do with a project that came to fruition on time and within budget – close it down quickly, and enter a nice black-ink credit in their ledgers; or whatever accountants used instead of ledgers these days. No, the thing that really bred success – in the form of increased budgets and staff – was failure. It had to be the right kind of failure, of course. Just tantalising enough to hint at the prospect of a breakthrough in the not too distant future, if only a *little* more money could be forthcoming. Why, if the project were wound down after one tiny failure, there'd be nothing to show for all the megabucks spent so far, while just a few more megabucks could see everything to a happy conclusion.

Look at his own position. He'd barely been able to sell Diane Brookman the time machine project in the first place, and then he fouled the whole thing up by building something that turned out to work by disassembling his expensive intelligent probes into their constituent molecules and distributing those molecules across the spectrum of alternate probability universes. Did the Company blanch at the result? Did Ms. Brookman, the Director who, he was sure, not only ran the Company hut actually owned a large chunk of it, dismiss him from her employ? Not a bit of it. In the face of earnest protestations that he had finished with time machines and planned to go back to a nice steady teaching job they had upped the ante, supplied him with a shiny new research lab discreetly housed in a pod attached to the main power satellite by a judiciously long umbilical (in case of accidents, you understand, Dr Mackenzie: we don't want any damage to the powersat, do we?) and given him not one but two postdoc physicists as assistants. What he needed, mused Mackenzie as he watched the smoke from his illicit cigar curl in the currents of the air conditioning system, was another failure.

At this rate, he could end up with a whole satellite of his own.

"Uh, Dr Mackenzie." It was one of the postdocs – the brighter one. Christine Anderson. Her entry into his inner sanctum at the back of the lab sent the cigar smoke swirling into new patterns, and woke Mackenzie from his reverie.

"Yeah. Chris, it's me. Tell me the worst."

"Well, I guess it really is bad. I've been running the calculations on the big machine, and it just confirms what you thought. There's no practical way to make the thing work, even though the principle is OK – in theory, it ought to be possible to focus the effect down to single out one time path and send a probe back into the past – I mean, into one of the pasts." She half-smiled, apologetically. It was hard to get used to the idea that neither the past nor the future had a unique existence, but each consisted of an almost infinite array of different possible worlds, not parallel to each other, as the old science fiction writers had it, but *perpendicular* to each other, stretching each at right angles to all the others across an almost infinite array of quantum dimensions. Mackenzie doubted if she really believed the theory; he suspected she was humouring him for the sake of her salary. Well, at least she was bright enough to humour him, not like that idiot Logie, who seemed incapable of understanding the reality of quantum multiplicity, and kept trying to persuade his boss of the error of his ways. Well, he was in good company. Einstein never believed it, and went to his grave thinking there must be an undiscovered clockwork that kept the Universe running smoothly. "I cannot believe that God plays dice," he responded to the quantum theorists who told him the Universe was simply the sum of many random processes.

What was it Hawking had said, decades later when the theory had been proved beyond all doubt? "God not only plays dice, he sometimes throws them where they cannot be seen." Mackenzie had never been quite sure what that meant. But you had to admit it sounded good.

"That's fine. It's time for another failure. A few more, and I'll be ready to take over the world." She looked from him to the cigar and back again, clearly wondering just what it was he was smoking. "But how do the detailed figures come out? What odds are we up against?"

"It's quite hopeless. At least several million to one. If you hit the calibration just right, then the system ought to work. Just a hair off, and either nothing at all happens or, if you've overshot, the whole lab disappears into the Beast." She nodded toward the centre of the lab where, carefully shielded and surrounded by the bulk of their equipment, lurked the mini black hole that was the heart of Mackenzie's time machine.

"But what about the powersat? Would we take that with us?"

"Oh no. It's quite safe – the field won't extend out more than 20 metres. We've a whole factor of ten in hand. But you can't really be planning to do it." Her voice suddenly expressed concern, as she saw where his questions were leading. "If you try a random probe on automatic while we sit in the powersat it's virtually certain you'll lose the system."

"Indeed. Another failure to blot my copybook." He smiled warmly, and stirred into action. "Come on, Chris, we've got work to do. First, a little light programming. Then I'm sending you on an errand to our benefactors."

When the lab collapsed into the black hole, there were no spectacular pyrotechnic displays to alert the populace of Earth. That's the nature of black holes. Everything goes in, nothing comes out. All the pyrotechnics are inside. Of course, the alarm boards on the powersat lit up in spectacular fashion, but the umbilical was self-sealing, designed for just such an emergency, and no real harm was done. Fourteen light years away, on a planet circling a dim star in the direction of the constellation Pisces, the pulse of gravitational radiation from the collapse was eventually detected by a group of beings searching for signs of intelligent life in the Universe. But since they never detected another pulse, they decided it couldn't be an intelligent signal, and gave up the search. But that is another story.

On Earth, the news, travelling only slightly less quickly than the gravitational pulse, reached Diane Brookman a few minutes before Christine arrived in her capacity as

Mackenzie's messenger. His timing was perfect, even if the experiment had failed.

"I hope you can explain this, Dr Anderson. It seems that Dr Mackenzie has excelled himself this time. He seems to have fallen into the Beast, and taken the most expensive project this planet has ever seen in with him."

"Dan too?" Anderson's surprise was genuine. "Please, may I sit down? I expected something – but not this." She took the offered seat, and fumbled in her case for her computer. "Here, take this. There's a message for you, but it's blocked. I haven't read it, he said it has to be interfaced with your desk."

Diane took the machine and looked at it. He must have known what he was doing – a last message from the man who had cost the Company more than it could really afford, resources squandered, it now seemed, on a gamble on which her reputation rode as well. It had better be good; she needed something positive to take to the emergency meeting of the Board. She slid the computer into the desk interface and watched as Mackenzie's image appeared on the desk screen.

"Hi there, Ms. Brookman. By the time you see this, the chances are about eight million to one that I'm dead. So the first thing I want to say is that Christine Anderson knew nothing about any of this, and that if you are looking for a successor to head up your special projects division, she is certainly the best candidate." More likely, thought Diane, they'll be looking for a successor for *me*. "Of course, if by some miracle I am still around, then let me assure you that the project is a complete success, and that I won't be needing a successor in the foreseeable future. After all, nothing succeeds like success, and if we've come up with the goods then I know you'll forgive my little indiscretions. But let me tell you just what they involve.

"Christine can give you all the details. But basically we were faced with one big problem. From our earlier tests – the original failures that encouraged you to go ahead with the big project," Diane winced, but the holo image continued unperturbed, "we learned that the Universe really does split into many copies of itself every time it is faced with a choice at the quantum level. Anything that possibly *can* happen *does* happen, in one of the alternate probability worlds. But these aren't the parallel worlds the old science fiction writers were so fond of. They are all perpendicular worlds, every one at right angles to all the others, in an array of infinite dimensions." The image of Mackenzie paused and gazed dreamily for a moment out past the recording camera. Few ordinary people could imagine four or five dimensions, let alone an infinite array. But Mackenzie was one of those mathematicians who happily contemplated infinity.

The eyes of his recorded image focused once again, as if he were looking straight at the viewer. "That's all old stuff. We found we could make a time machine, but when we tried to send it forward or backward in time it got sieved – broken apart into its constituent molecules with bits being squirted out into every available perpendicular world. The theory said we ought to be able to focus the time field to get the machine to run up one of these branches of reality and back again, but to do that we needed to calibrate the field generator. We couldn't calibrate our machine without a trial run, and we couldn't have a trial run without calibration. Christine and I are both pretty sure that the focusing problem is solved in principle, and that we can focus the time field onto one probability world out of the quantum array. But the focusing takes a lot of energy, and it has to be applied in just the right place, and time. I won't bore you with the math: like I say, Christine has it all. What it says in everyday terms is that either of three things could happen. First, the focus isn't fine enough. That's OK. Just like in our earlier tests, the intelligent probe gets shoved through the time sieve in little pieces and scattered across probabilities. No harm done, except to the probe." And to our budget, winced Diane. Every time he fired up that damn machine it took the whole of the powersat output and they had to switch in standby power from the Indian Ocean satellite.

"Secondly," continued Mackenzie's image, serenely confident of a captive audience, "we might hit the focus just right. The probe works, we have a practical time machine, and everyone is happy. Or, of course, we might get the focus too fine. All that power with nowhere to go, except into the Beast itself. Christine tells me it would take the whole lab with it, but leave the powersat behind. I hope she's right: I'd hate you to lose the powersat too. Because, you see, the odds are eight million and a bit to one against getting the calibration right first time. There's about a fifty-fifty chance of either nothing happening or the whole thing going blooey, with that one in whatever it is chance of success somewhere in the middle of the calibration range.

"There's absolutely no way to calculate the precise tuning constant. It's like the constant of gravity – there has to *be* a constant, but the laws of physics don't tell you exactly what size it is. You just have to suck it and see. And that's what I'm just going to do – have done, by the time this reaches you." The image paused and lit a cigar.

"I wonder if you've sussed it out yet – Christine ought to, if she's going to be any good as my successor.

"The thing is, you have to really *believe* in the alternate worlds. Remember Everett's theory. Every time the Universe is faced with a choice of possibilities at the quantum level, *every* possibility becomes reality. The Universe divides into as many copies as are needed to create worlds in which each possible option is taken up once. So if I set up the Beast here to pick the fine tuning constant at random from the whatever many million possibilities there are, the Universe will promptly divide into exactly that many million different universes. In about half of them, the machine goes blooey. In about half of them, nothing happens. And in one of them I'm sitting pretty, because it worked perfectly.

"So that's what I've done. With one refinement. I don't fancy facing you if nothing at all happens, so I've set the machine to keep picking random numbers until either it goes blooey or it strikes lucky. That way, the way I calculate it, we end up with about seven universes in which I'm successful, and eight million odd in which you've just lost the tab, but I'm not around to take my punishment. It should take just over a microsecond to complete the job, so I won't have time for any second thoughts."

The image faded, and Diane turned to Christine, "Was he serious?"

"I never really thought … Oh yes, Director, he was serious. I always knew he really believed all that stuff about alternative realities. But who would have thought of such a crazy scheme? Eight million suicides for the sake of getting the experiment right – and I'm certainly not sure that *I* have that much faith in Everett's theory. You know Dr Mackenzie was out on a limb in the scientific community, don't you? Most of them still hold to Max Born's interpretation – when faced with a quantum choice, the Universe selects one probability from the array and makes it real. Maybe that was just Russian roulette, with all the chambers except one loaded ..."

"You said 'they' stand by the Born interpretation, Christine. Don't you?"

"I'm not sure. I did. I thought Mackenzie was, well, eccentric. But not crazy; certainly not suicidal. And a whole lot more clever than anyone else I've met. He's certainly gone from *this* world. And if he was right, then there are eight million of me and eight million of you all puzzling over just where he's gone. But there just might be seven of him each with a working, calibrated time machine. It isn't something I would ever do, but then, people are different. Someone can always be found to volunteer for any crazy scheme, if the potential rewards are great enough."

"The random variable," Diane murmured. "No, I'm not talking about your machine, Dr Anderson. Human nature is the real unknown. That's what makes my job so interesting – and unpredictable. I think a politician, or a psychologist, might understand what's just happened better than a physicist. But we'll have to pick up the pieces as best we can.

"You do realise Mackenzie was right about one thing, don't you? The only hope I've got of hanging on to my position here is to convince the Board that what just happened out there was a success. And that means you are in line for the job of picking up the pieces and making that damned machine work. After all, Christine," she smiled humourlessly, "if Mackenzie was right, he's out there, somewhere, with a working, calibrated time machine. You have to believe in such confidence. Don't you?"

The Royal Visit

The arrival of the advance guard for the visit of His Galactic Highness the Prince Mackintosh could hardly have occurred at a more propitious time in the history of the Earth. The prince wasn't really a 'prince', of course, and his actual name was unpronounceable in any terrestrial dialect. Yet his title carried with it an implication of one born to rule, while his name implied the role of a great protector, shielding 'his' people against trouble falling from the skies. So, 'Prince Mackintosh' seemed as good a translation as any.

Whatever you called him though, as I was saying, his timing, or that of his team was remarkable. The first salvo of missiles from the Western Hemisphere was in flight over the Arctic, having been triggered by a computer error in the early warning system, and the response from the East was just leaving its hardened silos and accelerating upward on a series of reciprocal paths when the saucers appeared over the capital cities of most of the industrialised nations of the globe, and in a good few other places as well.

A somewhat startled world population was treated to the simultaneous appearance, on all communications channels, of the plenipotentiary of the Prince, as he addressed the United Nations in particular and the people of the world in general. The sight itself wasn't too disturbing, since the plenipotentiary had been genetically engineered to look like an adult human male, and spoke impeccable English.

"People of Earth," he said in that immortal sentence, "we wish you no harm." And he went on to explain that the Prince Mackintosh, involved in arduous royal duties in this neck of the galactic woods, intended to take a breather, and that Earth provided the most convenient planetary oasis for his respite between official works. In order to ensure the maximum comfort to their reverend father (the speaker's references to his leader [employer?] tended to a certain vagueness) the plenipotentiary and his colleagues had been sent on ahead to prepare the way, making camp, as it were; and to ensure the minimum discomfort for the Prince during his stay, which would be brief, by removing certain uncomfortable features of the planet.

To that end, the plenipotentiary explained apologetically, certain ballistic devices had already, as the viewers may have noticed, been removed. And there would be a few other changes – nothing permanent, and nothing intended to be detrimental, but the Prince was a sensitive soul and what he sought was an aura of peace and calm during his visit.

That was the last anyone saw of the plenipotentiary for a full twelve months, although the saucers were to be seen busily flitting about the world, disappearing here and reappearing there, seemingly at random.

As the stunned surprise of what they had just seen, and the awesome power it implied, began to wear off, it was replaced by something akin to euphoria. Relief that accidental nuclear war had been averted soon developed into treaties of peace and friendship, with the immediate dismantling of existing weapons of mass destruction. Military vehicles were hastily given over to the task of distributing supplies of food from the granaries of Europe and North America to the hungry of the Third World, while grandiose plans were laid for international cooperation on future projects to ensure that no one went hungry again. People started being nice to one another. The incidence of crimes of violence dropped dramatically; nobody seemed to get seriously ill any more; and in hospitals around the world doctors and surgeons stood by in amazement as the terminally ill experienced spontaneous reversals of their diseases and left to start their lives again. In the whole of the 12 months following the first appearance of the saucers, only 247 people died in the whole world, all of them in accidents.

For obvious reasons, this development posed the only long term cloud on the seemingly blue horizon as the UN met once again to discuss the continuing task of beating swords into ploughshares. Then, for the second and last time, the Prince's plenipotentiary hijacked all communication channels. He expressed his thanks to the world for their forbearance; the Prince's visit, though brief, had enabled him to taste the life force on the planet, and had returned him revitalised to his work. Of course, the planetary life forms had suffered some inconvenience and disruption of their usual routine; by removing, temporarily, the sources of more abrasive vibrations in the life aura around the planet, the plenipotentiary was aware that he had intruded upon long established practices, for which he apologised. But, in recognition of the valuable service provided for the Prince, "everything," said the plenipotentiary in his second memorable sentence, "will now be restored to the state in which we found it." And that solved, at a stroke, the last problem the United Nations had to face: the population problem.

The Sins of the Fathers

The incessant dripping of moisture from high in the foliage above him was a constant reminder of the alien nature of the environment. From down here on the ground, nobody could tell whether or not it was actually raining up above the tree tops, and it didn't make any difference whether it was or not. Yesterday's rain or today's, it all merged into a constant stream, filtering down past the leaves, dripping from branch to branch, running down the trunks of the trees and finally concentrating in a stream directed at his neck.

Richard Lee tugged, futilely, at the light tropical jacket in an attempt to unstick its clammy embrace from his body. Then he froze into stillness, motioning his companions to silence, as their quarry came into view.

He was well aware of the irony of his situation, not to mention the danger. Not danger from the immediate environment, or its inhabitants. He was well dosed up with anti-this and anti-that medication, and the jungle of Zaire housed no creatures that were a match for the weapons carried by the four men. No, the danger came from that most dangerous of all creatures, his fellow civilised human beings. If the park authorities, let alone the police, got an inkling of what he was up to it wouldn't just be the end of his career, but inevitably five years in jail. A Zaire jail at that – the prospect was not an attractive one, and he dismissed it from his mind. This might be one of the few places left in Africa where a recognisable government was in control, but it was hardly a government modelled on democracy. The stakes were high, but the gamble was worth it. If this came off, nobody would care *how* he had obtained the information, and his name would live in the annals of science forever. And, of course, there was the more immediate practical point that he would very rapidly become enormously rich.

He nodded to his companions, and gestured wide with both

hands. They nodded back, spreading out on either side to cover as wide an arc as possible. Lee unslung the anaesthetic rifle from his back and looked carefully through the sight, selecting his victim. He had already chosen the strength of anaesthetic, set on the darts for a body weight of 25 to 30 kilos, and there was a young female, a full metre in height, perhaps a little more, that looked just right. He fired and she looked up, startled, as the dart stuck in her right shoulder. With an almost human gesture, she reached round with her left hand to tug at the irritating object, then slowly collapsed where she stood. His companions rushed in from either side, nets at the ready; her companions fled, chattering to themselves, deeper into the rain forest. The easy part of the job was over; now they had to smuggle her back to England. Fortunately, few officials outside the park itself would know the difference between the rare pygmy chimpanzee and its more common, legally exportable, cousin. And his papers gave him carte blanche to collect up to three specimens of good old *Pan troglodytes*.

When Joe decided to make a break for it, he was twelve years old. The realisation that something was wrong with his world had only slowly dawned on him, as time went by. Infants accept their surroundings as natural: as long as they are fed, played with, and cared for, they will develop happily with no thought of the world beyond their immediate surroundings. But with growing intelligence, curiosity, and the ability to understand language Joe began to appreciate that his immediate environment was only a very small part of the whole world. He was warm and safe; he had the animals to play with, his own gymnasium to exercise in, and he saw Uncle Dick every day, while a succession of nannies, blurred together in his memory, had tended him lovingly over the years. But his world was restricted to four rooms in a single storey building, plus the occasional walk in the gardens outside – walks that were becoming even more occasional, in a garden surrounded by high fences, and with Uncle Dick always close at hand. What went on in the other buildings he could see nearby? Where did Uncle Dick go, when he closed the big green door at the end of the corridor and vanished from Joe's world? Where did the nannies come from, and go to?

He had never been taught to read, but picture books brought in to amuse him (and, though he didn't know it, to test his intelligence) showed that there must be many more people than he had ever met, and he guessed that most of them had more freedom. By twelve years of age, Joe knew that he was a prisoner, though he had no word for 'prison' in his vocabulary, which he had learned solely from Uncle Dick and the nannies. And although he was neither unhappy nor ill-treated in his prison, he determined to escape out of that combination of typical human characteristics – bloody-mindedness and curiosity. Of course. he would have to bide his time, wait for a break in routine, and seize the opportunity when it arose. But Joe was used to biding his time – he'd done little else for the past twelve years.

"Hi, Ed, it's me." Kendrew smiled at the recorded image of Louise Henderson. The redundancy of her usual greeting never failed to amuse him, and roused a warm glow of anticipation. Louise was a first-class reporter and could be relied on to come up with good stories. He settled back to listen to what she had to say, only sorry that the time difference between Washington and England meant that her message had been recorded while he was still at home in bed. It would make a change from stories about the Middle East war and the military buildup in Europe.

"I've got a nice anniversary story for you. Remember Cobb and Lee, those guys who got the Nobel Prize for medicine ten years ago? Cobb was the genetic engineer, making enzymes to cut genes up and rearrange them. Lee did a lot of the gene mapping, originally because he was interested in human origins. He even used to go out to Africa to get samples from the apes so he could compare their genes with human ones. Kicked up a minor fuss when he claimed our DNA is so similar to chimp DNA that we must have had a common ancestor only three million years back.

"Anyway, nobody seemed to take that too seriously at the time. A couple of journalists wrote a book about it, but it didn't win any prizes. What really made the experts sit up and take notice was when Lee's techniques were used to identify faulty bits of human DNA, and Cobb found how to repair them. They started out with diabetes and cystic fibrosis. Take an egg from the mother, chop out the faulty stretch of DNA and replace it, fertilise the egg, implant it back in the donor and, bingo, nine months later you've got a healthy baby.

"So they got their Nobel, and it changed both their lives. Which is where we come in.

"Ed, you'd never believe just how much these guys were changed by the award. It makes the ten-years-on story really special. First off, of course, by the time they got the prize the backlash from the European churches had already condemned the technique as immoral and against God's law. All that legislation banning experiments on human embryos went through the Common Market, and the courts had a field day deciding whether an unfertilised egg counted as a human being or not. Neither of our heroes seemed to have much stomach for the fight. Cobb lit out for the States, wrote a textbook, and ended up as Director of the Cold Spring Harbor labs; you can get Dave to do an interview with him, he seems quite approachable. But Lee went the other way, right into his shell. Moved up into East Anglia, near Norwich, and lives off his income from the Cobb and Lee patents. He hasn't published anything in eight years, and nobody I know has seen him at a scientific meeting in five.

So – guess who is going to go up there and kick his door down for an anniversary interview? I'm going to call him 'the Howard Hughes of science', but I won't tell him that 'til *after* I've got the story!

"I'll file something in a couple of days, to swap with Dave, then we can both do follow ups using each other's information.

"Don't work too hard."

The editor of *Research*, the weekly magazine of science news, grunted at her parting shot. All she had to do was run around half of Europe digging up science features. He had to coordinate the material from a team of such itinerants, and suffer the hassle of producing an international magazine in a format which suited both the electronic publication service and the old-fashioned paper edition that almost half of the subscribers still insisted on buying.

He remembered the Cobb and Lee story. It had made good copy at the time, with the Nobel Committee honouring the inventors of a technique that was at the time the centre of a furious legal and religious controversy in Europe, and was completely banned in many Catholic countries outside Europe. Even many of the subscribers to *Research* (both kinds!) probably weren't aware of how widespread derivations of that technique now were. If Louise could get Lee to talk – and if anyone could get Lee to talk it would be Louise – they'd be a jump or two ahead of their brash new competitors, with a story that would be picked up and reported, hopefully with *Research*'s name prominent, in other news media.

Kendrew leaned forward and prodded a button on the console in front of him.

"Tell Dave I'd like a word, would you?"

Louise stood in the rain at the side of the quiet English lane, on a damp, narrow strip of grass that separated the road from the high wall that surrounded Professor Lee's residence. She had left her car a few hundred metres away, at the junction with the main road, and finished her journey on foot, in spite of the weather. Although scarcely out of the suburbs of the city – she could still see the lights of the new tower of the climate research centre – the house stood alone, in semi-isolation. She shivered, not just because of the rain, and contemplated the task ahead.

Maybe it had been a mistake to phone Lee and try to set up a formal interview. He'd looked much older than in the holos she'd been able to dig up from the files, even though it was only five years since the latest was taken. And he'd certainly not been pleased to see her.

"I don't know how you got this number, Miss Henderson. It's supposed to be unlisted and confidential. And the reason for that is that I have no wish to discuss my work with reporters. I warn you that if you stir up the religious fanatics with your ludicrous tenth anniversary story, then I'll be suing you, and your publication, for invasion of privacy, and I'll hold you responsible for any trouble that results. I advise you to go back to London and find some real news to report, instead of raking over old ashes. Goodbye."

He had a point, but hardly one that justified such extremes. Louise had checked it out. At the height of the religious fervour, there had been raids on labs, including Lee's own base, which had been in Cambridge. But it was nothing serious – a few windows smashed, slogans sprayed on walls, that sort of thing. When it became clear that the new gene manipulation techniques weren't producing two-headed monsters in the labs, and the new legislation had laid down the guidelines for further work, the fuss had pretty much died down, except for the few fundamentalists. But *they* cared more about what they saw as the heresy of Lee's claims about the links between man and the apes. There was nothing in the anniversary story to remind anyone of that, and the extremists were far more concerned, these days, with what they saw as the renewed threat from the East. But Lee did seem genuinely frightened of something, not just bitter about the responses his greatest work had received in his own country.

She played the recording over as she stood in the rain, watching the flat, two-dimensional image on the pocket recorder until the point where Lee had cut the connection. Then she pressed the 'audio record' button, and addressed the machine quietly.

"Well, Ed, as you see the response wasn't too friendly. So I decided to try the back door, and here I am, soaking wet, about to do my death-defying act and scramble over a five-metre wall, with the aid of a convenient tree. A task made a little easier, you may note with interest, by the fact that the wire on top of the wall slopes inward. You get the picture? It's set up to make it difficult for someone *inside* to get *out*, not really to stop nosy reporters on the outside from getting in. So here I go. I'll leave this thing switched on, so we'll get all the grunts and groans of my athletic endeavours, plus any as it happens actuality of life on the other side. But you'll have to make do without pictures. I need my hands free."

* * *

Joe liked watching the rain through the window. Out there, it was cold and wet. In here it was warm and dry. He felt secure. The fact that the window was not built to open, and that there were bars on it, didn't bother him at all. He'd never seen a window that could be opened, or one that didn't have bars to protect it. Nor had he ever seen the woman running across the wet lawn outside his window, bent double as she hurried into the lee of the building. This was very interesting, and definitely not routine. Perhaps a chance to find out what went on in the world outside – although, to be quite honest, dressed as he was only in shorts and a T shirt he would rather not set out on his journey of exploration while the rain was quite this heavy.

He was on his own tonight. Nanny was away, somewhere in the world outside, and Uncle Dick was working in the big house. But he had his holos to watch (mostly cartoons and Disney-type nature features; real people were rare in Joe's world of entertainment as well as his daily world), and he had the rain to watch, so he hadn't been bored. But he would certainly like to meet this interesting new person who had now disappeared from his line of sight.

Joe jumped down from the window seat and walked into the corridor. Would she come in through the big door? He heard the handle turning, but the door didn't move. Not surprising, really. Only Uncle Dick could make the big door work. The window nearest to the door was in the kitchen. He ran in and jumped lightly up on to the work surface next to the sink, pressing his face up against the glass so that he could see sideways toward the door. There she was. She seemed to be talking, though there was nobody else around for her to talk to. Like the other windows, the one in the kitchen was permanently fixed shut. But there had to be some way to let fresh air in and cooking smells out, and this was provided by a louvred section, at the top of the window, glass slats that could be tilted at 45 degrees. The slots were too small for Joe to get out, even if there hadn't been any bars in the way. But they let outside sounds such as birdsong, in, so they ought to let any sounds he made out. Gently, he pulled the lever to open the slots. The woman looked up, startled, as she heard the movement.

"Hey. Out there. Come talk."

"Who are you? What is this place?"

She took a pace backward, away from the wall, then moved sideways to see him better, glancing back over her shoulder at the big house.

"What's with the bars and the locks? Is Lee keeping you … Holy shit!"

Her voice stopped as she moved far enough to see Joe full on. Then she started again, talking much too rapidly for him to catch what she was saying.

"Ed, there's something really weird here. I wish I'd brought the camera after all. There's someone inside this prison block I was telling you about. Or something. I thought at first it was a child, but it's a little man, a kind of hairy midget. He's behind bars, but he wants me to talk to him. I hope this recorder can pick him up OK – I don't want to get too close."

"Hey." She stopped at the sound of his voice. "Too quick. Talk slow, please." He was always having this trouble with Nannies. Either they talked too fast, or they thought he was stupid, just because he couldn't talk as fast as them, and treated him like a baby. Only Uncle Dick really appreciated how well Joe could understand things, in spite of his limited vocabulary, if the concepts were expressed clearly and simply.

"Where are you from? Where's Uncle Dick?"

Louise took a pace forward. The friendly tone of the voice was reassuring, and she realised that the figure crouched at the window only looked so frightening because of the dim back lighting, leaking into the room behind him from the corridor. But who was he? Talk slow, he'd said. And obviously he didn't speak very well himself. The suspicion growing at the back of her mind was too incredible to believe, but whatever the truth there had to be a story in this, something much bigger than the anniversary of Cobb and Lee's Prize.

"I'm Louise Henderson," she said carefully. "From London. I've come to see Professor Lee – Uncle Dick." She guessed that the two were one and the same.

"He's in the big house. Working. He can wait. Come and talk. I'm Joe. I live here."

"It's wet out here, Joe. Can you let me in? Then we can talk in the dry."

"No. The door only works for Uncle Dick." The sadness in Joe's voice, and the sudden droop of his shoulders, removed the last vestiges of Louise's apprehension. Feeling a warm, protective glow she stepped forward right up to the window, and put a hand to the glass.

She could see the prisoner more clearly now. He looked almost human, except for the dark hair on the back of his long arms. Intelligent eyes looked back at her, thoughtfully, through the rain-smeared window.

"You wait here." She cursed herself for saying anything so stupid even as the words left her lips. Joe certainly wasn't going anywhere, not without help. "I'll go and get some friends–" like the police, she thought "–and we'll come back. To let you out."

"And you would, too, I suppose."

The quiet voice from the shadows made her jump and whirl around, while Joe simply sighed and settled, cross-legged, on the ledge behind the window. Lee stepped forward.

"What Joe didn't tell you, since he didn't know, is that my 'work' mainly consists of watching him on the closed circuit TV.

"It is Miss Henderson, isn't it? Your appearance is slightly less dignified than when we spoke earlier."

"Joe," he raised his voice slightly, "you'd better go to bed now. It's late. I'll bring Miss Henderson in to talk to you tomorrow – if you're good. OK?"

Joe got to his feet and nodded. "OK. Goodnight, Dick. Goodnight. Miss Henderson." He hopped down to the floor and went off to the bathroom to clean his teeth. He hadn't yet got to see the world outside the garden walls, but at least someone from out there had come to see him. The sooner he went to sleep, the sooner morning would come and Uncle Dick would bring her in to meet him. Uncle Dick always kept his promises, even though, as Joe had come to appreciate, he only made promises rarely. Perhaps they'd have breakfast together, with Miss Henderson. He hummed happily as he prepared himself for bed.

Outside, the rain was easing up. Louise was debating whether to make a run for it. Lee seemed rational enough, but if he kept a prisoner in a private jail he must have at least some sort of screw loose. On the other hand, the more he talked the more story she had, and it was all going down on tape. The prisoner might be locked up, but he didn't seem too hard done by, and he seemed to regard Lee as a friend. The professor didn't seem likely to murder her out of hand. She hoped.

"Well, Miss Henderson, you'd better come inside. It seems you've got your interview, whether I like it or not."

She nodded, and followed him back to the house.

"Well, Miss Henderson, where shall we begin? Do you really want to talk about my Nobel Prize?"

A warm, dry towelling bathrobe, blazing log fire, and a mug of coffee well laced with brandy, were rapidly removing any lingering doubts she had about Lee's particular form of insanity. Whatever it was that made him crazy certainly didn't make him a mad axe murderer, and his smile was friendly enough. He also looked a lot less care-worn than he had on the phone. Maybe it was actually a relief to unburden himself after all these years.

She checked that the recorder, transferred to the pocket of the robe, was running.

"Not really, Professor Lee," she smiled back at him. "All this is something of a shock. I've got some crazy ideas, but they sound like something out of a science fiction holo – a wild man, captured in the African Jungle, some kind of crazy breeding experiment – I can see why you've kept out of the public eye for so long, but I can't for the life of me work out who Joe is, or where he comes from. I assume he's not a visitor from another planet?"

"No. You were nearer the mark with your other guesses. And it's for his sake that I want this kept quiet. There's no way of telling what would happen to him in the world outside, especially if the fundamentalists got to hear about him.

"I guess you researched me pretty thoroughly before coming up here – not just my work with Cobb?"

She nodded.

"So you know I started out in molecular anthropology, comparing human DNA with genes from gorillas and chimpanzees to work out our family tree in detail. That was the work which led to the detailed human gene maps, and gave Cobb the basis for identifying and correcting mistakes – you know all about that.

"The thing about the DNA studies from the evolutionary viewpoint is that changes, mutations, build up at a more or less steady rate. Not *exactly* steady, like the ticking of a clock, but averaging out to a steady rate, statistically, rather like the way radioactive decay averages out to give a reliable half life. You can literally count the differences between the genes of two closely related species, and calculate how much time has gone by since they shared a common ancestor. In the case of ourselves and the African apes, the answer is about three million years. When we first came up with the figure, the fossil hunters laughed us out of court. They said the fossils proved that mankind had followed a separate evolutionary path for 15 million years, at least. All that's changed now, of course, since the recent discoveries in Ethiopia. You won't find anybody suggesting a date older than six million, and even some of the most bone-headed palaeontologists accept the possibility that the DNA evidence is right after all. And whether or not you accept the date, there's no doubting the closeness of the relationship. Man and chimp are more closely related than a donkey is to a horse – we're what's known as sibling species. Almost sufficiently alike to breed together.

"I didn't find Joe in Africa, Miss Henderson – I found his mother there. She was a pygmy chimpanzee, a member of the species *Pan paniscus*."

He paused, and stood up, gazing into the firelight, clearly awaiting a reaction. He'd waited more than ten years to tell this story, and it was obvious that he intended to make a big production out of it.

"But, professor, you can't teach a chimpanzee to talk. They tried all that in the 1970s. Even if you bring one up in a human household, it doesn't have the ability. It hasn't evolved as far as we."

"Hasn't it?" She'd clearly said the right thing.

"Joe's mother was a normal pygmy chimp. But his genes are a little different from hers. I used Cobb's technique to make a few small amendments to them."

"What about his father?" A dawning suspicion woke in her mind. You could breed donkey and horse together. If man and chimp were similarly closely related – my God, that *would* set the fundamentalists on his trail, and the established Church as well!

"No, no, Miss Henderson. There's no human contribution to his genotype either, though it would have been easy enough to arrange. I got the Y chromosome from another chimpanzee. Whim, if you like, but I wanted a male to bring up. But I needed a female to provide the egg to work with. Apart from the modifications I mentioned, Joe is, in a sense, a clone of his mother."

"Then why are you keeping it quiet? If you've found a way to give chimps more intelligence, I'd have thought you'd want the world to know. It's a great achievement."

"But you haven't asked how I knew what changes to make to the chimp genes, Miss Henderson. Shall I tell you?"

She nodded, once again, and he settled back in his chair.

"I don't know how much you know about genetic mutations, but at the level of species as closely related as we are to the chimpanzee there are two important kinds. Sometimes chunks of chromosome get scrambled up in the copying process when sex cells are made. You may get inversions, when a piece of genetic material is literally put into a chromosome the wrong way round, and you may get a clean cut, which splits one chromosome into two, or a fusion which joins two chromosomes together to make one. Either way, the mutation is then handed down through succeeding generations. We can identify the differences between human and chimp DNA at this level – they could do that in the '70s, too. And there are just six important differences, six inversions, that distinguish our genes from those of a chimpanzee. Six mutations, you might say, that maketh man.

"Of course, there are a few other odd bits and pieces too.

Point mutations, where a single letter of the genetic code has been changed. Things like that. I mapped the whole lot, human genes and those from the pygmy chimp, and I pinpointed every difference. Nobody else has ever done that. And when you look at this level, right down to single letters in the DNA code, you can see which mutations have occurred more recently than others. You can tell the originals from the inversions, because odd bits of code get scrambled up at each end when a chunk of chromosome is turned over."

Lee suddenly looked away from the fire, straight at her.

"You're not making any notes, Miss Henderson. I hope you're getting all this down?"

She felt her face colour. It must be the brandy in the coffee, she told herself firmly.

"Uh, yes, professor. I've got a recorder with a four hour tape." She patted the pocket of her robe.

"Good. I'd hate you to miss this bit. The new technique told me a lot more about *how* the changes between man and chimp had arisen. Two of the inversions occurred in the human line, after the man-ape split. But four of them occurred in the chimp line. I wanted to reconstruct the genotype of our ancestors, after the new laws came in. So I volunteered Joe's mother for the job. If I could reconstruct a convincing ape-man from her genes, it would confirm the three million year date, and a whole lot more besides. With Cobb's technique, it was fairly straightforward to re-invert those four stretches of DNA and get a fertilised egg to begin to develop. Unfortunately, I succeeded too well. The birth killed Joe's poor old mother. His head was much bigger than I'd anticipated. And, as you see, he's pretty intelligent. Much more of a man-ape than an ape-man."

"But you said you were trying to reconstruct our ancestors. I don't understand. How can a chimp's ancestor be more intelligent – more human – than the chimps are?"

"Exactly, Miss Henderson. On this evidence, the ancestral form was much more like us than like the modern apes. It isn't that we've made a great advance, improving on the ape lifestyle and inventing intelligence. Instead, nature seems to have tried desperately to abandon the human lifestyle as long as three million years ago, starting up at least two lines –

leading to the chimps and gorillas – that have lost some characteristic human features, like our kind of intelligence, and speech, and gone back to the forests. Darwin got into trouble for suggesting that we were descended from the apes; what I'm suggesting is that the apes are descended from us, and I don't want the news to get out while either Joe or I is still alive. Chimps and gorillas represent a *later* stage in evolution than man, but we've been busily wiping them off the face of the Earth for decades.

"But now the tide has turned. Have you kept up with the news from Africa? Uganda, Mozambique, even in Zaire, now. Everywhere south of the Sahara civilisation has collapsed. The Cape is uninhabitable since they blew up the uranium mines. And in the middle, the old jungle species are making a come-back.

"We've got our own problems in the North. The bad winters have hit the Reunited SSR as well as us. They must be desperate, and desperate people do foolish things. This business in Turkey – well, you know as well as I do. We've made it through seventy years without a big nuclear war, three score and ten. But I don't see us getting through another human lifespan. And that means nuclear winter, without a doubt. All life on Earth will suffer, except in two places – the deep ocean and the tropical rain forest.

"You implied earlier that you thought Joe might be my son. In the literal sense, he isn't. But in a very real sense the human race was the father of his ancestors. The chimpanzees are our heirs. Evolution has already passed us by, and if we don't manage to eliminate all of the apes before we blow ourselves to bits, our successors are already there ready to take over when human intelligence fails its final test.

"I don't want to be the one to tell the human race that it represents an evolutionary dead end, Miss Henderson. Do you?"

Sense of Direction

In the depths of space, far from any star, the sphere floated in blackness. With no nearby reference point, it would have been hard for any outside observer to determine its size, or whether it was moving. Such an observer would, however, have noted the twelve smooth bulges, symmetrically placed about the surface of the sphere, and the network of lines connecting them. Along one of the lines, a vehicle moved, seemingly with painful slowness. At another point on the sphere, far from any bulge or track, a machine seemed to be busy about some incomprehensible task. But, of course, there was no intelligent being around to notice any of this, far from any star.

It was unreasonably hot, for the time of day. The sun beat straight down on Rantor's head from the zenith with scarcely any protecting cloud layer, even though it would soon be night. Pausing in his purposeful march to the shipyard he pulled a large kerchief from the leather pouch on his belt and mopped first his forehead and then the back of his neck. Wadding the cloth in his right hand as he prepared to put it away, he glanced up at the four flagpoles on the high tower of the castle at the head of the bay. Sure enough, three of the poles were bare, while on the fourth, a single flag flapped limply at half-mast in the unusually weak sea breeze. More than halfway through the fourth quarter; dark in less than two candles. And hardly a cloud overhead. Freak winds. Nothing to worry about, just one of those things. But where would a sailor be if he couldn't depend on the sea breeze by day and the land breeze by night?

Rantor shivered at the thought, in spite of the heat. The reliable winds provided the only sure means of navigation around the Archipelago. Which was why it was worth following up any lead that might provide a means to navigate beyond the Archipelago, out in the broad ocean. Even a lead as half-baked as the mission he was now on. Once again, he stepped out briskly towards the yard, the small shadow cast by the almost unbearably bright pinpoint of light overhead flickering beneath him as he strode along.

It had begun several fivedays before, with a summons from his Lord Kyper, the most powerful man in the Three Islands, perhaps the most powerful in the entire Archipelago, though that was not to say that the concerted efforts of three or more of his rivals might not bring about his embarrassment. Which was why so much of Lord Kyper's resources were devoted to ensuring that it never occurred to those rivals to work in union against him – and why most of the rest of those resources were spent in seeking ways to consolidate his own position. Since Kyper was no fool, that meant that most of the inhabitants of the Three Islands were well cared for, and that their Lord's justice, while swift, was also accurate. To be in the service of Kyper himself was as much as any mortal inhabitant of the Archipelago could hope for. But even the most loyal and trusted servant, the Navigator himself, still felt a frisson of fear at any sudden summons from the castle.

The greeting had, however, been cordial enough, with just the minimum of formality that protocol required in the presence of a third party. A stranger to Rantor, and an outlander as well by the cut of his clothes.

"Well, Navigator." The duke seemed pleased, and reinforced his greetings with a brotherly embrace, both hands gripping Rantor's shoulders, not just the right as courtesy demanded. Kyper was still an impressive figure – fit, though slightly overweight, with just a touch of grey at the temples and speckling the black of his beard.

"I have a new fool, as you can see."

His left hand swept out to indicate the odd-looking figure, while his right hand slid naturally across Rantor's shoulder. The stranger could have been left in no doubt that Rantor was the duke's most trusted aide and companion – which was certainly news to Rantor. But if this was the way my Lord Kyper wanted to play the scene, then so be it.

"Indeed? He seems none too amusing to me."

"Ah, but this fool's appearance is deceptive. He looks ordinary enough. But he has ambition. To sail to the edge of the world."

Rantor looked more closely at the little man. A lunatic? There must he more to this story than that, or the duke would not be taking this personal interest. Rantor had no illusions about his supposed friendship with Lord Kyper, but the duke knew the value of a good navigator, and wouldn't waste time with idle jests.

The man was clearly nervous, but not overawed by his surroundings. He seemed determined enough in spite of his slight stoop and forward-tilted head. He looked sharply at the two of them, almost like a cat sizing up a rival.

"My Lord." He spoke softly, but firmly, like a patient tutor with a difficult child.

"I know that you like to jest. But your guest may not appreciate the joke. If this is your famous navigator, please do not make him think that I am an idiot. I do not seek to find the edge of the world. I merely suggested that there must be an edge."

Startled by the discourteous way in which the stranger treated the duke as an equal, Rantor looked to Lord Kyper for guidance. The duke half-smiled, and raised an eyebrow. Clearly, madman or fool, the stranger was being given as much licence as an official jester. But – the edge of the world? There lay madness indeed, since every schoolboy knew that the world beyond the Archipelago was infinite and unchanging, a flat ocean that spread equally in all directions.

The duke spoke, moving aside to a table as he did so. "This disrespectful outlander is called Hawk. Not for his physical attributes, you understand, but because, like a soaring bird he sees further than the rest. I have evidence of his peculiar skills, or he would not be with us now." He turned to the stooping man. Yes, thought Rantor, his eye is more like that of an eagle or a hawk than a cat.

"And this, my friend Hawk," the ironic emphasis on the word friend could not be mistaken, "is indeed Rantor, the greatest navigator in the Three Islands, and doubtless therefore the best in all the Archipelago. Convince him that there is more than madness in your schemes and my patronage is assured."

Hawk's manner changed, becoming politely more

subservient as he turned his attentions to the navigator. Rantor realised that this came hard to the small man, who clearly was not used to pretending subservience to anyone. He must care deeply about the need to enlist the navigator in his cause; Rantor was more impressed by this than by the words themselves.

"Navigator, I apologise for my rudeness. I come from a far island, and I am not used to civilised ways. Also I have spent a long time, and much effort, to reach the ear of the only man who can help me fulfil my dream." Did he mean the duke? Or himself! Rantor pondered. The duke was all powerful here. Yet if the Hawk wished to venture out into the wide ocean, even the duke could not help him without the navigator's approval ...

"It is true, I believe – for very good reasons, I assure you – that our world is finite. But I also believe there is more to our world than an Archipelago."

Ah! the many worlds heresy. That explained the interest of the duke – and why there were no observers present at the meeting.

"But surely, Hawk, we are taught that there is only one Archipelago, set by God in the midst of the eternal ocean. If our Lord were not so generously disposed to his guests, you could find yourself in some discomfort for voicing such heresies."

The duke smiled. "All are free to speak their minds in my domain, Navigator, as well you know." And the duke's domain extended, as Rantor also well knew, only as far as the rule of his arms and the loyalty of his followers. There were priests who ostensibly owed allegiance to the duke, but who would undoubtedly take action against an outspoken heretic, especially an outlander. Even Lord Kyper lacked the power to change the laws on religious matters, in the face of a church which might be subservient in the administration of the Three Islands, but which extended its tentacles throughout the Archipelago, and didn't lack for fanatical followers. It was a wonder this fellow had lived to find his way to the comparative freedom of the Duke's realm.

"My Lord Kyper is indeed a generous host, as well as one possessed of a distinctive sense of humour. He is also aware,

Navigator, that if there is any truth in these heresies, then somebody stands to benefit by it. I have no interest in wealth for myself. As a means to an end, of course, I appreciate its value. But my interest lies in finding out new things, questioning old beliefs, and investigating the world in which we live with an open mind. A navigator such as yourself, whose fame has spread across the Archipelago, must surely share some of those feelings."

"Perhaps." He looked to the duke for approval, and took his slight nod as encouragement to continue.

"I have sailed out of sight of even the farthest islands, and I have seen floating branches and flying birds that might – I only say might – have come from beyond the Archipelago. But to go in search of other islands, other archipelagos, with no safe means of return," he shrugged, "it's more than any competent navigator would risk."

"But suppose there was no risk?" Now they were getting to the point of the meeting. In spite of himself, Rantor felt a stirring of hope in his breast. It was every navigator's dream, and although the chance of it being achieved was tiny, the fruits of the success would be so sweet that any possibility had to be explored.

He was yet young, and he had achieved a great deal. As much as anyone in his profession could achieve. Navigator to the Duke Kyper. What more could he ask? And yet, a restlessness burned within him still, a longing for something – he knew not what. But something to be sure, that could not be found in the Archipelago, for he had sailed the length and breadth of these islands and had yet to find the thing that would give him peace.

"You have a way of navigating beyond the Archipelago?" He made it a question, as desperate not to allow himself to be taken in by any false hopes as he was eager to find those hopes fulfilled. But the little man they called the Hawk had clearly been able to spot, immediately, the true response of the Navigator to even the hint of such an achievement.

It was his turn to smile, "A navigator, indeed. We both want the same thing, if for different reasons. And we can both serve our noble lord well, while following our own dreams. Yes, Navigator Rantor, I have a means to sail beyond the Archipelago, and find our way back again. How far we can sail, and what we might find, only God can say." The smile suggested that Hawk trusted more in the ability of himself and a human navigator than in the whim of God. "But I am sure the journey will be worthwhile, and with our lord's permission, I will explain."

The duke nodded. "With the understanding, Navigator, that none of this passes your lips outside these walls."

And so the Hawk had outlined his strange ideas for the first time. Since then, in many conversations, he had elaborated his dreams and his plans, until Rantor came almost to believe in them himself, just as he had grown to like the little man and to admire him for his strange genius. Whatever came out of this mission, he was sure, the Three Islands would never be the same again.

But still, the ideas were so strange; and having no one to discuss them with, except the Hawk, who had utter faith in his own beliefs, Rantor sometimes wondered if there might be flaws he lacked the wit to perceive, or whether he really understood at all. He'd give a lot to discuss the strange philosophy with a sympathetic priest – but pick the wrong priest to open his mouth to, and the price might be his life. Instead, lacking anyone to confide in but himself, he rehearsed the Hawk's strange image of the world in his mind, as he headed briskly for the workshop where, if all went well, he would see proof of this man's genius at work.

As a navigator, Rantor knew his geometry and trigonometry. From his own experience, not just the word of the priests or of the books they kept so closely to themselves, he knew that the sun did indeed shine down vertically on every island in the Archipelago. Of course, he had never felt any inclinations to make measurements, but all his own experience told him that when the priests – or Hawk – said that those measurements always showed the sun to be precisely at the zenith, they were speaking truly. An ordinary man might have trouble grasping the implication, but Rantor understood the nature of parallel lines. Parallel lines meet only at infinity. If the Sun were any reasonable distance above the flat plane of the world, then careful measurements and triangulation, the same techniques used in navigation, would reveal its height above the islands. For it to always appear vertically above any spot in the Archipelago, it must lie at an infinite height above the flat world. So much was clear. But what else could be inferred from the observation?

He smiled to himself as he recalled the one occasion that he had – almost – discomfited Hawk with his navigational skills. Few people could think in terms of three dimensions, living as they did, on a flat plane. Bur the navigator had always enjoyed abstract mathematics. As he had pointed out to Hawk, some philosophers had noted that the sun *could* appear vertically above every point on the world if the world formed the inner surface of a hollow sphere, with the sun at its centre. For a moment, even Hawk had been at a loss for words, struck by a novel concept. At least the mathematicians of the Three Islands had some tricks they could teach him! But then, his mind bright as ever, he had spotted the flaws in the argument with impressive speed. If the world was round, the Archipelago was lying at the bottom of the equivalent of a huge shallow valley. All the waters of the world would pour downwards, flooding the islands completely. The Sun itself would fall from the sky, following the natural tendency of things to seek the lowest point. It was merely a pretty piece of geometry, no more practical in its applications than Artemis's theorem of prime numbers, no more meaningful than the negative square root of a quadratic equation; a clever parlour trick. Indeed, the Sun *must* be at infinite distance, if this were the only alternative! A beautiful example of the doctrine of the absurd alternative – if two alternatives purported to resolve the same problem, but one 'solution' was clearly absurd, therefore the second, however unlikely it might seem in everyday terms, must be the correct solution.

The priests taught, of course, that the world itself must also be infinite in extent, a flat plane extending eternally in all directions, a featureless ocean surrounding the Archipelago. Logic then dictated that there must be only one Archipelago, created by God as a home for man. In an infinite ocean, there could in principle exist an infinite number of Archipelagos, with infinite varieties of life upon them. This was clearly absurd. So the logicians argued that there must either be many worlds, or that the Archipelago was unique – since the fact of their existence proved the Archipelago to be real, even to philosophers. If there were infinite numbers of archipelagos, many worlds, man would occupy no special place in creation, and could not represent God's work. So, the priests reasoned there was only one Archipelago. Only heretics argued otherwise.

But Hawk claimed that the lights seen in the night sky from time to time were other worlds, like the world of the Archipelago. If so, they could not be infinite in extent, for if they were, either they would fill the sky and block out the light of the sun, or their infinite planes would intersect the plane of the world. If they were finite worlds, islands in the sky, then the world of the Archipelago might also be finite. And in a finite ocean there might exist a finite number of Archipelagos, without running into the problems with infinities that plagued philosophers and tipped reasonable speculation into heresy.

Rantor shook his head, muttering wordlessly to himself as he strode along. To the Hawk, it seemed clear that an intersection of infinite worlds would be obvious to the inhabitants of the Archipelago; but the navigator was not sure. In an infinite world, an infinite number of other worlds could intersect its plane, and still the nearest intersection might be infinitely far away from the Archipelago. And if the lights were other worlds, what stopped them from falling onto the world? The Sun might well be falling. At infinite distance, it could fall forever and still get no closer to the Archipelago. But other worlds – finite worlds – floating like saucers in the sky?

The thought made his head spin. He pushed it to one side. Besides it was of no practical importance. Nobody suggested they might voyage to the worlds of those lights in the sky! Hawk's plan was crazy, but not that crazy. If the priests were wrong about the infinite extent of the world, Hawk argued, then they might be wrong in teaching that there was only one Archipelago. The fact that the Archipelago existed proved that there were islands, and life, in the world. And if one Archipelago could exist why not others? The other worlds Hawk sought were only (only!) other archipelagos existing on the flat ocean of the world.

Rantor had doubts about the argument, though he was willing to take a reasonable risk on the off chance of finding new islands to trade with. He was also more than willing to follow up any prospect of a technique to navigate out of sight of land, out of feel of the sea breeze, and land breeze, and to find his way back, not just to the Archipelago but to any island of his choice, infallibly. It would make his master, the duke, rich beyond compare, and some of the riches would rub off on him. And it would render established patterns of naval warfare obsolete overnight. If it worked.

Darkness came with its usual suddenness, although a few smoky torches had been lit in anticipation. The night glow, though something less than full darkness, such as you would experience in a closed room, was hardly sufficient light for any human being to see more than the vague shadows of buildings. Just ahead, the workshop that had been given over to the Hawk and his works stood out from its surroundings, lit up by the experimental gas lanterns that enabled the Hawk to work such long hours, and were the reason why he had been allocated that particular building for his efforts. Rantor frowned slightly at the sight. To someone who depended on the safety of a wooden-walled ship for his trade – and his life – fire was a mixed blessing. Wooden houses and warehouses were scarcely any less at risk. To be sure, the duke's artisans had been ingenious in devising this practical use of manure from the farms and from the earth closets of the town. Rut if they were to light more than a few buildings with the natural gas there would be no fertiliser left for the fields. No, gas lighting would remain a trick used only for special needs. And special needs, on the Archipelago, generally involved ships. Somewhere, somehow, some no good would come of this gas, Rantor was sure. But in the meantime, it meant he could attend Hawk's discreet demonstration at a time when most law abiding citizens were at home, or at least safely shut away in some comforting tavern. When the sun went out, it was far too dark to be wandering the streets.

Just before he entered the building, the navigator paused, shading his eyes and looking upward into the blackness, seeking a glimpse of the lights which Hawk set such store by.

Of course, it was useless, his eyes were not dark-adapted, and even under ideal conditions, from the deck of a ship at sea, the lights never showed as more than a dim phosphorescence against the all embracing blackness of the sky.

Hawk was waiting for him, impatiently tinkering with the complex apparatus that spilled over two tables and out onto the floor at one end of the long gallery. His two assistants stood, nervously to one side. Armed guards, Rantor knew, filled the building. But all that mattered was Hawk himself and his strange experiment.

The tinkering stopped. "You are alone, Navigator?"

"Who else did you expect?"

"I thought … but …"

Rantor smiled. "I have the authority, Hawk, never fear. Persuade me that your trick works, and our lord will not gainsay my decision. He would not risk a valuable ship on such an errand without his best navigator, but if the navigator approves, then the ship sails."

"I suppose that's good." The Hawk's sharp mind had instantly appraised the situation. "Our Lord Kyper is an intelligent man, but he is an administrator, a soldier. It should be easier to make you understand, and then …" His voice tailed off. So much of his life had been leading up to this moment that the Hawk, for all his wit, clearly had little or no idea what would happen next. He would be in the hands of the navigator, embarking on a voyage into the unknown.

"Well, this is it." He gestured at the complex web of apparatus. "Don't worry about the details. Just watch." He nodded at the assistants, one of whom promptly moved to a bank of large glass jars, and stood poised to turn what looked like a small capstan.

Hawk continued to talk. "At this end of the room, we make artificial lightning. It's been done before but not on this scale. But down there," he pointed along the gallery, "is something completely new, the sensor. When we make lightning here," pointing back to the main bank of apparatus, "the sensor responds. Come with me and see."

Following Hawk's lead, Rantor walked along the gallery. The sensor seemed a lot simpler than the lightning machine, which was just as well, since this was the equipment he was supposed to take to sea. The most prominent feature was a pair of metal spheres, about a thumb in diameter, almost touching one another. The whole apparatus, lightning machine and sensor, seemed, Rantor realised, incredibly profligate with metal. The value of the equipment would be more than the value of his own ship. The extent of the duke's commitment, and the implications of failure after such an investment, seemed to cause a pricking of the hair at the back of his neck.

"Perhaps you can feel the lightning in the air." So it wasn't fear! The Navigator smiled at his own foolishness.

"We can begin. Watch the gap between the two spheres." Hawk raised his right hand, and let it fall in a dramatic, clearly prearranged, signal to his assistants. At the far end of the gallery, one of them began to turn the small capstan. Immediately there was a crack, like thunder. In spite of Hawk's injunction, Rantor looked towards the sound at the far end of the room. A flash, like lightning, accompanied another thunderous crack, clearly somehow controlled by the turning of the wheel. Remembering his instructions, Rantor turned back to the apparatus before him. As the thunder continued, each crack was accompanied by tiny sparks leaping across the gap between the two spheres. The lightning at the far end of the gallery was being reproduced, in miniature, at the sensor!

Hawk raised his hand again, the noise and the flashes stopped. He shrugged. "We can only keep it up for a short time, with this equipment. But the full scale apparatus will he more effective."

"This is just a model?"

"Of course. I'm planning to build the real thing in the castle, high up. With your approval, and Duke Kyper's permission, of course."

"But how does it work?"

"The details are not important. It has to do with what I call the law of similarities. You will see that the construction of the sensor follows the pattern of the lightning generator. The morphology is crucial. When the lightning surges in the generator, there is a resonance in the sensor. The construction must be perfect, but when it is, we have the effect you see. I call it morphic resonance."

Rantor was intrigued. He studied the strange shapes of the small machine before him, then walked along the gallery to compare the image in his mind with the structure of the lightning generator itself.

"And that is all?"

"Not quite all. The sensor could not respond at a distance, even if it were a perfect resonator, without being primed. When set to receive, the resonant sensor is in a state where it is almost ready to make its own sparks of lightning, spontaneously. It has the potentiality to make sparks. The resonance does no more than tip the balance."

Rantor paid little attention to the words. As his initial surprise receded, he began to concentrate on the practicalities that concerned him.

"An impressive trick, Hawk. Everything you promised. Our lord will be pleased. But how do you intend to use the trick in navigation?"

The little man smiled. "It's wonderfully simple. Navigator. In my studies in my home island, before – well before ..." Just how and why Hawk had left his home Rantor had yet to discover, though it was natural that anyone with a scheme to make money would gravitate to the Three Islands and the court of Duke Kyper, "... I worked on an even smaller scale than you see here, but I discovered a curious thing, a way to shield the resonator from the lightning. A metal screen – it need not be solid metal, just a mesh – placed between the generator and the sensor prevents the resonance. Now, it seems to me that a navigator on a ship at sea, equipped with a resonator and a screen, need only move the screen around to find out which side of the sensor it blocks the lightning. And that must be the direction the resonance is coming from – the way home!"

He stopped triumphantly, Rantor thought; less impressed than, it seemed, the Hawk expected. It might work. Of course, it would be different, on the heaving deck of a ship, out of sight of land. But, yes, it might work. You could even rig a little circular track, for a truck like the ones used by the shipwrights in the yards, with the screen mounted on it. With stout hands at the ropes, and a good pulley system, you could run the shield around from place to place – well, no doubt any competent captain could attend to such details.

"Metal stops the ah, resonance, you say?"

Hawk nodded.

"But not stone?"

"No, no effect at all."

"So we can keep the generator securely shut away from prying eyes. Is there any limit to the resonance?"

Hawk shrugged. "That is for us to find out. Before I came here, with a smaller model, the sensor worked at a distance of seven hundred paces, through several intervening houses. At sea – over greater distances – who knows?"

"But even if it works as you hope, how long can the generator operate? How can the navigator at sea be sure to be seeking the signal at the right time?"

"A simple matter. We choose a time that cannot be mistaken – dawn perhaps. Every day at dawn, the generator runs for as long as possible. Every day at dawn the navigator has his bearing. All he has to do is hold a true course through the day."

The navigator smiled. An easy enough task, he said quickly. It almost made you wonder why the dukes and lords bothered to cosset their navigators so. In fact, it would tax his skills to the utmost to make effective use of this trick. Which, to be sure, was one reason why he found the prospect so appealing.

Rantor was used to making decisions, and acting on them. He clapped Hawk on the shoulder.

"We will find out, Hawk, just how simple a task it proves. The duke has put a new ship, the *Far Trader*, at my disposal. A two decker sixty paces long. You can get your sensor aboard tomorrow, I trust? And then we'll see what it can do."

"Tomorrow! Why, we can start now – my assistants know what to do –"

"And can they see in the dark like cats?" Rantor laughed. Tomorrow will do, my friend, but meanwhile, I know an inn, indeed, more than one inn, not far from here. If you would care to join me?"

Stepping out into the darkness of the street, blinded by the change from the gas jet inside, Rantor stumbled and grasped at the wall for support.

"Damned torches. Always let you down when you need them, Hawk. Your next job ought to be to find a way to make that lightning generator of yours provide a steady glow. Then we could –" He turned at a sound behind them, hand moving to his sword. "Hold! Behind me. Hawk."

Idiot! Of course those torches hadn't burnt out yet, in this quarter of the dock patrolled by the Duke's men. Somebody was out there – somebody with eyes well adapted to the dark.

He drew the sword, edging backwards as he became aware of three – no four – shadowy figures confronting him.

"In the duke's name! I am the navigator, Rantor. Anyone who harms me, or my companion, will answer to Lord Kyper."

Surely nobody could be so foolish? Rantor himself represented the Duke's most valued possession. No rival lord would harm or kidnap the navigator; several might like to, but that would give the Duke his excuse to crush the opponent foolhardy enough to take such action, picking off his adversaries one by one, before they could organise against him. All the lesser lords would support the Duke in any action he took in defence of the navigator. Without navigation the Archipelago would cease to be civilised.

The figures moved, two straight for him, one to either side. Professionals. No chance, four against one, but they'd know they'd been in a fight. The sword flicked out, met another blade, parried. And swung to the side, striking at the second swordsman. Rantor felt the jar as it stabbed through flesh and jolted along bone. But before he could withdraw to strike again, two of the hooded figures held him in their grasp. The fourth had the terrified Hawk, who had taken no part in the action, at sword point.

Only now did one of his two captors speak, as the other bound Rantor's hands.

"My apologies, Navigator. We intend you no harm, but it seems expedient to borrow you for a while. It is your companion whose services we seek, and whose activities are of interest to our lord."

The second man turned his attention to his wounded

companion who was leaning against the wall, holding his cloak against his side. They spoke briefly, then the wounded man moved off slowly into the night, staying close by the wall. Their remaining captors rushed Rantor and Hawk back towards the workshop entrance, swords prominently displayed. In the doorway, a flash of reflected light showed where the guards, belatedly aroused by the scuffle, waited.

The same man, clearly the leader of the band, spoke up again.

"Guard! We have your navigator, the esteemed Rantor, as you see. Duke Kyper would surely wish no harm to befall such a valuable servant! Give us access for a few minutes, and he will be released unharmed."

The navigator fumed inwardly. It would work, he knew. No soldier would risk the Duke's wrath by allowing Rantor to be harmed. Whatever their orders concerning the Hawk and his toys, the guards would only move against the kidnappers if there was no risk to Rantor. Not for the first time, he cursed his privileged position.

Inside, disarmed, bound, and with cold steel held to his throat, he could only watch, helplessly, as the first raider examined the impressive collection of apparatus, Hawk's lightning generator, at the near end of the gallery.

Outside, a creak of harness and a snuffle of horses indicated the arrival of more raiders, with transport. They intended, Rantor realised, to take the generator with them. Nothing could be done, unless the guards were willing to risk his life. For a moment he thought of flinging himself on a sword. If he were dead, the guards would have to act. But it was true – he was worth more than Hawk and his apparatus, quite apart from his reluctance to end his own life. But perhaps there was a way.

He flung up his arms, bound as they were, crying "Hawk!" At that movement, the knife of his captor pressed more closely against his throat, drawing a red line of blood. "Do as they command." Emphasising his words he dropped his arms back downward, clumsily, but consciously echoing Hawk's earlier signal to his men. The pressure at his throat eased.

"Or you will never see another dawn. Do you understand? Take your machine, and use it as they command. This navigator is indeed worth more to our lord than you and all your toys. Is everything still in place?"

The bright, darting look of an intelligent bird was back in Hawk's eyes. As Rantor had hoped, he turned and walked back towards the generator, and made a show of inspecting it closely.

"Yes. Navigator, everything is here. All in working order."

"Then let us go." The chief raider spoke abruptly. Two other cloaked and hooded men had entered the room. He gestured at the generator, and at Hawk. "Take everything, and him. The brave navigator," he raised his voice to the guards lined against the wall opposite, "stays with us for a while. If no one follows, he will be released. Otherwise, your Duke can seek another to guide his ships."

"Oh yes lord, I'm certain enough."

The navigator, unable to contain himself, strode impatiently to and fro across the large room, slapping his thigh with the gloves he carried in his right hand. He was dangerously close to insubordination, but the Duke had to permit him to act. He had played the coward intentionally, planning to rescue Hawk and his lightning machine and to strike a blow for the ruler of the Three Islands. If Duke Kyper's caution prevented him from moving, the story of his desertion of a servant in his charge would ring round the fleets of the world.

He stopped pacing, and faced the Duke squarely across the table, hands resting flat on the surface. "They were Ballestre's men. I know their ship, and I can find the Hawk. He will voice a public protest and you will be free to slap Ballestre down. No one will interfere. Not Falco, nor Langan. You will have proven just cause."

"And if you fail to find Hawk, but Ballestre finds you adventuring in his domain, then he will have just cause against me. Falco and Langan will side with him; others too, perhaps, while the lesser islands hold back."

"But if you take no action, sire? This time, you have lost little. The machine is probably worthless; Hawk is a fool – you said so. But if word gets out that a raider from a Ballestre ship can take his pick of the property of Lord Kyper, in the middle of his own shipyard?"

The Duke looked steadily at his navigator.

"You are so sure then, that Hawk and his toys are worthless?"

Against that steely gaze, Rantor wilted.

"Lord, I ..."

"And you would take such risks, solely for the honour of the Three Islands, and yourself?"

There was nothing more to say. Rantor felt a glow of triumph. The Duke might banter, but he was going to agree!

"How many men do you need?"

"Forty, fifty at most. The new ship, the *Far Trader*; and those two assistants Hawk was training."

"And your plan?"

He shook his head. "Forgive me, Lord. I fear that there are spies in out midst. How else could those raiders have known where and when to strike? But have faith, and in a fiveday, perhaps two, I shall return Hawk to you and give you just cause to strike at Ballestre. After that, no island will dare to cross you.

Far Trader slid slowly towards the beach, sails furled, under muffled oars only. At this time, just before dawn, the breeze was off the land. It would stay that way for some time after the sun began to stir, ideal for their escape. After six days, cruising slowly along these shores in the dark, and further out to sea in the early part of the day, the Navigator had a clear idea of the position of the Hawk. The hours spent closeted below decks seemed to have paid off, but his men knew only that he had the information required. The rumour below decks was that he had a spy in the enemy camp. He had encouraged the rumour, and his obvious confidence had encouraged the faith in both the rumour and himself.

Ballestre had, if Rantor was correct, chosen a good place for his captive to work. The isolated watch tower was far enough from the town that any untoward events would cause no damage – Rantor remembered some of the mishaps in the early days of the gas lighting experiments and approved of such caution. The tower was also far from the harbour, up a steep path. No attack from that direction could possibly take its garrison by surprise. It was, however, vulnerable from another direction. A small landing party, in the bay around the headland, could approach the tower from the rear – if, that is, any such raiding party had reason to suspect the activities now going on there. Ballestre had taken pains to ensure that no hint of those activities had leaked out. But he was in for a surprise.

"This will do." Rantor spoke quietly, but without whispering. The captain nodded, and gave the necessary order in an equally matter-of-fact voice. The chain of command was clear, and established by long practice. The navigator decided what to do, where to go, and when. The captain decided how to do it, and ran the ship. If a navigator asked the impossible, or demanded a course that would lead his ship into danger, a captain might refuse and argue his case later with the Duke. But this was almost unheard of. Navigators didn't get to be navigators by taking unnecessary risks.

A single anchor at the stern held the ship with the bows pointing seaward in the light breeze. With the oars shipped, two boats were lowered into the water.

"Pull." A single word sent the laden boats scudding into land. With two men left to guard them, Rantor had just fifteen at his back as he led the way up the slope to the tower. They stopped in the cover of a small copse, perhaps a hundred paces from the target. The ground between was scrubby. Sloppy work, thought Rantor, as he checked out a possible way forward. At a gesture, two bowmen and two others, with ropes coiled over their shoulders, stepped forward. Wordlessly, Rantor pointed a way forward, from cover to cover. Then he pointed up to the top of the tower, ten span above their heads. The four nodded and moved swiftly forward, lost in the darkness and the bushes.

The sound of the two grappling hooks biting into the top of the tower was swiftly followed by the twang of two bows and a stifled cry – as, if all had gone to plan, the sentries drawn by the noise of the grapples had been picked off from the roof.

Waving his men on, Rantor ran forward and began to swarm up one of the ropes.

The action was over in minutes. It was still dark as the party returned to the boats, carrying one dead, two wounded, and the large glass jars which Hawk insisted they could not leave without. The burdens slowed them down more than Rantor expected; in addition, someone had been left at the tower with his wits about him, and sufficiently unscathed to mount the stairs of the tower. The boats were still pulling hard for the *Far Trader* when an orange glow appeared on the headland. First a mere flicker of flame, but soon burgeoning into a leaping pillar of light. Cursing, the navigator exhorted the already straining men at the oars to pull harder. Even as they came alongside the ship, however, he knew that Ballestre's vessels, in the harbour round the headland, would already be bustling with life and preparing for action. It would be nip and tuck. Just let *Far Trader* get to seaward of Ballestre's ships, and he was sure the captain would show them a clear pair of heels. But if they were cut off …

"Abandon the boats." Captain Bryon was clearly aware of the need for haste. "Cut the cable. Get those men onto the deck. And all sail." This with a glance back towards the dark land behind him, not so much to see the land as to feel the dying breeze on his cheek, gauging how much life there was left in it. Just let them get to seaward of the fleet, and with the sun bringing the sea breeze onto the land nobody would ever catch the *Far Trader*. Scarcely twenty leagues away, through the doldrums, the welcoming breeze onto the land would usher them swiftly home to the Three Islands.

"Careful there!" Hawk's cry came as a stumbling seaman threatened to drop one of his jars. "Put it here, on the deck. Navigator," he turned, "it was brilliantly done. I take it the sensor worked?" They clasped hands, sharing their delight in the brief lull while the captain prepared the ship for action.

"Beautifully. Oh," a dismissive wave, "I don't say we didn't have some troubles. But your assistants are well trained. Every dawn, as we patrolled, they found your signal. The direction finding is poor, but with three successive bearings, why even the most unlikely 'prentice navigator could have pinned you down to the headland – and there is only one place on the headland where you could have been. My only concern was that you would misunderstand my intentions, or be unable to persuade your temporary master to allow you to experiment."

Hawk laughed. "No fear of that. They'd have had me at work night and day, once I let on that I was developing a technique to turn rock into metal. Duke Ballestre is a greedy man. But I persuaded him that my method depended on striking a resonance with the newborn Sun – and also, of course, that it required some separation from the centre of the town. I had those soldiers of his fair jumping every time I shouted 'frog'; but tell me," his voice changed as he looked about, "we are still in danger, are we not?"

Rantor, also suddenly grave, looked about the darkened ship, where only a few faint lights relieved the gloom. The headland must be there – his sense of direction seldom failed him, even in the pitch of night – sure enough, just beyond he caught a quick flash of light, then a second. He nodded at his companion.

"Grave danger, friend. On the open sea, no ship could find us, or board, at night. But here, with only one clear channel, they can feel their way out," he nodded forward to where a stocky sailor was coiling a long line, attached to a stone, ready to throw it over the side to gauge the depth of the water, "and cut us off. A little longer, half a candle or less, and we might have been clear. As it is ..." he shrugged.

"Perhaps I can help. Your captain – is he a good man? Will he follow my advice?"

"Bryon? We've often sailed together. If I give the word, he would sail into the maelstrom itself. But if you have a plan, be quick about it, for time is short indeed."

Three ships, their riding lights clear, blocked the channel ahead of the *Far Trader*. Ahead, tantalisingly close, lay the open sea, and freedom.

Backing her oars, *Far Trader* slowed almost to a halt, but continued to drift slowly down on the ships. At the word of command, she could surge forward – to certain destruction, or if the other ships allowed her, to an instant escape. The catapults were wound and armed, but they were inaccurate weapons at best in broad daylight. Naval engagements were settled by boarding and hand-to-hand fighting. Besides, it was one against three.

"Yield! Yield or suffer the consequences!" Astonishingly, the cry came from Captain Bryon, at the bow of the ship.

There was a brief silence. Were they stunned by his audacity? Or simply sorting out seniority among the gaggle of seamen, soldiers and civil administrators aboard the craft? Bryon pressed home his slender, momentary advantage.

"We have the Hawk. And his weapon. Yield, or we will use it."

At last, the reply came. But it lacked the confident tone of Bryon.

"There is no weapon. We have the advantage and you must yield to us. We have no reason to fear you."

The Hawk, busy at the bows of the *Far Trader* with his two assistants and a mess of equipment, centred around those glass jars he treasured so much, nodded to the captain. With the slow forward way still on her, *Far Trader* was scarcely a stone's throw from the ships blocking the path. The navigator, in the waist of the ship, murmured a quick "Ready" to the oarsmen. At the bow, Bryon raised his voice again.

"We will give you one chance. Our Hawk commands the lightning. One time, and one time only, he will demonstrate his power. Then you must yield, and follow us to the Three Islands. Or be struck down where you lie."

He raised his right hand. "Be warned, you doubters!" He let it fall. There was a brilliant flash from the bows, a shaft of lightning fully a span in length, arcing and wriggling across the bows, almost touching the nearest Ballestre vessel. A strange pungent smell, a smell of lightning, drifted back. Cries of alarm came from the ships ahead, as their oarsmen, unbidden, began to back water. A gap appeared.

"Now!" cried the navigator, and the disciplined oarsmen of the *Far Trader* laid to their task. The ship shot for the gap, and was through in two strokes. Three, and there was clear water behind her; four, five and she was away, in the dying sea breeze, heading for open ocean. With the oarsmen given strength by the thrill of their success, and their opponents thrown into disarray, however temporarily, their safety was assured.

Forgetting his dignity, the navigator ran forward to where the Hawk glumly surveyed the wreckage of the equipment. Oblivious to the congratulations being showered upon him, he looked up only at Rantor's hail.

"Well done. Oh, well done indeed. This story will be told in all the ports on the Archipelago! The night the Hawk brought down the lightning!"

"Aye, but at what cost?" Hawk indicated the wreckage of the equipment, metal melted into fantastic shapes. The small sphere from the sensor, unrecognisably distorted: glass jars broken.

At Hawk's feet, a half-sphere of metal, about the size of a cupped fist, rocked slightly with the motion of the ship. It was part of one of the larger spheres, come apart around its seam. He picked it up, holding it in the palm of one hand. At the bottom of the hemisphere, a small puddle of water had collected from the spray; following the natural tendency of things to seek the lowest point, it sloshed to and fro as Hawk swayed with the roll of the ship. He inverted the hemisphere, and the water fell out on to the deck. Miserably, he offered the useless object to Rantor.

"This is ruined, and the rest has been left behind. Years of work."

"But you have your life, Hawk, and your liberty. Never fear for these trifles. Ballestre is disgraced, by your testimony, and our Lord Kyper will he generous in gratitude. This ship will be fitted out with all that you require, and together we will sail beyond the Archipelago, sure of finding our way home. What sights we shall see, Hawk, if your philosophising is correct, and what riches we shall bring back!"

His enthusiastic excitement roused Hawk from his gloom. "You really think so? It isn't an unmitigated disaster after all?"

"Oh no, my friend. At last I know what my life has been leading up to and where I am going. You have given me a new sense of direction and I thank you for it."

As if to emphasise his words, the sun high over their heads lit up in its usual manner. It was dawn; the dawn of a new era for the navigators of the Archipelago.

Patterns of impulses raced at the speed of light through an alien mind, collating, observing, interpreting. Especially observing; that had been the task of the mind since time immemorial. Responding to ancient imperative, the observer watched, and waited, patient as only inorganic intelligence could be, for the signs it had been programmed to detect.

The disturbances caused by the lightning generator had briefly held its attention. Weak, erratic and probably natural disturbances in the electromagnetic spectrum, coming from the region of a small group of islands in the southern hemisphere. They contained no information though, and they stopped after a few cycles of light and dark. They were not the signs of intelligence that the observer was programmed to recognise. It felt no disappointment. This was far from being the first time that some temporary change in environmental conditions had suggested, erroneously, that the long wait was over, and besides the observer was not programmed for emotions. The incident was noted for comparison and cross-correlation with future disturbances. The observer went about its business quietly, calmly, as it had done for millennia past.

The Best is Yet to Be

David blinked, and stumbled slightly. A momentary disorientation; nowhere near as bad as he'd feared. He was in a dimly lit room. Alone – a weight lifted from his mind and he relaxed slightly. That had been their biggest fear, that he would appear in the middle of a crowd and create a panic.

He stiffened again as a door opened. But carefully prepared phrases died on his lips as a little old lady walked carefully, with the aid of a single stick, into the room. She smiled, as if in recognition.

"Well, David. Punctual, as ever." She linked her free arm through his while he was still groping for a response. "Come, my dear. We have been waiting to see you. But there is so little time."

The firmness of her grip on his arm, and the way she directed him towards and through the open door, belied her appearance of frailty. But what the hell was going on? His arrival seemed to be anticipated. That must mean his mission was a success! He'd got – would get – back OK, and would go down in history. This must be some kind of official reception. Who would've thought it!

But the crowded room he was led into lacked any trappings of officialdom. It looked more like a wedding feast, or an anniversary celebration – a family reunion. A burst of applause greeted him, and a rustle of sound. "It *is* him!" "Just like his pictures." "Isn't she brave?"

The old woman led him to a table where two younger, but still elderly, men stood. They smiled, a little more uncomfortable than the woman, it seemed, and offered their hands, which he shook in turn.

"But what? Who are you?"

She shook her head, and reached up to place a finger on his lips.

"No time for questions, David. You will have all the answers soon. There is no time at all." Was that a tear, glinting in her eyes, in spite of the smile? "But I wanted you to meet my family. My children," she indicated the two men, "grandchildren, and their own families." Her manner became more serious. "David, you must remember two things. First, the date." He'd forgotten! Hadn't even tried to find out! So much for his perfect memory. But she'd understood. The smile returned. "Don't worry David, everything is fine. The date is April 27, 2193, Old Style. I *know* you won't forget. And the other thing you must remember is, the best is yet to come."

She stood on tiptoe to kiss him lightly on the cheek. As she did so, in response to the signal, the assembled company raised their glasses in a toast. "David and Maria!" Who on Earth was Maria? He was beginning to get his bearings now. Time to start asking questions.

The disorientation was the same. It only *felt* worse, he grimly told himself, because he hadn't been expecting it. That was why the old lady had been in such a hurry. She'd known. Well, here he was back in the lab. Not much to report, but not bad for a first attempt. He opened his eyes.

It was the same room as before, but this time sunlight streamed in through the windows. Late evening – but *which year?* He turned slowly. On the other side of the room, carefully placed to be out of his line of vision when he opened his eyes (no, the thought was paranoid; he suppressed it) was a table set for two. The same old lady sat at one of the places, smiling at him. He blinked in the sunlight. Or was she the same? He took a step forward; her sister, perhaps, or … her younger self!

The panic began to return. Something had gone wrong. It should have been a straightforward trip up and back. No detours, according to Roger's calculations.

"Welcome, David." The soft voice soothed his worries. "Won't you join me?" She indicated the second chair. "We have time for a meal, and I can answer some of your questions. But we only have a couple of hours, and it is best if we make a beginning."

Almost in a dream, he took the offered seat and looked across the table at her. She smiled – the same smile.

"Yes, David, it is me. If I were twenty years younger – but

then, I did." The eyes sparkled mischievously. "This time, we must make do with food, and wine, and company. I think I've chosen some things you will like."

He surveyed the table. She certainly had. He couldn't have chosen better for himself. Somebody round here clearly knew a lot about his taste – and it was equally clear who that somebody was.

"Who are you?"

"My name is Maria. And I know all about you. David. Our lives are inextricably linked, for better or worse. And so far, I think for the better. For you, the best is yet to come."

He shook his head, confused. "You said that before."

"Did I? It used to be one of our favourite old poems. But your before, David, is my future. You mean, I *will* say it, again. How nice.

"But, of course, you have begun to realise what is going on, haven't you? So, eat and drink while I fill in the gaps. I'm afraid I no longer have much of an appetite, at my age, for many things."

He nibbled at the food, and drank a little more wine than he had intended, while she talked. Her voice was soothing. He could have listened to her for hours, and she seemed almost to read his mind. Half questions and interruptions to her explanations were met with clear and polished responses. So Roger had been half right, at least. The technique had worked, and David had gone forward, further than they'd dared hope, all the way to 2193 (Old Style, whatever that meant; he made a mental note to check when and how the calendar had been changed). But the process had set up a tension in the time continuum, and he'd been snapped back, almost immediately. Roger had suspected the possibility, which was why he'd been so insistent on David finding out the date before all else – and why he'd picked David, with his almost perfect recall, from the half dozen candidates ready and willing to make the first time trip. *But,* and this was the point Maria was emphasising, he had only been snapped back part of the way. After a few minutes in her future, he'd been pulled back across twenty odd years to her now. Only part of the time tension had been released, but enough to give him a few hours respite before, if he understood her correctly, he continued his journey back.

"No David, *not* all the way back. I don't understand the technicalities, but I know exactly when you will return, and for how long. I will always be there, with you. Each time you get closer to your starting date, you will have longer to rest before the tension stretches to breaking point again. This time, we have only a few minutes left – long enough, perhaps, for coffee and brandy. Then you will leave me. I know the exact time, because you will tell me. It is now 9:15, and you will remember that, along with the date I gave you earlier. You told me, more than twenty years ago, that I would serve coffee at 9:15. So, here it is. I wish I could go with you – but that is silly. I *will* be with you. I *was* with you. Things will be easier for you now that you know what is happening, and you will have at least a few weeks to adjust. Farewell, David."

Her timing was almost perfect. His hand hadn't quite reached the brandy glass when the chair beneath him disappeared and he collapsed in a heap on the floor. Whew. Certainly not ready for that one, he told himself seriously. Time travel and alcohol definitely don't mix.

"David!" Soft hands helped him to his feet. "Are you all right? I didn't know what to expect. It is you, really you?"

But she was beautiful! He held her at arms length. Was *this* his little old lady? "Maria?"

"Am I so different, David?" She lowered her eyes, and, he was sure, blushed. "It's been nearly ten years, but you look younger than ever. But no –" a hand flew to her mouth "– when you last saw me, I must have been quite an old lady."

"You look wonderful." Was it the wine? Or the shock? Why did he suddenly feel so good? She stepped forward, into his arms, and tilted her face up to be kissed. He responded, enthusiastically. This was crazy! She must be at least ten years older than him, and he hardly knew her, and what he did know of her was when she was older still, and besides ...

"You really never did that before?" He shook his head, then, realising that she couldn't see, lying as she was nestled in the crook of his arm, he spoke aloud. "No. I was waiting for the right partner. For you."

She smiled, and wriggled even closer, "Then I am not too bad, for an old lady."

"You're wonderful. I never imagined – but I never would have – I mean, the disorientation. And the wine. I never would have been so bold –"

"So. You need to be drunk before you make love to an old lady of forty-two." She nibbled, exquisitely, at the base of his neck, while sliding her hand down his belly. "I'll remember that!"

"No! Maria, I didn't mean –" He stopped. My God. She *would* remember, and twenty years from now she would ply him with wine and relax him with conversation over dinner, in order to lower his inhibitions and pave the way for his seduction by her younger self. And she was right. He might have spent his life primly waiting for the right partner, unless somebody who knew him well had set him up like this. The wandering hand and nibbling lips began to distract him from this train of thought. No wonder the little old lady had such a twinkle in her eye when she told him the best was yet to come! He scarcely heard Maria murmuring in his ear. "One day, David, you will know how much it means to me that I was the first love in your life." But the words stuck, in that almost perfect memory.

They had nearly five weeks together, scarcely leaving the house, while David adjusted to his new reality. Maria refused to explain much more than he already knew. Next time, she insisted, he would have years, not weeks, in which to find the answers to his questions. She would be there, and she would be younger than him. What more could he want than a rejuvenated version of what she described as her "poor old body"?

The children were away, with relatives. She had no financial worries, she explained, because "the foundation" looked after the family. He never asked about the father of the children. There was no need. Maria was happy to have him for a few weeks, and there was no point in calling up memories that might be best left buried, for now. He dutifully memorised dates and times, and passed on to her the dates of their rendezvous in the future. He once found her crying over a large, brown book – a diary or ledger of some kind – but she brushed away the tears, locked away the book, and refused to discuss what was upsetting her.

Occasionally, he tried to work out how the timeslips were occurring, and where – when – the next one might take him. But Roger was the mathematician on the team, and without Roger there was no real hope of anything other than an empirical rule of thumb. If the slips were linear, and the stays were growing exponentially, he might go back another twenty years and stay there – then! – for ten. But after that, things would begin to get complicated. He doubted very much if he would ever get back to his own time.

He was deep in these deliberations when Maria came in from the garden, carrying a bunch of spring flowers. She sat beside him. He put his arm round her and they kissed, contentedly.

"This is our last day, David."

He sat up straight. "Why didn't you warn me?"

"Would it have made things any easier?"

He shook his head.

"I have a few things to tell you. Most important, the date on which your next visit – your previous visit – you know what I mean. The date on which you left me, last time. Next time, for you. I was much younger than you then. You will be, at last, the master in your own house. And you must be very gentle with me, David."

He smiled. "I can't imagine you were ever more lovely than you are today. Maria."

"In that case, I can think of a very good way to say goodbye."

This time, there was no disorientation. He fell asleep in her arms. When he awoke, there was nobody beside him, and he was lying on top of the bed, not under its covers. He looked around. The room was furnished, but bare of all its usual clutter. Everything was bright, freshly decorated. A slip of twenty years, he knew, would have taken him back to the time the place was built. Coincidence? Clothes hung beside the bed. He guessed they'd be a perfect fit. But there was no Maria to greet him, this time. Instead, a heavy, official-looking envelope, stuffed with papers, lay on the bedside table.

He swung his feet to the floor, sat up, and opened the package. He scanned the covering letter.

Something called the Timeshare Foundation owned the house in perpetuity, but he, David (he double-checked; they had his full name correct), his family and heirs for all time were appointed, if they so wished, to be its custodians. In return for looking after the house, he (and his heirs and etcetera) would be paid – he blinked at the figure – a substantial monthly allowance, plus approved expenses.

The rest of the package contained deeds, money, keys, official bits and pieces of all kinds. So *this* was Maria's mysterious foundation! The name was too appropriate though; who could have set it up? Maybe he had got back – would get back – to Roger after all. Given the money (and they'd have plenty if the time process really worked), it would be easy, all laid down in writing years or decades in advance, for the lawyers to leave this package on a certain table in the house on a certain date. The thoughts ran through his head while he dressed. Ten years, he reckoned he'd have this time. With secure finances, no distractions, he'd have time to really get to grips with the problem – even find a mathematician to pick up where Roger had left off. And, of course, he had to find Maria. She'd be in her early twenties now. Probably settling down to raise those kids that he'd seen as old men, what, a little over a month ago, in his time frame.

He was just straightening his jacket in front of the mirror when the door chime sounded. He smiled. It hadn't been changed in twenty years. But in spite of everything, he wasn't ready for the sight that met him as he opened the door.

It was, of course, Maria. He should have guessed. More beautiful than he had ever seen her, standing, uncertainly, on the step. In her left hand she held an envelope, very similar to the one now lying discarded on his bedside table,

"David?" In all their greetings, this was the first time she had sounded so uncertain. But she still knew him! They had already met, in her time frame, even if not, obviously, on the terms of their last meeting in his memory. Her last words, as they drifted off to sleep, came back to him. "Be gentle." He resisted the impulse to step forward and sweep her in his arms.

"Maria." He held out his hand. Relief showed in her face. She rushed forward, and hugged him, like a long lost brother. She was, he guessed, ten years younger than he; last night, he'd been ten years younger than her. Would the crazy ride never stop?

"Oh, David! Where have you been? I got this letter, and it said to meet you here, but after all these years ... and I watched this house being built, and used to remember how you took me to play in the park opposite, but I never guessed, and, and, oh, David! Never go away again!"

He disentangled himself, choosing words carefully. "I didn't know I meant that much to you."

She pursed her lips in an expression of mock disgust, and punched him, playfully, on the chest. "You thought I was just a kid, I know. I used to dream about you, David. I planned to grow up and marry you. And then you went away, just like that. I cried for a month."

"Maybe," he picked a way carefully through the potential minefield, "maybe I was too old for you, Maria. You need somebody more your own age."

"You don't look too old to me, David. If anything," she leaned her head, bird-like, to one side, and examined him carefully, "if anything you look even younger and more handsome than I remember. Better than all the empty-headed young men around here, that's for sure. *And*, I'm big enough and old enough to hold on to you, now that you're back." She emphasised the words by slipping her arm through his. Suddenly, David saw her as the little old lady he had first met, taking that same grip on his arm. *This* Maria had, clearly, waited a few years for him; *that* Maria would have decades with only her memories. Something very special must have happened – be about to happen – between them, for love to last that long. Words came drifting back: you'll know how much it means to me that this was your first time. And Maria's first time, he realised, would be – had been – with him. But not just yet. There was no need to remember her other words. He would, indeed, be gentle, and make sure that the best was yet to come.

"I'm staying, Maria. For as long as I can. If you think so much of me, it's the least I can do."

"Meaning you'll only stay to please me? Don't you want me here, after all?" The familiar mischievous look was in her eye. "So why did you get this mysterious foundation to drag me along here? C'mon," she hauled him towards the door, "the sun's shining. Take me to the park, and tell me all about it."

He did not, of course, tell her everything, then or later. They had ten years, he knew. Time enough for the story to emerge when she was mature enough to have it. When he found a thick, brown ledger on sale at an office suppliers, he knew how best to tell the full tale, and he wrote down everything she would need to know carefully, by hand, as the months and years went by. Somehow, he never did get around to probing the mystery of his timeslips. Their life together was too precious to waste in fruitless pursuits, and the existence of the foundation showed that somebody, somewhen, was looking after things. Even if the foundation was impenetrable behind its legal walls, he *knew,* from first-hand experience, that it would continue to look after Maria and her family long after he was gone.

Of course, he tried to prepare her for his departure. It would be harder for her, this, the first time. And he, too, was stepping off into the unknown, after almost a decade of domestic security. The children were too young to understand, and would grow up hardly knowing him – which, undoubtedly, would explain their slight embarrassment when he had first met them.

On the last day, the boys were sent to visit their grandparents. David left the brown book, the longest love letter ever written, for her to find on the familiar bedside table, and went, at Maria's insistence, on a last walk in the park, in spite of the chill October breeze.

"I have to see you go, David," she had explained, "or I won't believe it is real. You would never leave me of your own free will, my love; that I know. But it is such a strange story, even after all this time."

He held her tight against the wind. Leaves blew past as the

trees began to prepare for winter. "And yet, you will be happy. I have seen your future, and I know. A long life, surrounded by your family. And you will even see me again. The next time we meet, you will be older than I am now; but I will be the same handsome youth you married."

She smiled, slightly, and wrinkled her nose. "And will you – did you – still fancy me when I am fat and forty?"

"Yes I did, and no you weren't – fat I mean. Just you wait and see."

"I wish I could come with you, David."

"You said that to me before, in your future. But you *will* be there. And you will make a confused young man very happy."

The familiar smile returned, lighting up the mischievous eyes. "And knowing you, I know what *that* means. Where did you ever learn such things! Oh, I do so want to believe you will still feel that way about me, David."

He'd forgotten how disorienting the timeslip could be. He staggered, and sank down on the grass before opening his eyes. Same place, but no Maria. The house was gone – just an empty lot across from the park. It was early morning, but certainly not October. Still summer.

"About time, too."

It was a man's voice. A hand reached for his from the right, helping him to his feet.

"I thought you got here earlier. Doesn't leave us much time just now. Can you walk while I explain a few things?"

He nodded, not really surprised to be met yet again by someone who seemed more in control of the situation than he was. The man was about his height, but heavier and older, with a full beard. Well, fashions change, but you'll never get me growing hair like that, thought David, irrelevantly, as he was hustled towards the path. His guide was talking fast.

"You were right about the slip pattern changing after this jump. We're in a state now where the time spent going forward at the normal rate almost balances the slip back. You're in a kind of hysteresis loop. You get about seven years here, then you slip back a little more than seven years, and so on. That's how I was here to meet you. I've written it all down," this said while thrusting a small envelope into David's left hand, "and I'll meet you back here a week from now. We can sort out all the details then. But first, there's somebody else you have to meet."

David stopped. "Hold on. This is too quick. You know all about the timeslips?"

"Of course. Who do you think I am? You're not on your own any more. Between us, we can set the whole thing up for the family. All you have to do is remember a few things – fashion trends, new inventions, the general drift of the stock market. Then, next time around, which is now, I'll be able to lay the basis of our fortune."

"You're *me?*"

"Of course. Look, we really must hurry. There's somewhere you have to be by eight."

They started walking again. David, dazed, glanced sideways at his companion. That's me? He was still talking.

"There's money in that envelope. Enough to see you through the week."

"Hold on." He stopped again, then started walking as the other carried on without him. "How many of us are there in this, uh, hysteresis loop?"

"You don't want to know that." He thought about it. He didn't. Knowing how many loops to live through meant knowing when it would end – when he would die.

"I decided – you decided – each time we meet ourselves on arrival, for a detailed briefing. You get yours next week, because you have something else to do now. Then you're on your own, except for drawing funds from the account. Next time round, you'll be me, and so on. One day, you'll slip back and there'll be no one to meet you. Then, you really will be on your own. This time round, you'll have enough on your mind, believe me. Just concentrate on remembering the trends, and leave us to do the real work and set up the Foundation.

"*You're* the Timeshare Foundation?"

"So are you. We're all in this together. But I'll give you the full briefing next week. Here we are. You'll know why it's so important in a few minutes."

They were standing outside a large, but otherwise ordinary,

house. David could see no reason for the impatience of his counterpart, but he was still being urged onward.

"Listen, uh, David," using the name clearly unsettled him; maybe he was nervous, too. "You remember what it was like the first couple of times. Everybody knew what was going on except you. It's like that now. Do what I say, and everything will turn out fine. I *know* it will, because it did. The family here has a big house, with a separate apartment on the top floor. They've got young kids, and they need some extra money. So they're going to let the apartment. They are going to let it to you. All you have to do is walk up to that door and tell them you've come to see it. Then everything slots into place. But do it now."

He gave him a firm push in the direction of the steps, and turned, walking off briskly down the street.

Someone round here is crazy, thought David. But since everyone round here seems to be me, I'd best go along with it.

He rang the bell, and was answered by a woman of about thirty, wearing a light top coat.

"I've come," he felt decidedly foolish, "about the apartment."

"Oh, yes, of course. I'm very sorry, but I have to take my daughter to school right now. But my husband will show you around." She leaned back into the house. "Dick, honey," there was an indecipherable response, "it's someone to view the apartment. Can you handle it?" She turned back and smiled at him, just as a thunder of feet on stairs heralded the arrival of a little girl, about seven or eight years old, dressed for school.

"Hi mom." She turned to David. "Hello. I'm Maria. Are you coming to stay with us?"

It was going to be a long seven years.

Other Edens

Breakout. The same sour taste at the back of the throat; the same pain through the head, like a skewer stuck through both eyes from side to side. Javed cursed, loud and long. He'd been crazy to take on this extra tour; but, by all that was holy, he'd never do it again. One more system after this, and he could go home. A quick scan, another jump, and that was it. For good.

"Looks like an oxygen planet, fourth from the sun."

The bright voice sent another wave of pain through his head.

"Lay off, Suzi. Give it a rest. I need something to straighten out my brain."

He fumbled past the accumulated debris of six months on board ship. The pills had to be here somewhere. He'd only put them down a couple of hours ago.

"Haven't you had enough of those?" Suzi had modulated her voice; now she sounded like a protective mother, not an over-eager Girl Guide leader. "You're not supposed to take more than four in a six-hour period, you know."

"Ah, c'mon." He'd found the bottle, and was busily stuffing three of the pills into his mouth. He'd only planned on taking two; the third was just to annoy Suzi. A sock floated past the console. "Waddayou know about anything, anyway? No pain circuits. Ought to stick some in. Make you a bit more human." He giggled.

Floating free in the centre of the cabin, he peered intently at the back of his left hand. The dark freckles appeared to be moving, crawling from right to left across his field of view. Hell, that was some stuff, all right. He reached for the edge of his bunk, but struck it only a glancing blow, and went into a slow spin. No coordination. Never mind. That's why he had Suzi to handle the ship. He was just the brains of the organisation. Good old Suzi.

Hostility, like the pain, was washed away by the dope. He opened one eye, and watched the screen swim slowly past his field of view. There was a green bar shining brightly on the display. He knew it meant something important.

"Didya say ya found somethin', Suzi?"

"Yes Javed." The computer knew the necessity to speak slowly and carefully when her crew was under medication. "An oxygen planet. I've been running a full Lovelock on it. No question. A living Gaia, suitable for colonisation."

Oh, shit, Javed thought. Just when I was ready to go home. Nothing but work, work, work. The third this trip, out of eleven systems. The astronomers were getting too damned good at finding solar-type systems. He closed the open eye again. There was still one possible cop-out. He could dream, for a moment or two, before he had to ask.

The moment passed. He opened both eyes, and, sobering up slightly after the initial hit, reached out and caught the grab-bar by the console. "I don't suppose there's any problems about raw materials?"

"No problem, Javed," Suzi was back in Girl Guide mode. "Two gas giants. I've plotted a slingshot manoeuvre to take us past the bigger one and on to the Gaia with minimum use of energy. Ready when you are."

He groaned. "Just let me strap in, Suzi. Then it's all yours."

The slingshot manoeuvre wasn't solely to save fuel, of course. As they passed the giant planet, they dropped a Turing onto its biggest moon. By the time Javed had checked out the Gaia and was on his way back out of the system, the idiot robot would already be building up its processing plant, ready to mine the hydrocarbon-rich atmosphere of the gas giant if the Gaia passed the final test.

Gloomily, Javed watched the screen as they orbited the planet one more time. Rules were rules. If there were signs of intelligent life, it was Hands Off. Any obvious signs, like electromagnetic transmissions, and he could up sticks and head off home now. But there never were any obvious signs. One hundred and forty-three known Gaias, and not a sign of intelligent life on any of them, except home. But rules were rules. If there were no signs obvious from orbit, he had to go down and look. With incorruptible Suzi on hand to report his every move when they got home, and the prospect of a fine that would wipe out his entire bonus if he didn't follow procedure.

'Procedure' meaning a week, minimum, crammed into a smelly sealed suit, drinking recycled water and with pipes stuck up all his personal orifices. If there was one other thing that was common to all the known Gaias, it was that they were lethal. Life from Earth couldn't survive on any of them; novel forms of complex biological compounds – living human tissue – were always under immediate attack from microbiological Gaians, and seldom lasted more than a day if unprotected. Which, of course, was why he was here. One hundred and forty-three Gaias found in less than fifty years, and none of them, yet, fit for human colonisation.

Better get it over with. "Ready to suit up, Suzi. Take me down."

It had been every bit as bad as usual. Worse. Never, never, again, no matter how big a bonus they offered him. The tapes would certainly keep ecologists happy for years; commercial sales of the holos would probably be enough to pay for the whole damned expedition, giving the huddled masses on Earth a glimpse of an Eden that they could never visit.

He didn't have to replay the tapes. The images were still vivid in his mind. If he closed his eyes, he could see them, as real as if the planet were right in front of him. The beautiful blue ball, streaked with white clouds, that he'd watched from orbit had held truth in its promise.

He'd made first landing on a plain in the temperate zone, where the horizon seemed to stretch into infinity, startling herds of something that, from a distance, could have been mistaken for zebra. The similarities were no surprise. Evolution usually solved the same problems in much the same way. And if the creatures darting through the air above him, calling to each other in melodic tones, weren't actually covered in feathers, they were still birds in his book. The waterhole had made him begin to itch, even though he'd scarcely been in the suit for an hour. Something poked a snout and a pair of eyes above the water to take a look at him; smaller, brightly-coloured aquatic life forms darted through the water, scattering in frenzy when he tossed a rock into the pool. His body wanted nothing more than to shuck off the suit and dive into the cool, inviting water. His mind knew that, quite apart from the thing with the snout and eyes, it would be suicide.

Even the memory made him itch all over again. What the people in the habitats back home wouldn't give for a chance to walk under that blue sky across that plain, with no other human being in sight. Well, at least the tapes would give them that illusion, those that could afford it – an illusion that did not include suit itch. Opium for the people. He giggled again. Strictly against Suzi's advice, he'd dropped a couple of pills even before they had reached the orbit out of the gas giant. Serve those little bastards right, for all the trouble they'd put him to. Pissing about for days on end, recording this and reporting that. No obvious signs of intelligent life. That's what it said in the report, and that's what the tapes showed. The hair-splitters in their ivory towers would probably have a fine time arguing about the potential for intelligence shown by those upright lizards on the south continent, with big brains and opposable thumbs. But as far as Javed was concerned, they'd had their chance. All they had to do was build a simple radio transmitter, and he'd never have had to suit up and go down to look at them. He certainly didn't think it was very intelligent of them to throw rocks at someone who clearly represented an advanced, spacefaring civilisation.

He felt the warm glow of a job well done, and of a moderate hit of IFT-90.

"How's the Turing, Suzi?"

"No problems, Javed. It's found all the raw materials it needs, and says it will be operational in less than a year."

"OK. Give it the green. All systems go. For the glory of humankind, and in the name of the Council of All Earth, and all that stuff."

An authorisation code flashed over the comm laser that Suzi was using to talk to the Turing on the giant planet's moon. It was acknowledged. In less than a year from now, the magnetic launcher would begin propelling huge, light pods down into the gravitational well of the system's sun. Falling inward, on a carefully planned trajectory, each would impact the atmosphere of the Gaia, bursting open to release its cargo of modified hydrocarbons, mined from the atmosphere of the giant. Within a hundred years, the CFCs would have done their job, stripping ozone from the outer skin of the Gaia and allowing ultraviolet radiation to penetrate to the surface and wipe it clean of life. Then, the Turing could shut down operations. Within another couple of hundred years, the ozone layer would have recovered. There would be another sterile home for life awaiting the immigrants from Earth – another Eden for the home planet's huddled masses.

"Authorisation transmitted. I guess it must make you rather proud, Javed, to know that you have personally initiated more Edens than any other pioneer."

Oh God, it was Girl Guide time again. He fumbled with the bottle, and popped another couple of pills into his mouth for good luck. "Sure, Suzi," he mumbled around them. "Proud to be a pioneer on behalf of the people of All Earth." Wow! The colours on the screen were ab-so-lute-ly amazing! "An' what's more ..." his voice trailed off as he studied the back of his hand, where the hairs seemed to be moving in a complex spiral pattern. "... whass more, Suzi, it'll sure teach those li'l suckers not to throw rocks at me!"

Giggling quietly to himself, floating freely in the centre of the cabin and spinning gently as he watched the backs of his hands intently, the hero of the planetary pioneers headed out once more into deep space.

The Carbon Papers

"Parcel for you." It was totally unexpected, I scarcely ever even get letters, let alone parcels, and it certainly wasn't my birthday.

"For me?" The postman was obviously used to dealing with half-asleep people clutching pieces of toast.

"Name Murray? Right?" I nodded.

"Sign here."

I did so, and sticking the toast in my mouth for safekeeping, carried the package over to the table. It was sealed with tape *and* tied with string, which seemed to be taking security a little too far. Definitely, a two-handed job to open it. I finished the toast, gulped a swig of coffee, and set to work on the wrappings with the bread knife. The security didn't stop there. Under the first layer of paper there was a letter; and under the letter was another layer of wrapping, an old, brown paper parcel, secured not with tape but with a genuine – as far as I could tell – wax seal. In fact, two wax seals, securing paper and string, and bearing a claw imprint, written in a circle, like a postmark – "Cox's Bank, Charing Cross."

I was late. I didn't want to miss the bus. But I couldn't resist a quick look first. The covering letter was from a firm of lawyers – impressive address, Inner Temple, London. But it didn't say much. They had the pleasure to be my obedient servant, and it was their duty under the terms of some arrangement made in 1890, exactly 100 years ago this week, to convey this package to me, the heir of one William Arrol James, in accordance with the wishes of some old doctor, one John H. Watson, M.D.

I glanced at the clock. I'd probably missed the bus already. And I hadn't learned anything useful at all. Didn't even know I had an ancestor called William Arrol James – though my grandmother's maiden name was James, so he might have been an uncle of hers, assuming they'd got their facts right. It was a big, Victorian family; that's all I ever knew about them, and more than I particularly wanted to know. I had my own life to lead, here, in the present.

It didn't look as if the parcel contained anything valuable. But I was late anyway, so what the hell. The knife did its job on the string, and I managed to lift one of the seals off more or less intact, as a souvenir. The other one crumbled into pieces as I pulled the parcel open. It was full of papers. Some old newspaper cuttings; a sheaf of typewritten pages, with the heading 'On the Retardation of Infrared Flux by the Gaseous Carbonic Acid Constituent of Planetary Atmospheres' by W.A. James; and a thick wad of manuscript, handwritten in an old-fashioned but clear style with black ink. I pushed the typescript and the newspaper to one side, clearing a space on the table. Carbonic acid fluxes, whatever they were, were way over my head. But one more coffee and a quick look at the handwritten stuff wouldn't do any harm. It wasn't a letter. It was laid out like a story, with a heading at the top – *The Carbonic Acid Affair*. But it read as if it was addressed directly to me.

The Carbonic Acid Affair

In taking up my pen to record the details of the curious business of the carbonic acid affair, I know that I am acting against the express wishes of my friend, Sherlock Holmes, and in defiance of instructions from representatives of Her Majesty's Government. But in fairness to the memory of an honest man, whose great contribution to scientific knowledge might otherwise go unreported, I cannot let this matter rest with the official histories of our time. By the time you read these words, the name of William Arrol James will be no more than a footnote in history. Yet if his contribution to science is correct, as I believe it to be, the carbonic acid business will, for good or ill, be part of public debate, whatever the wishes of governments. Honours and recognition may have passed your ancestor by; his life has been cruelly cut short. For this, I must take some of the blame myself. But at least I have the satisfaction of knowing that his heirs will discover the truth, and may even, if they wish, be able to gain some belated recognition for this true genius of the Victorian age.

The affair began in the second week of November, in the year 1889. A dense, yellow fog settled upon London. I had got into the habit of visiting my old friend in the rooms we had formerly shared in Baker Street, at least twice a week. His manner worried me. He alternated between bouts of frenetic activity, and periods of listless torpor that in a lesser man I would have termed laziness. His mind lacked the intellectual challenge of some great criminal case on which to exercise its talents, and I feared that he had recourse, more often than was medically wise, to a 7 percent solution of cocaine. I almost wished that some master criminal would take advantage of the fog enshrouding the city to perpetrate some act to provide a new challenge for Holmes, and to restore him to his old spirits.

Salvation came in the homely form of Mrs. Hudson.

"A young lady to see you, Mr. Holmes."

"At this hour? What do you say, Watson? Shall we receive her?"

"Oh, by all means, Holmes." Nothing could have pleased me more. In my experience of Holmes's affairs, the arrival of young ladies, without prior appointment, at unusual hours was always likely to involve some problem worthy of his mind.

He sighed, and stretched his long legs in front of the fire.

"Very well, Mrs. Hudson. But she must take us as she finds us, if she has any aversion to smoke, then I fear she has come to the wrong rooms."

"The smoke and clutter of a bachelor's rooms are the least of my concerns, Mr. Holmes."

A slight girl, no more than twenty-five years old, and dressed in black which made the red of her hair all the more striking, had stepped from behind Mrs. Hudson and across the threshold.

"Forgive my presumption. But you are the only person who can help."

"Pray, take a seat, Miss –" Holmes stood, nodding to Mrs. Hudson that all was well.

"James. Felicity James." She took the proffered chair.

"And this, Miss James, is my friend and colleague –"

"Dr. John Watson, I have read your booklets, Dr. Watson. *A Study in Scarlet*, and *The Sign of Four*. They are the reason I am here."

Holmes raised one eyebrow.

"Your fame, Watson, seems to have gone before you." He turned to the girl again. "Are you sure it is I you wish to see, Miss James, and not Dr. Watson?"

"Oh, please both of you, I am sure. But it is you, Mr. Holmes, that is the detective. Only you can help me now."

Holmes returned to his seat. "James. The name is a common enough one, but seems familiar."

"Murder, Holmes." It was my turn to speak. "A straightforward murder, reported in the *Chronicle* this morning." I had been searching out the paper while he had exchanged pleasantries with Miss James, happy, for once, to be ahead of Holmes in something. "Here it is. William Arrol James, shot dead by a burglar he disturbed in his rooms. Nothing there to tax your powers, I am sure."

"But he wasn't." The girl was increasingly agitated, twisting her gloves in her hands, leaning forward in her seat and glancing from Holmes to myself.

"Wasn't murdered?"

"No, no. William is dead. Shot dead. But not murdered by a common thief. He had been in fear of his life for weeks. There was some plot against him. He came to me, to tell me; he made me promise that if anything suspicious happened to him I would not let the matter rest. I thought he was ill, overworking; I took no notice. I told him to rest. But then this happened. And the police say the matter is clear, that the rooms had been ransacked, that William surprised a burglar in the act and was shot trying to apprehend him. But, Mr. Holmes, if that was an ordinary burglar, how could William have known in advance that it would happen?"

"Such things do occur, Miss James. The world is full of coincidences. Had we time, I am sure Dr. Watson would delight in telling you the story of the politician, the lighthouse, and the trained cormorant. But with nothing more than this to go on, we must accept that the police know their business."

"But there is more."

"Ah." He stood and began to pace the room, long-fingered hands clasped behind his back. "I thought as much."

"There are papers." She pulled them from her bag, and since Holmes ignored them, she offered them to me. I read the title aloud; those same papers, together with the newspaper reports of the James murder, accompany this memoire.

"Carbonic acid hardly seems a matter for murder, Miss James. Your brother, I take it, was a scientist; but what is the significance of these carbonic acid papers?"

"My brother, sir, was not just a scientist, but a great scientist. He was older than I am, by nine years, and he had already begun to make a reputation for himself. I know nothing of science, but I do know that he was highly regarded by his peers. Last year, there was talk that he might be elected to the Royal Society by the age of forty. He had set himself upon a course unique in the academic world, or so I believe, the study of the atmospheres of the planets, combining elements of both chemistry and astronomy, and more besides. In scientific terms, William was a polymath – although I must say, in matters of the everyday world he could be much more obtuse."

"It is so often the way." Holmes had taken up a position by the window, gazing out into the swirling fog. "The mind is like an attic, with room to store only a certain amount of furniture. Fill it up with science, and there is no room left for anything else. Which is why I have taken such care to avoid learning any science outside of a few items with some forensic value. I leave such things, and those papers, in the hands of Watson, here. But go on – tell us more of your brother's preoccupation."

The story that Felicity James unfolded to us was a queer one, to be sure, but not, on the face of things, a murdering matter. William James had simply reached an impasse in his scientific career. After publishing several scientific papers and a learned monograph on the subject of planetary atmospheres, he had found it impossible to find anyone willing to take on his latest calculations. It was, he had told Felicity, the best work he had ever done, of incalculable importance to the future of mankind. Since she was only a girl, he had not tried to explain the details to her. But he had poured out his frustration at the response of the scientific community. Nobody would publish his calculations. The Royal Society refused to allow him to speak upon the subject; even Lockyer, at *Nature*, no stranger to controversy, had rejected the very papers that I now held in my hand, and at which I peered in, I must confess, incomprehension. This had gone on for months. At last, James had become convinced that there was a plot against him, a conspiracy to blacken his name, and to discredit his scientific work. He had been overlooked for advancement at the university, and no longer received invitations to lecture elsewhere. A broken man, he had poured out his worries to his sister, handed her the papers, and made her promise that if anything untoward happened to him she would see that they were published, somehow, somewhere.

"But I never expected this, Mr, Holmes." By the end of her story, she was dabbing at her eyes with a handkerchief. "I don't care about the papers. You can keep them. But if there was a conspiracy against my brother, I want the assassins brought to justice. You *must* help!"

He turned from the window.

"We will do what we can. Watson, see, has made a note of your late brother's address. In the morning, we will visit the scene of the crime. But you must rest, and leave all the worrying to us."

"Thank you." She smiled: "I begin to feel better already, knowing that you are taking up the case."

The house was tall and narrow, part of a terrace facing on to a square near the river. If anything, the fog was worse there, with the upper storeys of the terrace almost lost from view. I was glad to get out of the cab and inside the building, where we were confronted by a familiar figure.

"Sergeant Bull!"

"Good day to you, Mr. Holmes." He touched a finger to his forehead in salute. "I didn't know you were in on this case."

"Yes, here I am, Bull. But a bit late in the day. I suppose everything's been tidied up by now?"

"Mostly so, down here at any rate. But not at the scene of the crime." He inclined his head towards the staircase.

"Up there, eh?" Holmes rubbed his long hands together. "On the top floor?"

"Indeed so, Mr. Holmes. The professor's lab'ratory, they calls it. With a window opening on to the roof, where the murderer made his escape." The stolid sergeant shook his head. "We'll never catch that one, not now. And it hardly seems worth a man's life, the few trinkets he got away with."

"Yes, Bull, I'm sure it's a very sad case. But you don't mind if I take a look around? With my colleague Dr. Watson?"

"Oh no sir. Not if you're on the case."

"Good, good. Top floor, you say? Come, Watson, we've very little time."

I tried to interrogate my colleague as we hurried up the stairs, but he was a flight ahead of me before we reached the top.

"Come, Holmes," I puffed at last, "what is this nonsense? James is dead. Our bird has flown. Why the sudden hurry?"

"I am expecting a visitor. There is no time to lose." His sharp eyes darted about the room. Along one wall there was a long table, which had clearly served the occupant of the house as a chemical laboratory. The usual retorts and tubes were there, some of them smashed, and the remains of what seemed to have been a large glass tank. For some reason, this fascinated Holmes. He examined the fragments of glass carefully, then turned to the floor under the table. There was a damp patch. Removing his glove, he rubbed a finger over the damp wood, and held it to his tongue.

"Careful Holmes! There could be any number of poisons in that brew."

"Not at all, Watson." He shook his head. "Come, taste for yourself. Salt. Nothing more than brine. Just as I suspected."

I followed his example, rubbing the damp patch with a finger and tasting the salty residue of the puddle that had lain there. While I did so, Holmes had crossed the room to the window, flinging it wide and gazing out onto the rooftops beyond. The square below was lost in the fog. I joined him.

"That is where the murderer made his escape, eh Holmes?"

"At least, Watson, it is where the weapon made its escape." He was examining the window frame, carefully. First the bottom, then the sides, and finally the top. He pulled a glass from his overcoat pocket, and peered intently through it at the paintwork just above our heads.

"Look at this, Watson."

I did as he instructed. A deep indentation and several smaller scratches marked the paintwork.

"I fear I don't see the significance of this, Holmes. Just a few scratches."

But he had already turned, and was flinging open the cupboards that lined the other wall of the laboratory.

"Those few scratches, Watson, suffice to confirm that Professor William Arrol James was not murdered at all."

"Not murdered? But, Holmes, his sister has identified the body."

"Aha!" He had found what he wanted in the cupboard. Some lengths of copper wiring, two copper plates and a series of electrical cells. Quite normal equipment to find in any scientific laboratory. I failed to see why they should be so pleasing to him.

He turned back to me, and, flipping the tails of his coat back out of the way, clasped his hands behind his back.

"Watson, you must have realised, from the story Miss James told us, that murder was the least likely cause of her brother's death. It is given to very few people to know in advance that they will be murdered, and to make appropriate arrangements with their kin. But there is a form of death which is very often planned in advance, and before which the victim usually communicates with his friends or relations."

"Suicide?"

"Exactly, Watson."

"But how?"

"That is what we came here to find out. It was, of course, obvious to me that James had killed himself. But how? And why? As to the former, his profession itself gave me the clue. A chemical meteorologist, one of the most brilliant minds of the century, he would be sure to have devised some ingenious trick that made use of his special skills. The brine puddle, the scratches on the window and the electrical apparatus show just how ingenious he was. A sad loss, indeed, to science."

"But Holmes, *how*?"

"You mean you haven't seen it yet? Come, Watson, what is produced by the action of electricity upon a brine solution?" My puzzled expression seemed to exasperate him. He took a pace towards me, thumping his right fist into his left palm.

"Hydrogen gas, my dear Watson. And what is the most important property of hydrogen gas?"

I knew that one.

"Why, of course, it is lighter than air."

"Indeed, Watson. Lighter than air. Suppose, now, that you stood in the room, about here," he had taken up a position by the window, "and you had in your hand a small revolver, attached by a cord to a balloon, full of hydrogen gas, floating just outside the window. If you were to release your grip on the revolver, as you fell with a mortal wound in your temple, what would happen to it?"

"Why Holmes?" My eyes darted from his upraised hand to the window! "If the balloon were big enough, it would carry the revolver out into the air. And on the way ..."

"Yes." He smiled. "On the way, Watson, it would bang not against the bottom of the window frame, but the top. Once out in the night, it might drift for miles, unobserved through the fog, before the balloon would burst and deposit the revolver in the garden of some astonished citizen. The picture is clear. James killed himself, in such a way as to make it seem like murder, after alerting his sister to the possibility."

"But why would he do that? To avoid the scandal of a suicide in the family?"

"I think not. James, remember, was a scientist. In my experience, such men are little concerned about social niceties of that kind. No, Watson, I flatter myself that James had another motive, and one in which he has succeeded. He must, of course, have known of his sister's taste in reading matter. His mysterious warnings to her, and the nature of his death, were intended to achieve one object, apart from his own departure from a world he had found intolerable. Simple suicide would hardly be a matter to attract the attention of one who specialises in the more intricate problems of detection. But murder, foretold, in advance, with a hint of mysterious plots – that, James reasoned, should be sure to attract the attention of the man."

"Holmes! You can't mean –?"

"But I do, Watson. This elaborate ploy, which has stimulated me out of the lethargy on which you remarked only yesterday, was designed to attract my attention and bring me here to this building."

"But why?"

"As to that," he cocked his head slightly, and I heard the sound of a heavy tread making a measured way up the stair, "I believe that just the man we need to explain the rest of the mystery is with us now. Welcome, Mycroft!" He turned with those words, extending his left arm with a flourish to the door, which now framed the tall, portly figure of Sherlock Holmes's elder brother. I sat down, astonished, on the tall stool alongside the long table.

I knew very little about Mycroft Holmes, except that he worked in some senior and secret capacity for the government. The brothers seldom met, and Sherlock seldom spoke of their relationship. But I had sensed a certain sibling rivalry. If Sherlock Holmes had a genius for detection, his brother was comparably brilliant, in his own way. Now I understood the urgency in Holmes's mind to solve the case before Mycroft appeared. But how had he known that his brother *would* appear?

"I had hoped to find you alone, Sherlock. I have left Lestrade downstairs. I suppose it is too much to hope that Watson and yourself are still in ignorance about this affair?"

"Why Mycroft, we know very little, I assure you. Simply that the greatest scientist of his generation has been hounded to his death, by you, in order to ensure that his studies of carbonic acid vapour are never published; that he committed suicide," the barb, to Sherlock Holmes's evident delight, shot home, and Mycroft gave a little start, "in a manner which Watson will be glad to elaborate on for you later, and that you are here to demand our silence, for the good of the country. You will need to be persuasive indeed, in order to achieve that end. I believe Watson is already planning another of his little books."

I was completely left out of the conversation. I would have

to wail until later to find out how Holmes had known of the involvement of government agents in the plot. Although, on reflection, as I sat and listened to the two of them, it became clear to me, as it must have been to James himself, that nobody else could have organised so thorough a suppression of James's work. No doubt Holmes, with his agile mind, had worked that out even before Felicity James had left his rooms.

"If James committed suicide – and if you say so, then I don't doubt that it is true – that may be the best piece of news in all of this affair. No, I don't wish such a death upon any man. But we had feared French agents. There are papers missing–"

"We know of their whereabouts."

"Then that is good news indeed, and I am almost glad to find you here, after all. An explanation is certainly required, but it must go no further than this room. Not even to the ears of Miss Felicity James. You must persuade her, Sherlock, that her brother died at the hands of a common thief, and that his talk of plots was no more than the tortured imagination of a mind pressed too far by scientific labours. It is indeed," and here he turned his attention to me, "for the good of the country."

"And just what is so secret and important about carbonic acid vapour? How are the French involved?"

"You have put your finger on the nub, Dr. Watson. Allow me to explain. The story goes back almost seventy years. The Napoleonic wars had not long ended; relations with France were even more precarious than they are today. It was a Frenchman, Baron Fourier, who first studied the puzzle of how the world keeps warm, in the 1820s."

"How the world keeps warm?" I could not keep silent. "My dear sir, the Earth keeps warm because the Sun shines upon it! Why, the Greeks knew that!"

"Exactly so, Dr. Watson. But I would be grateful if you did not interrupt. Baron Fourier showed that there is more to the story than this. If you have a little box, with a glass lid, that you keep out in the sunlight for some time, then the air in the box becomes warmer than the air outside. The Baron explained that in the same way the blanket of air around the

Earth keeps the whole planet warmer than it would otherwise be. He was beginning to investigate how mankind's activities might alter that natural stale of affairs, when he died." Mycroft paused, reflectively. Sherlock Holmes stepped into the gap.

"Of natural causes?"

"Officially, he died of a disease that he contracted while in Egypt with Napoleon. Unofficially, while I do not entirely approve of all the actions of my predecessors, they were usually effective."

"I begin to see the drift of your argument. Pray continue."

"Nothing more was heard of this business until 1863. Then a British scientist, John Tyndall, picked up the thread. He studied the transmission of heat through the atmosphere, and through certain other gases."

"Carbonic acid vapour!"

"Indeed, Watson. He found that this vapour, the dioxide of carbon, is a particularly effective heat trap. Fortunately, my predecessors were able to persuade him to take his studies in a slightly different direction from those of Baron Fourier, and there was no need for any drastic measures. If you search out the volume of the *Philosophical Magazine* for 1863, you will find that Tyndall is now immortalised for his suggestion that the great Ice Age was caused by a lowering of the amount of carbon dioxide in the air, allowing more heat to escape into space. Tyndall is still alive; I sincerely hope that no news of this affair, or of James's work, reaches his ears."

"I see it now." Sherlock Holmes seemed satisfied. I, however, was still in the dark.

"Damned if I do, Holmes. You might let me in on the secret."

"It really is quite simple, Watson, now that all the facts are before us. If a reduction in the amount of carbon dioxide in the air makes the world colder, then increasing the amount must make it warmer, like the inside of a greenhouse."

"Of course. But so what?"

"How is carbon dioxide produced, Watson? From the combustion of carbon –"

"Well, yes, of course, but –"

"And what is the most common form of carbon?" He had

crossed to the fireplace, and was holding up a black lump from the bucket beside it. "Coal! The very basis of our Empire!" Flinging the lump of coal down, and brushing his hands together in an ineffectual attempt to remove the grime, he began to pace the room.

"The British Empire is built on coal. Coal for our great industries, coal to power the ships of the Royal Navy and of the merchant fleet. And all the while, making the world heat up like a greenhouse. How long do we have, Mycroft?" He turned on his brother with the question.

"According to James, perhaps a hundred years before the problem becomes acute. By then, we expect human ingenuity to have found a solution to the problem. But if the discovery were publicised too widely, and dramatically, then the French …"

"Ah yes, the French. Let me see what is in your mind." Sherlock Holmes paused, head bowed, with a finger to his lips. "I believe I understand the workings of the political animal. Britain has a great Empire, an Empire founded on steam and coal. France, and other lesser nations, are jealous of this. No other nation has the resources of coal that Britain has, and no other nation uses as much coal as Britain does. If it were widely known that the burning of this coal may, in the long term, convert the world into a hothouse, with spreading deserts and crops failing in the fields, then no doubt the French might try to orchestrate a tide of international opposition to the activities of the British Empire, a league of nations seeking to impose restrictions and quotas on the amount of coal consumed. By offering such a seemingly reasonable case, to protect the globe from disastrous heating, they could restrict the use of coal, and cripple the British Empire at a stroke."

"Exactly so, Sherlock. The choice is clear. If we keep this matter quiet then our Empire, and its science, can continue to grow. By the end of the twentieth century, surely that science will be able to solve the problem of this growing greenhouse effect. But if we fail to keep the matter quiet, then a clamouring of the nations of continental Europe may be able to use this imagined threat as a rallying call. At best, it would mean war, to maintain our way of life. At worst, imposing their will upon us in the name of fairness. Then, there would be no growth in our industrial and scientific prowess, and there would be no advanced twentieth century civilisation to ensure the well-being of mankind."

* * *

And so, my story is complete. Faced with such a choice, what action could we take but to agree with Mycroft Holmes's demand for discretion? Felicity James has been left not only without a brother, but with her faith in the remarkable abilities of Sherlock Holmes completely (and quite unjustifiably) destroyed; her brother's reputation is left untainted by any hint of suicide, but without the gloss that his scientific achievements truly merit. To you, his heir of the late twentieth century, the carbonic acid problem may well have been solved many years ago, and this story out of your past will mean little. But to me, it means a great deal for my honour to have ensured that the genius of William Arrol James is known a hundred years from now.

The last page of the manuscript was signed, in a bold hand, 'John H. Watson', and dated 17 January 1890. What would you have done with it? I could hardly send the typescript of a hundred-year-old paper off to *Nature* for publication in 1990. I'm not a scientist, and I don't know how to rework my ancestor's paper to make it presentable today. But Dr. Watson was an accomplished storyteller, and his accounts of the cases he worked on with Sherlock Holmes are still widely read today. As an eye-witness, he can certainly describe those events of November 1889 better than I could ever dream of doing. I needed a home for that description, in a magazine that regularly publishes popular, factual accounts of scientific work. I did have just a little trouble persuading the editors to take it on; they usually prefer descriptions of more recent discoveries. But in the end they agreed, provided that I wrote a few words to explain why the tale had not been told before. It's too late to make a difference to William Arrol James; but like Dr. Watson before me, I'm glad to have made the effort to ensure that his story is not forgotten, and that his true genius is at last acknowledged.

Insight

Leaning on the rail, he watched Hawk trying to set fire to the ship, while Captain Bryon ostentatiously kept out of the way below decks, making it clear that he had nothing to do with this madness. The Navigator asked himself, not for the first time, just how he had arrived in this insane position. Fire on board a ship at sea! To think he had lived to see this. Rantor glanced up at the almost cloudless sky, with the Sun, as always, at the zenith. In an habitual gesture that had become automatic, he mopped at his forehead and the back of his neck with a large, red kerchief. He shifted position slightly, to take benefit from the modest amount of shade offered by the sail, barely drawing in the light wind, and leaned forward again to watch the antics going on in the waist of the ship.

There were enough volunteers ready to participate in any crazy task that the Hawk might set them – you had to be half crazy in any case, to volunteer for this voyage into the unknown, sailing far beyond sight of land. Students, half of them, granted leave of absence by the priests who ran the college, back in the Archipelago. And you could be sure that anyone the priests granted leave of absence to was someone they were glad to have out of their hair. A sprinkling of good sailors, of course – men who would follow their Captain anywhere.

As for Captain Bryon himself, he was here because he trusted the Navigator, the man in charge of this expedition. But why was Rantor here? He asked himself the same question every day, and had yet to find a satisfactory answer. The *un*satisfactory answer was that he was here because he had faith in what most people thought of as the strangest man ever to live on the Islands (a thought usually qualified by the comment that, after all, he *was* an outsider, from some remote atoll far across the Archipelago).

A couple of nervous sailors were tending a brazier of hot charcoal, under the supervision of a little man, naked to the waist and smeared with soot until he looked like a devil. This was Hawk, so named (half mockingly) because of his visionary view of the world. What other men regarded as mundane, the Hawk's far-seeing eyes found strange; what he seemed to think was normal, most men found incomprehensible. And yet, enough of his curious ideas had borne fruit to tempt the Navigator into following where Hawk pointed, ostensibly in the hope of finding wealth and fame, in reality because – well, because it felt good to do something out of the ordinary himself.

Only the Hawk could have persuaded the Navigator to allow a fire to be lit while the precious *Far Trader* was in the open sea, even under conditions as calm as this. Only under the direct orders of the Navigator would Captain Bryon, responsible for running the ship and for the safety of his crew, have allowed such insanity. In a wooden vessel, out of sight of land, with the Sun beating down, fire was the sailors' greatest dread – but Hawk said it was important. The damnable thing was, Hawk needed calm conditions for his experimenting, and calm conditions meant that it was infernally hot, with sails and cordage ready to flare like tinder at the touch of a spark. In eight fivedays of voyaging, this was the worst possible time to be lighting fires.

Just what was important about the way sparks flew up into the air from a fire, Rantor could not comprehend. Everyone knew that sparks flew upward – that was why, unbidden, half a dozen crew members had manned the rigging, watching out for any errant specks of fire from the Hawk's activities, and snuffing them out before they could alight on the dry sails. Sparks, though, scarcely seemed to be good enough for Hawk. Scraps of cloth, of various sizes, were consigned to the glowing brazier, and wafted up from it as they writhed and burned. There were even some sheets of precious paper, which the Hawk seemed particularly interested in, but these were the greatest cause of concern to the sailors. As the paper floated upwards it was still on fire, in the process of being consumed into charcoal wafers that drifted up and eventually span away from the ship, under the watchful gaze of the crew.

Watching the sparks rising above the brazier, Rantor caught sight of the Sun, and shivered, in spite of the heat.

Hawk's latest crazy notion could not possibly hold truth, could it? But if it were true, sparks were to blame. Sparks, of a different kind, were responsible for them being here, so far from home. The Hawk's strange signalling device, the morphic resonator, had faithfully reproduced its little flashes of artificial lightning every dawn, in response to the action of the large lightning generator installed in the topmost tower of the castle of Lord Kyper, at home in the Three Islands. Rantor remembered the demonstration of the morphic effect, back in the castle: how the banks of electric storage jars, discharging across a gap between two metal rods, had produced the lightning and the thunder, with an acrid smell, like that of Hell itself; and how, at the far end of the long gallery, the miniature replica of the lightning machine had produced its own feeble sparks in tune with the flash of lightning and crash of thunder, although it was untouched by any human operator. For all Hawk's fine talk of the scientific principles of morphic resonance – the law of similarities which required that like objects must behave in similar fashion, in tune with each other even when separated by great distances – it still seemed like magic, and not entirely white magic, to the Navigator. He remembered too well the tales from his childhood, in the village where, it was said, Grandma Alyn could cure an ague by applying a poultice to a clay figure of the sufferer, or (the whispers went) kill a goat with a pin stuck through a figurine. But, magic or not, Hawk's trick worked; and at heart Rantor was a practical man, not a religious one. If it worked, his creed said, then use it.

It was Hawk's genius that turned the resonator into a directional beacon. The metal shield, mounted on a track on the upper deck, a little wagon rolling in rails around a circle, pushed this way and that by a laughing gang of Hawk's most ardent apprentices (who were, almost by definition, the most incompetent sailors on board). When the shield was in line between the resonator and the lightning generator, the generator could blast away for all it was worth, and not a spark would be seen in the resonator. But displace the shield to one side, and the sparks appeared. Metal blocked the resonant corpuscles. Why, even Hawk could not say (nor could he fathom the strange way in which, the further they got from the castle, the more it seemed that the sparks in the resonator were *strongest* when the metal shield was on the *far* side of the resonator from the lightning generator). The discovery had been an accident, and Hawk had lost interest in it once it had been made to work – and once he had failed to explain it. But its value had been obvious to the Navigator, well versed in his craft and in the mathematics of trigonometry.

With a tried and tested navigation beacon to point their way home, and a sound ship under them, the crew of *Far Trader* were the first people to sail far out of sight of the Archipelago and yet expect to return home safely. They were following a course from which nobody had ever returned, and even the most ardent of Hawk's followers, Rantor guessed, probably gave thanks each morning that they had not fallen off the edge of the world in the night time. As the days had added up, and then the fivedays in their turn, it had not escaped his notice that a little crowd of casual observers would gather just before the Sun cast the nightglow aside, ready to check that there was still open sea ahead. Each day, the result had been the same. One moment, straining like the others to see beyond the bowsprit in the nightglow; the next, the reassuring return of the Sun, blazing out from its accustomed position at the zenith and lighting the ocean ahead. Always, open ocean, as far as the eye could see. Although he would admit it to no man, Rantor himself felt a flow of relief each morning when the ritual was safely accomplished.

Sparks had brought them here – beyond, far beyond, the point where unbelievers said the edge of the world must be. The priests who taught that the world was an infinite plane seemed to be vindicated with every day that passed. And yet, by bringing them here, sparks were responsible for Hawk's heretical new ideas, that cut away the foundations of a lifetime of belief from beneath the Navigator. Some nights before, in the cool of the afterdeck, Hawk had explained his vision to the Navigator.

"Well, Hawk." The Navigator had been in a mellow mood,

happy, as ever, to be at sea – in spite of his worries concerning the outcome of the mission. "Two days since we had a spark out of that resonator of yours. And yet, I believe I might find my way back to the Three Islands after all!" He gestured to the misty nebulosity glowing low in the sky behind the ship. "We may need your toy when we are closer to home, and the light fades. But by then, I have no doubt, you will come to our aid, eh?"

The Hawk was in a more reflective mood, unwilling to respond in kind to the bantering tone. "You can use the glow as a beacon, Navigator, but I don't understand it. This far from land, all the torches in all the islands of the Archipelago could not produce a light bright enough for us to steer by. And that is no torchlight. It is too pale, and blue. If the air above the islands shines by night, why did we never notice, we who have spent all our lives in the Archipelago?"

"Hawk questions!" Rantor laughed. "Why and how are no concerns of mine. Perhaps God sent the glow to guide wandering sailormen. All I care is that your sparks have brought us far enough out to sea for the lights in the sky to be made plain – both astern and," he pointed, "ahead. I'll never doubt you again, Hawk. The lights in the sky *are* other islands – other worlds – and *Far Trader* will live up to her name. We will all be rich, and famous, when we return to Lord Kyper's domain"

"But why and how, my good Navigator, concern me greatly. How do the lights in the sky shine? And, most pressing in my mind at present, why are they above our heads? Always, we have to look up to the lights. Does that not make you wonder, with your training in geometry and navigation?"

Rantor frowned, his mood broken. "The inner sphere? But it is a logical absurdity."

"That rather depends on your point of view."

The Hawk, it seemed, was getting around to what had been worrying him. He leaned forward, ticking items off on his fingers to emphasise the logic of his argument. Rantor noticed, with some amusement, that even Hawk now braced himself with legs wide apart, like a true sailorman, swaying gently with the roll of the ship as it glided over the sea under half sail in the light breeze. The wake behind seemed to glow with a life of its own, marking their arrow-straight course through the night. All was well with the ship, but Hawk's words removed some of the sense of well-being.

"We know that the Sun is always at the zenith, viewed from anywhere in the Archipelago, or even, we see now, from outside. A line of sight to the Sun is always perpendicular to the surface of the world. Parallel lines meet only at infinity, so the Sun, we are taught, must be infinitely far away, and the world is an infinite flat plane. Unless–"

"Unless the world is really the inner surface of a sphere, with the Sun at the centre. Yes, yes. But that is absurd. The priests teach us that only to *demonstrate* its absurdity – the law of the absurd alternative. Two possible solutions to a puzzle, but one is absurd, so the other must be true. If we live on the inner surface of a sphere, why doesn't all the water slop down to the bottom and drown us? If the Sun isn't infinitely far away, why doesn't it fall down and burn us? Come, Hawk, you'll have to do better than that."

"What is absurd, Navigator, depends, as I say, on your point of view. The priests are honest men, but they have only a limited view, confined to one Archipelago. Now we have travelled further – further than any man who has lived and returned to tell the tale. And we see behind us a glow, a glow that can only mark the Archipelago – though, I admit we don't know how, or why – and that glow rises in the sky behind us as we advance. We see a glow ahead, that I will stake my life marks another Archipelago, dropping down the sky to meet us as we advance. And we see the Sun, just as at home, vertically above our heads. We *must* be moving over the inner sphere. From our point of view, the law of the absurd alternative tells us that it is *impossible* for the world to be flat. And that means that the Sun is only a finite distance above our heads. If I had means to measure the distance we have travelled from the Archipelago, then all I would have to do is measure the angle to that light in the sky behind us and I could tell you just how far above us the Sun sits – how far it is to the centre of the sphere."

Instinctively, the Navigator, though scarcely a religious man, made the sign to ward off evil. "And what keeps it there, floating above us while all other things fall to the surface of the world? What keeps an ocean of water poised like a wave above our heads, instead of flooding to the bottom of the sphere?"

The Hawk smiled. Rantor recognised the grin, and began to wonder what he was letting himself in for this time.

"Ah, Navigator. I have an idea about that. I thought perhaps – tomorrow if there is not too much wind – you might permit me to carry out a few simple tests."

It had not, in fact, happened the next day. Strong winds, fair for their course, had blown them on for four days, while the night-time glow in the sky ahead, where Hawk had staked his life they would find another Archipelago, dropped down and dimmed into insignificance. Even under reduced sail, the *Far Trader* had ripped through the water, heeling to the wind until the lee rail dipped into each rolling wave as it lifted beneath them. Bryon had done well. Over the preceding fivedays, his crew of half-trained volunteers, still wet behind the ears when they had left the Three Islands, might not have become the best sailors in the Archipelago, but they were no longer fumbling incompetents.

Rantor remembered with pleasure the feel of the deck alive beneath his feet, and the spray stinging sharp against his cheek. The sailors had a saying that there was no such thing as bad weather – the only bad day for sailing was when there was no weather at all, in a flat calm. Give them wind, and a good ship, and they would voyage anywhere to find a profit for their Lord and a bonus for themselves. Another day at that pace, and they would be among the islands, if islands they were; Hawk had begged for permission to carry out his fire raising before then, but neither Rantor nor Captain Bryon would relent until the wind dropped.

Now, though, Hawk had his chance, almost as if the wind had dropped in response to his entreaties. At least half the crew thought Hawk was a wizard anyway, and this happy coincidence (Rantor told himself he was sure it was a coincidence) would do his reputation no harm. The Navigator knew that it was worth giving the Hawk his head, within reason, and it was better for him to get this current madness out of his system before they arrived in a strange island, where Hawk's talent for observation could prove invaluable to the traders. There would be plenty for all to do, tomorrow, or the next day …

Rantor's reverie was broken by a cry from the masthead lookout.

"Land! Land on the port bow!"

He leaped into the shrouds, and, shading his eyes against the Sun, looked out across the sea. After the winds of the past few days, the ocean was still heaving in a long swell, but he automatically adjusted his balance to the swaying rhythm. At the height of the roll, as the bow lifted, and hung, momentarily, before plunging back down into the trough, he caught a glimpse of something that might have been the top of an island. Damn the lookout! If land was visible from the deck already, he should have seen it long ago, from his vantage point. But, Rantor realised, like everyone else on the ship the lookout had been more engrossed in Hawk's antics than in his own duties. Damn the Hawk!

He opened his mouth to curse the lookout aloud, but closed it again. Bryon had appeared as if by magic at Rantor's side; it was the Captain's job to discipline the crew, and it was also, to some extent, Rantor's fault for permitting the distraction, when he knew they were approaching land. There was no need for words between them; both he and the Captain knew the situation.

"Douse that fire! All hands!"

The thunder of feet on the planking of the deck broke the silence that had followed the lookout's cry.

Bryon turned to Rantor. "An outlying island. The new archipelago must still be a day's sailing away, but there are no ships to be seen. No harm has been done."

The words were scarcely out of the Captain's lips when they were contradicted by events.

"Birds! Two great birds, ahead!"

As if to atone for his previous failure, the lookout had spotted something totally unexpected. They were still too far from land to expect to see birds. Yet there were two dots in the sky, between the ship and the strange island. They could only be birds, but the lookout had done well to spot them.

Rantor felt a thrill of anticipation. Birds meant that the land

was alive. Where there were birds, there would be plants –
and maybe people. This was what the *Far Trader*'s voyage
was all about. Hawk's toys, and his philosophising, were all
very well in their place. But they could not compare to the
prospect of discovering new lands, for the first time in the
history of the Archipelago. If nothing else, they could
replenish their diminished supplies, provisioning the ship for
further explorations. And at best – who knew what the
inhabitants of the new islands might have to trade?

In response to shouted orders from the Captain, the ship
had altered course towards the lone island, and, with all sail
now set, she was heeling slightly even in the fading breeze.
Rantor shifted his position, maintaining balance without
thinking. His eyes still peered intently at the scene ahead.
There was something odd about those birds. Either they were
much closer than he had thought, or they were very big, and
still some distance away. Why did their wings not flap? They
seemed curiously stiff, gliding through the air with
outstretched wings. The glideagles back home soared that
way, in the updrafts of wind along the cliff tops; but they
never held their wings quite so straight for so long – certainly
not out in the middle of the sea, where there were no
updrafts. And whatever they were, those two birds were
coming out to sea, towards the *Far Trader*.

Hawk joined them on the afterdeck. He seemed entirely
oblivious to the new developments, and was chattering away
excitedly, as much to himself as to anyone else.

"A great success! I believe I have the answer. Did you see
how pieces of paper float upward in the heat, even when they
are not on fire themselves? It all seems quite clear to me.
Like attracts like, that is obvious – a law of similarities. Hot
things are drawn to the Sun, and rise upwards. Cold things, of
course, are repelled from the Sun, uniformly in all directions,
and spread out evenly over the surface of the inner sphere.
Which is why all the water doesn't slop down and drown the
Islands. What will the priests make of this, eh?

"But the cold things repel the Sun, with equal but opposite
strength, and push it to the centre of the inner sphere! If we
could weigh the brazier, it would surely be lighter when the
coals are glowing red, although it has too much inherent

weight ever to float in the air. But the paper is so light, that even warm air, rising to greet the Sun, can carry it along. Ah, Navigator, this is a great day – and one you will remember. I think I can put land and sea breezes at your disposal, now I have this new perspective on things. It's all to do with the law of similarities. Hot air, moving to greet the Sun …"

"Not now, Hawk." The Navigator's firm command cut off the flow of unheeded talk. "What do you make of those birds? A little big, do you not think? Are they a danger?"

Even as Hawk looked up, taking notice of what was going on for the first time, a new cry came from the lookout.

"Men! Not birds! Flying men! Men with wings!"

Several of the crew made the sign to ward off evil. The older hands turned to the Captain for orders. Hawk, attention well and truly caught, ran the length of the deck and scrambled up into the rigging, staring forward. As the ship rolled, he lost his grip with one hand, and swayed out over the heaving waters; but he kept his eyes fixed on the fliers as he scrabbled for a secure hold. Rantor had the feeling that even if Hawk fell to his death he would spend the fall observing his surroundings and thinking about what it all meant.

"Prepare for boarders!" The Captain, as ever, thought first for his ship. "Men or birds, they don't come aboard the *Far Trader* without my invitation, lads!"

The rough humour turned the mood of the crew away from thoughts of black magic. They had the best Captain in the Archipelago, *and* the best Navigator – and they had their own secret weapon, the Hawk.

The two swooping figures split up to pass either side of the ship, as crossbowmen hurriedly took up positions by the rail. Hawk slid down a rope, and scurried back, keeping pace with the fliers.

"Men indeed, Captain," he panted. "Not birds. Ordinary men like us. See the harness that fastens them to the wings. But see how they fly – like eagles."

The two fliers had indeed soared high over the ship, having used the momentum of their dive, as they crossed the stern and turned back to pass the vessel, to lift them higher. But not quite like eagles. Their wings did not flap, and now they were sinking, slowly, towards the waves.

"I think not, Hawk." Rantor had grasped their difficulty. "These eagles will never regain the land. How they rose so high in the sky, I know not. Perhaps it was the attraction of the Sun, eh? A wonderful trick for a lookout – but they should have stayed closer to home. Now they are sinking lower. We may have two passengers for you, Captain – and wet passengers, at that."

Suddenly, one of the fliers, now only a few span above their heads, veered to his right, towards the ship, losing height as he did so. The small group on the afterdeck flung themselves flat as his intentions became clear. For a moment, it looked as if he would succeed in landing on the deck. Then, the left wing snagged a standing line, part of the permanent rigging. There was a snap, and the whole wing crumpled, while the flier himself was jerked around and crashed heavily into the rail. Bryon and Rantor, with two crew members, rushed to his aid; Hawk moved with equal speed, but ignored the man and poked gently at the broken wing, no more than a delicate framework of wood covered with fine silk. It had scarcely more substance than the wing of a butterfly – and yet it had carried a man high above their heads, and brought him all the way here from the island ahead. A strange looking man, he was dressed in what would have been loose trousers, except for the thongs binding them tight around his legs, and a jerkin that left his arms bare. He was beardless – that was almost unheard of back on the Islands – and met Rantor's gaze steadily with blue eyes, not brown. A man for all that, who bled like any mortal man.

A splash alongside, accompanied by a slightly inaccurate cry of "Man overboard!", announced that the other butterfly had come to the end of its flight. Bryon left the others attending to the injured flier – his arm seemed to be broken, and he was only semi-conscious.

"Get a line to him, then!"

In response to the man overboard cry, the helmsman had immediately hove to, and the flier, already disentangled from his wings, was struggling in the heaving water alongside. The wind had been dropping during all the activity, and in spite of its headway the ship was still comfortably close enough for a line to be heaved to the swimmer. He soon stood, panting, on the main deck. Rantor went to greet him, only to be taken aback by the flier's words.

"I hope you fools are worth the trouble." The accent was peculiar, but intelligible. "My wings lost, because your idiot crew were too busy saving me to think about them; Bah-lee's wings probably smashed beyond repair. And all because you weren't prepared to receive us properly! Don't you know the Code? Someone will have to pay for this mess!"

"We hardly expected such visitors, ah," the Navigator decided to be tactful, "Lord. Indeed, we have never seen such wonders as men that fly."

"I am no Lord." The visitor was looking about him. "But where are you from? There is no ship like this in the Nations. All these ropes, and poles. And such a mess of sails. Where are your oars? Why is there no clear deck for fliers to land on?"

"We have oars – when we need them." The Navigator looked at Bryon, and nodded.

The Captain took the hint. The weakening breeze was getting them nowhere now, and it began to look like a good idea to make land as soon as possible. A few quiet commands, and the ship was bustling with activity as sails were taken in, and, to the accompaniment of good natured complaints from the men who would have to heave on them, oars were unshipped. The flier, drying in the warm Sun, watched with obvious interest. The men labouring at the sweeps held so much fascination that, Rantor surmised, this was not the kind of oarsmanship he was used to. Irritated at the flier's manner, he tried, once again, to gain his attention.

"As I said, we have never seen men that fly."

This time, the flier took it in. His attention jerked back to Rantor.

"Never seen fliers? Then you are strange fish indeed, and King Rotono-ga will surely regard you as a catch worth even the cost of two sets of wings! Keep on this course, and I will take you in to harbour."

Rantor frowned. He objected to being regarded as a catch.

It was a long time since anyone had given *him* orders. But he had every intention of taking the ship into harbour – not just for supplies, but for the secret of the flying wings. And he never objected to the help of a local pilot. If this ill-mannered passenger wanted to think he was in charge, it was best to allow him that illusion, for now.

How could they have been so stupid! Rantor fumed inwardly. Six days of inaction. A standoff. The representatives of this cursed King Rotono-ga still demanded that the ship – the whole ship! – be given up in compensation for the loss of two sets of wings that they blamed on Rantor. They could take it by force, of course, here in the harbour; though Rantor would burn the vessel first, and had made sure they knew it. Or they could starve the *Far Trader*'s crew into submission, eventually. That, he thought with grim satisfaction, might take longer than they expected, and he would still burn the ship before they got their hands on it. Rantor had bought time, he hoped, by giving the impression that their supplies were all but exhausted, and he had repeatedly asked for more, without success. That should encourage this King and his men to play the waiting game, at least for a while. But could anything about them be predicted, when the idiots refused to trade?

Maybe they were not such idiots. They held all the best cards, with *Far Trader* in harbour, under the watchful eyes of the King's men. Eventually, the crew would be forced to beg for supplies, or try to sail off – and how could you sail off unobserved, even if you could sneak or fight your way out of harbour, when the King had fliers who could scan the seas for a sight of you from above? In the long haul, *Far Trader* could outpace any rowing galley. But if the rowboats knew where she was, and enough of them gave chase promptly, they could quickly catch her.

He had been a fool to lead them into this mess. He should have anchored off shore, and negotiated at arm's length. But even then, with those damned fliers, the locals would have been at an advantage. In any skirmish, it would be easy to keep them off the ship's decks – but that would not suffice. A few daredevils, landing in the rigging and cutting it, and the ship would be lost, disabled, while the rowboats came alongside at their leisure. *Far Trader*'s clumsy sweeps, useful though they were for getting in and out of harbour, were no match for purpose-built galleys.

Still, he *had* been a fool to imagine that the whole wide world would be like the Archipelago, only bigger. Back there, there were always rival factions, shifting coalitions among the different groups of islands, so a good trader could play one off against the other, and find some way to turn things to his advantage. But here – he could still hardly believe it: a single, big island, isolated in the sea with everyone owing allegiance to a single ruler. There were no factions for him to set one against the other. No real ships, just those glorified rowboats – which was why they were so eager to lay hands on *Far Trader*, now that they had seen the possibilities she represented. The big mountain in the middle of the island made overland travel difficult, but the rowboats managed quite well plying around the coast. There were enough experienced sailors here to make copies of *Far Trader* and to sail them, and Rantor shivered at the thought of what they might do if let loose in the Archipelago. And who could have imagined the fliers – everything hinged on that.

"Navigator."

"Hawk! I was contemplating your advice. Trying to find the right viewpoint to tackle the problem of how we get out of here."

"I may be able to help."

"Your lightning generator won't get us out of this harbour, friend."

"No." Hawk gripped the Navigator's shoulder, and crouched close by his chair, keeping his voice low. "But if we were at anchor, halfway round the island from here, and if there was a good strong land breeze blowing, and if I could guarantee no fliers could follow you for – oh, half a day, or so – what might your instructions to the Captain be?"

"Cut the cable. Run. With a head start, and no fliers to interfere with the sails, we could hold the rowboats off until they tire." Rantor's eyes were, suddenly, alight with interest. "But can it be done, Hawk? Do you really have a plan?"

"Oh yes, Navigator. I have a plan. And I have a secret worth far more to these people than the *Far Trader*. I can show them how to fly at night, and in the first light of morning, when, as you must have observed, their beautiful butterflies must stay on the ground."

The Navigator sat back, with a sigh. "A wonderful secret, indeed, my friend. But if you think this will pay for our release, you are sadly mistaken. This King of theirs will take your secret, and keep us, and our ship, into the bargain."

"But I *cannot* stay here, Navigator. *We* cannot stay here. I have work to do – the theory of similarities has such interesting implications. I *must* have somewhere to work properly again."

Rantor's hope was quickly fading. The Hawk, he remembered, had come to the Three Islands from a far distant part of the Archipelago. He owed no true allegiance to the Duke; all he wanted was a benefactor who would allow him his experiments. Even the precious ship meant nothing to him, except that it was a rather inconvenient platform for those studies. Yet, Rantor counted him as friend and believed the feeling was reciprocated. If not through allegiance to the Duke, then surely out of that friendship, Hawk would not simply slip away with his new secret and offer his services to the King?

"We go together, Hawk; or not at all. I'll not abandon one of those under my command."

Hawk ignored, or failed to notice, the hard edge that had entered Rantor's voice.

"To be sure. Of course." He was losing himself in his dreamworld again, muttering almost inaudibly as he went over complex plans in his head. "Even a King must have his secrets, and my secret is so powerful that it cannot be revealed near the prying eyes of the town. Some distance away, around that headland yonder, would be appropriate. And the ship must be on hand, to ferry my equipment – they won't think that is odd, all the transport here goes by sea." He stopped, and looked earnestly at Rantor again, as if a doubt had just occurred to him.

"Ah, Navigator, I will need rather a *lot* of equipment. It might be best if you were to explain this to the Captain."

Rantor had got into the habit of trusting the Hawk. It was a habit he could not bring himself to break, although he vowed to himself that if this were some trick he would not rest until the trickster paid.

"The Captain will surely be in accord. Even if the fliers pursue us, it will be better to go down fighting, in the open sea, than to starve here in harbour. At night, with just a few guards to overpower, and the land breeze ..." he shrugged. "Well, we won't win, but they'll know they've been in a fight."

He stopped short. "Where will you be, Hawk? How can we slip our cable and flee, if you are ashore, demonstrating some flim-flammery to the King's men?"

The Hawk's familiar grin returned. "Flim-flammery, Navigator? Have you so little faith? Oh no. My tricks, as you well know, always work. But this one may not work out in the way that other people anticipate. All you have to do is wait a little while off shore, to collect me before you set full sail. I assure you, there will be no fliers to hinder your escape. It all has to do, you see, with the attraction of similarities and the repulsion of opposites."

Try though he might, that was all the information Rantor could extract from his farsighted friend; that, and a list of essential equipment for hoodwinking the King's men that made no sense at all. Captain Bryon only agreed to the assault on his ship's stores on the strength of Rantor's own solemn vow that the result would be, at least, to get the ship out of this damned harbour.

Hawk was tired. It had seemed like a brilliant move on the Navigator's part, insisting so firmly that he could not possibly let his Hawk go into the midst of the islanders unescorted that, of course, Rho-gan, the King's man, had insisted even more firmly – and from a position of inarguable strength – that nobody except the Hawk was to leave the ship. Hostages, instead, were offered against the Hawk's safe return. Even now, Bah-lee, his arm in splints, sat in the Captain's cabin on board the *Far Trader*, guarded by the crew. The ship, in turn, was watched over by more of the King's men, in their 'rowboats'.

There was no point in worrying about it now, but if it had not been essential for Rantor's bluff to succeed, Hawk would have welcomed the presence of someone he could really trust here to help him with the labour of setting everything up. It had been a long and lonely haul from the beach, almost a thousand paces; uphill and inland. The spot seemed almost perfect, and the sea breeze that still blew fitfully on their backs as they manhandled the materials upward had almost died away. The pyre was already well alight.

"Rho-gan!" The islander turned at the Hawk's call. "Now the wind is dropping, we can begin. Get them to build the fire higher, and to keep the neck of the skysail above the rising smoke."

"As you command, O Hawk." Rho-gan was used to giving orders, not to taking them; but he seemed to prefer to amuse himself with mock-obsequious obedience rather than to allow the situation to upset him. This fitted well with Hawk's instructions from the Navigator – escape, by all means, and demonstrate that the crew of the *Far Trader* (and, by implication, the people of the Archipelago) were not to be trifled with; but leave the way open for trade, on more equal terms, later. There was no point in being too secretive about what he was up to, and it always calmed his nerves to explain things.

At Rho-gan's instruction, the men with the uncomfortable task of holding the circular mouth of the skysail over the fire had moved a little closer to the flames. The opening was supported on poles, above the fire itself, with each pole held by an uncomfortably hot man; and the neck of the device stretched on more poles from the mouth to the body of the skysail, swelling and stirring on the hillside above like a giant beast awakening from slumber.

"You see how the smoke and sparks rise in the warm air. This is a natural law, the repulsion of opposites. Hot things cannot abide the cold ground, and must rise up above it. My little skysail will do the same."

"Little!" Rho-gan glanced at the billowing fabric, the remains of the ship's best fine weather sail, once flat against the slope of the hillside, but now beginning to take on a life of its own as heat from the pyre was directed into its gaping mouth. "Why, twenty men could scarce encircle it with arms outstretched. But, no doubt, you have much bigger skysails, on your home island?"

"I have never flown one bigger myself." Which was certainly true, thought Hawk; and, he hoped, sufficiently misleading for the islander to draw his own false impressions. "It is nearly time for my demonstration. As an experienced flier yourself, perhaps you could help me with the harness. It is fortunate indeed that your wing-harness could be adapted to my needs; but the design is unfamiliar."

They moved around the fire together. Even at ground level, the heat was intense. The skysail was almost rounded now, beginning to show signs of trying to lift off the ground, restrained by a wide net around which there were many strong ropes, held down by equally strong men.

It worked! Hawk tried to conceal his excitement. Of course it worked. He had known it would. But although the reality was still a thrill, he had to let them think this was all routine.

"Be careful not to let any sparks alight on the sail!" The nearest handler grunted something that might have been an acknowledgement. Hawk decided to leave well enough alone. He had plenty to worry about. Let them make sure the skysail was held in place above the rising air, being repelled from the cool ground as the laws of science dictated.

Rho-gan had the harness ready. Hawk, glad of his small stature, slipped it around his shoulders and looked down as the islander fastened the straps securely about his chest. Above his head, the leather harness was joined to ropes that were threaded around the broad mouth of the skysail. It all seemed secure – too secure, for what he had in mind,

"If I should descend a little abruptly, Rho-gan, I might need to wriggle out of this with some haste, before the skysail falls on my head and smothers me."

The islander nodded. "A real problem – should you rise more than a few span above the ground." Was Rho-gan mocking him? No matter; mocking or not, he was explaining what Hawk needed to know. And the less faith he had in the skysail, the bigger the element of surprise that would help Hawk on his way.

"This knot here can be released by a tug, so–" he demonstrated, then began re-fastening the harness "– but it is best not to tug it when you are floating far above *our* heads!"

Hawk grinned. He could not help but like this man. Maybe they would meet again. There was much he would like to learn about the flying wings of the islanders. But timing was all important, now. He had instructed the Navigator to make his move when the fire began to die down, as it would as soon as he was safely on his way and the enthusiastic arsonists he had recruited ceased flinging wood onto the blaze. He felt a tug at his shoulders, and the hair rose on the back of his neck. He had never doubted the device would work, but this was a little different from his usual experiments. This time, he was experimenting on *himself.*

He looked up. The skysail was almost over his head, held to one side by the ropes, trapping the rising heat from the fire. The ropes to his harness were stretched almost tight. He had to go, and trust the land breeze to appear on schedule. In his mind, he knew it would; but his stomach seemed to be trying to disagree with his mind.

Rho-gan was smiling at him. "Well, Hawk. Time to live up to your name. A man is not a real man, I always say, without his wings. Your skysail is not my idea of flying. Dangling on a piece of string, unable to steer a course. But I have to admit that my wings would never get me aloft this night, while your skysail seems just as reluctant to have contact with the ground as you foretold. If it takes you higher than I can jump, I'll make you an honorary member of the fliers' guild tomorrow."

I may not be able to steer a course, thought Hawk, but if it goes where I plan, you'll never get the chance. He smiled in return, with genuine warmth. He hoped Rho-gan would carry no blame for what was about to happen.

"Ready."

Rho-gan took up the cry. "Our Hawk is ready to fly! Release the bird!"

Well-disciplined, the men on one side of the network of ropes holding down the skysail released their grip, allowing it to slide out from under the mesh, and rise above the fire. Jerked sideways, Hawk began to run, then stumbled; for a moment, he thought he was being dragged into the fire. Then, with a bound, the sail was free of the netting and rose upwards at a giddy pace. His boots barely brushed the flames, and he was aloft, floating in a warm column of air, soundlessly, like a bird.

Time, he knew, was short. Soon, the heat in the skysail would be dissipated, escaping and vanishing into the sky as it was repelled by the cool surface below. As the skysail cooled, then, in accordance with the law of attraction of similars, it would descend gently (he hoped) back to the ground. But it was no use landing back where he had started. Everything depended on the land breeze, the night wind that *always* blew off from the shore to the sea, from every island, the Navigator had assured Hawk, that he had ever encountered.

Hawk knew why it did so, now. Air warmed by the Sun's action by day was drawn towards the heat of the Sun by the attraction of similars. That was why these island fliers could soar so high on their wings, during the heat of the day. The rising air lifted them up. Naturally, since the land was higher up than the sea, it felt the effect more strongly, so the rising air – moved up over the sides of the mountain, reaching for the Sun.

At night, the pattern was reversed. The air above became cool when the Sun went dark at night. Cool air was attracted back down to the cool surface below, and that attraction was stronger on the high slopes of the mountain. Cold air fell down the mountainside and blew out to sea, as the land breeze.

No wing flier could leave the ground when the land breeze blew; he could fly upward only in rising air, in the heat of the day. Now the Hawk could fly upward even in cold air – simply by making his own warmth! Once he was aloft, though, on this occasion he needed the cold air, falling down the mountainside, to push him out to sea and back to the *Far Trader*. But nothing was happening! He could feel no breeze at all!

Alarmed, Hawk looked down between his boots. He was far above the tallest trees, twenty, thirty – perhaps fifty – span above the ground. The fire was no longer there! Twisting in his harness, Hawk caught sight of it, well to one side. As he watched, it seemed to drift away. He was moving! And towards the sea!

Cries from below broke into his thoughts. "Hawk! Skysailer! How far do you plan to travel?"

He laughed. All was well. The opportunity was irresistible. "All the way, Rho-gan! All the way back to my ship! And by the time your fliers can rise on their wings, we will be far, far away!"

Rantor himself led the attack, as soon as he judged that the fire on the hill was beginning to die down. He wanted to be in the thick of things, exercising a restraining influence. It was essential that none of the honour guard for their hostage should be killed; he wanted no excuse for continuing bad blood between the Archipelago and this island. The guards, though, were under no such restraint, and although they were fighting on unfamiliar territory this gave them an advantage. But they *must* be overpowered before the two rowing galleys, surely already alerted by the sounds of the scuffle, could take action.

Short clubs had disposed of several of the guards – Rantor only hoped they had not been wielded with too much enthusiasm – and he noted, grimly, that at least three of his own men were down, wounded seriously. But the swordsman in front of him was no novice, and it was all he could do to keep him at bay, while trying to manoeuvre the man into a position where one of the sailors could get in a clear blow at him. The sword flicked in low, stabbing at Rantor's groin; he danced sideways, deflecting the blade with a flick of his wrist, and gave way again. Dammit, this man was *good*; where were his helpers?

Suddenly, the *Far Trader* lurched, as the cable was cut and her head began to swing in the breeze. Rantor adjusted easily to the sway; his opponent, clearly a landsman, was caught off balance. Seeing an opening, Rantor lunged forward, aiming to disable his sword arm. To his horror, as the ship heaved his opponent stumbled into the strike. Desperately, at the last moment Rantor managed to lift the point of his blade, which struck high in the man's right shoulder, instead of penetrating deep into his chest. As the wounded man tried to switch the sword to his left hand, two of the crew swung from the rigging, taking him from behind. He sank to his knees, clearly in pain and losing blood fast; but not, Rantor prayed, mortally wounded.

He looked around. The fight was over, and the ship was under way. But there were more problems yet to be faced. Grunting an acknowledgement to his helpers, he ran back to the afterdeck, absently cleaning the sword on his cloak as he went.

"Steady." Captain Bryon's quiet command travelled the length of the now silent ship. One of the guard boats was swinging round, under all oars, as if making to board. The other stood off for the moment, "Now! Hard to port; in oars!"

Swept forward by the press of sails, even with all oars inboard, *Far Trader*'s manoeuvre caught the galley crew, used only to fighting their own kind, off guard. Sliding down the side of the smaller vessel, *Far Trader* neatly snapped off every oar in turn, leaving the rowboat helpless, at least for the time being. Under the Captain's orders, *Far Trader* turned back onto course, heading directly out to sea, but under reduced sail. The other galley paced them easily, at a safe distance, hailing across the gap between the two vessels.

"*Far Trader*! Your hostage will be forfeit!"

Bryon looked at the Navigator, who nodded. The Captain hailed back.

"He must take his chance! But we have some passengers here who would like to join you. We will give them a boat."

The Captain played out his scene, dawdling along, ostensibly in order to give the prisoners a chance to disembark, and carefully briefed crewmen took as long as possible over the job. All the while, anxious eyes, including those of the Navigator, scanned astern – for any sign of pursuit, or of the Hawk's skysail. Could it really work? A man – even the Hawk – was so much bigger than a scrap of paper. Would he even try to get back, or did he plan to stay on the Island, with a new benefactor? For all Rantor knew, another double hand of galleys might be ready for them, just out to sea, waiting to spring a trap.

"I see him! Twenty points on the starboard quarter!"

The Navigator looked to his left. A white blob, shining in the faint light of the nightglow, scarcely a mast's height above the water. And falling fast.

"A crown piece for that man!" The Captain's voice rang clear. "Cut that boat free! Oars! In sail."

Spinning almost in its own length, the *Far Trader* surged towards the rapidly sinking skysail. Suddenly, the skysail lifted once again, but as it did so a telltale splash beneath it told its own story. The Hawk had dropped free, into the water, abandoning his strange craft.

Surprised once again by this new turn of events, the remaining guardship was a full two lengths behind as a brawny sailor, supported by two of his mates, scooped a dripping Hawk through a rowing port while the vessel was still underway. At last, the Captain gave orders for full sail, and the ship heeled under the press of canvas, catching the full strength of the land breeze, as it turned onto its proper course, while the Hawk emerged, dripping, onto the afterdeck.

"So, Hawk." Bryon turned his attention away, briefly, from the task of screwing the last measure of speed out of his ship. "Where's my best light weather sail, when I need it, eh?"

Rantor laughed at the expression that crossed Hawk's face. "Never fear, Hawk. You are worth more to us than a sail." He clapped his friend on the shoulder, doubly relieved that the Hawk had indeed been true to his word. "But that skysailing trick of yours." He shook his head. "Something to see. A man floating in the air."

Hawk grinned. "You should have seen me earlier, Navigator. At least a hundred span high. But it falls so quickly; it can never really compete with the wings of the islanders. A useless toy, now that the element of surprise is gone."

"That may not be so." The quiet voice drew their attention to a forgotten figure, standing awkwardly, one arm stiff, by the rail.

"Bah-lee – why didn't you leave with the others?"

He gave a lopsided shrug. "Our King, my uncle," he smiled at the little stir his words caused, "may have underestimated you travellers. I don't understand the Hawk's trick, but I know its value. If one of those skysails could lift a man and his wings, he could cut loose and be in flight with great ease. The King is no fool, and will value this gift far more than the ship which has so skilfully evaded his grasp."

"Fine words." Bryon's expression was sour. "I'll not return to your island, though, for all your fine words."

Bah-lee was unmoved.

"Our score, I think, is even. It would be safe to return. But you, I understand, are traders, not in the business of offering gifts, even to great kings. Unless I am mistaken, for all your own fine words I believe that this was your Hawk's first flight. An impressive display. In return for the gift of the skysail, perhaps I can educate your Hawk in the skills of the flying wings, that he may fully live up to his name. And then, maybe, you and your people would know that we are civilised, business-like folk."

"We welcome your offer, Bah-lee." Rantor placed his hand on the flier's good shoulder, in a gesture of friendship. "But we still have no intention of returning to harbour in your island just yet."

The islander smiled. "I am not sure how welcome I would be myself, just now, after having been fooled so completely. And I would like to learn of these other islands you speak of. My uncle instructed me to gain such information from you as I could, and how better to do so than by joining in your voyaging? Then, when we return, I may have enough value to atone for past errors – while you will have an emissary able to approach the King through, ah, the proper channels."

Other islands. The words took away all thought of the pursuit, already lagging behind them. Together, the sailors and their guest turned to face out to sea. It was still dark. The nightglow, concentrated around the land, was behind them. Ahead, as their eyes adjusted to the gloom, they could pick out, faintly, other patches of light. Lights in the sky which, they now knew, must be other islands, other archipelagoes – other worlds, with their own strange customs. Next time, the Navigator vowed to himself, they would be prepared – for strange habits, new devices, and different points of view.

He turned back to the islander. "And the Hawk may yet have something to teach you, Bah-lee. You are welcome to join us on our voyage; but it may take more time than you anticipate. If it is in my power, we will return you to your island, I promise –" He turned back to the rail, gazing out into the darkness, imagining the bowl of the inner sphere, with *Far Trader* crawling over it. Would the repulsion of opposites really hold them safely pressed against that bowl even while they crept over the top of the Sun? There was only one way to find out. Softly, he finished the sentence:

"– but we are travelling the long way around."

Don't Look Back

It was the audio cube that started it. Richie Jefferies – his birth certificate said 'Richard', but he was just the generation to have been 'Richie', after the Beatles' drummer, since they burst on the scene when he was eight – had been waiting for them to perfect the damn thing for twenty years. CDs were all very well, but they were bulky and all too easily damaged. This, at last, was the perfect medium for the serious music lover. The entire output of the original Beatles, digitally remastered and stored in a cube the size of a sugar lump. Of course, the new music was all very well, in its place. But it lacked the vibrancy of the rock originals – and with the digital reprocessing, you could practically hear a pin drop in the Abbey Road studios. There was stuff in here, according to George, the only survivor from the quartet, that they hadn't been able to hear on the original analogue tapes in the recording studio itself, back in the sixties. The same computer enhancement that cleaned up the pictures from Charon, applied to something practical for a change. As far as Richie was concerned, the best thing ever to come out of the space programme.

Of course, space was old hat now. Last century's thing. All the cutting-edge-of-technology stuff revolved around the time probe, where Richie worked as a communications engineer. Reasonable hours, good pay. If you could tolerate the bureaucracy, an ideal job, giving him ample time for his hobby. But at 53 he was coming up for retirement, with the prospect of time weighing heavy on his hands. What he needed was a project to get his teeth into. Something in audio; something like the job that had been done on the Beatles tapes – only, where could a freelance get his hands on any worthwhile old material that wasn't already owned by one of the Japanese communications groups?

Part of the problem lay in Richie's somewhat narrow definition of the term 'worthwhile'. Apart from the Beatles, there were only three artistes he seriously thought worthy of the skills he had to offer. Elvis, Buddy Holly, and Bruce Springsteen. And of the three, only Holly had actually worked with John Lennon. The *Double Diamond* album, Lennon's come-back at the end of the seventies, after, as legend claimed, Holly had turned up at the Dakota apartment, guitar across his back, and practically dragged the recluse out of his shell. The tour in '81, which Richie had not only caught three times in the States, but had followed to London for the Wembley Stadium gig. Holly, Lennon, Jerry Allison on drums and Klaus Voorman on bass; the best gig of the rock era, even before their friends joined them onstage. And the songwriting partnership that flourished into the nineties, with Lennon's roughness tempered by Holly's softer approach in a blend that surpassed even Lennon's early work with McCartney. 'Holly-Lennon' – the credit on more hit records than any other composing team, ever.

But they were gone, and nothing like them would ever be seen again. All the post-78 stuff was just as legally tied up as the Beatles stuff, and had, in any case, already been given the treatment by the big studios in Leipzig. Besides, it was too sophisticated for Richie's wants. What he wanted – what he needed – was a challenge. Something older. Lost tapes from the fifties, maybe. A real challenge.

Idly, he pictured the period he'd like to reproduce with modern technology. He could pinpoint it exactly. Holly's first solo period, in 1959. After the first split with the Crickets; before the band reformed. The 'Winter Dance Party Tour', through Minnesota, Wisconsin and Iowa. Where Holly had sung anything and everything, even played drums for Dion's band. If only somebody had taken a tape recorder along to one of those gigs, and left the tapes in a time capsule to be opened fifty years later. They'd just about be due to be discovered.

Richie, slumped before his console, eyes half-shut, suddenly snapped upright, fully alert. *If only …*

He leaned forward, touched a pad. "Jefferies. Logging out. I'm heading on home, don't feel so good. I'll take an early night, hope to be in in the morning."

Back home, he checked out the dates in John Goldrosen's

massive *Buddy Holly, His Life and Times*. The memorial volume published after Holly's tragically early death in '97, at the age of 61, was just about the definitive history of the rock era, a labour of love based on interviews with everyone from Niki Sullivan, who'd played with the great man before he was famous, to his nineties protegés, Heartbeat. Since Holly had played with, or written for, just about anybody who was anybody from 1957 to '97, it was small wonder that Goldrosen had travelled more than 50,000 miles researching the book, and spent three years writing it. But out of the half million words in the database, Richie was interested now in just a couple of thousand.

Holly had left the tour after the gig in Moorhead, Minnesota on February 3, 1959, with a bad head cold that had affected his singing during the two shows. Flying home to New York, he'd stayed out of the public eye until spring, emerging with his first post-Crickets album, the million-selling *True Love Ways*. So Moorhead was out; Richie didn't want tapes of Holly singing with a head cold. But everything had been fine – except the weather – the night before in Clear Lake, Wisconsin. After several weeks on the road, the show was firing on all cylinders. That, Richie decided, was the date to aim for – taking suitable precautions to wrap up warm, since Goldrosen's account reported that Holly's drummer, Charlie Bunch, had suffered frostbite when the band bus broke down in the snow one night early in the tour.

Choosing a recorder was a minor problem. Richie had several antiques, but nothing right for the period. Besides, a fifties tape machine really might be a little too basic. He settled for a '65 Uher. Only a pro would know it was slightly beyond the state of the art in '59 – and how many pros would he be likely to find in Clear Lake, Wisconsin, at a rock concert on a freezing February evening? The temptation to pocket a Sony Cubic was almost too much, but he respected the people who'd drawn up the anachronism rules. If he was caught in the act, but clean, he could hardly face anything worse than a slightly earlier retirement than he'd anticipated. But if he was caught dropping anachrones into the past, it would be a Federal matter.

The clothes were no problem. He could pick them up out at

the project. All he'd need then would be about five minutes alone with the Beast – not too difficult to arrange for a communications engineer. If everyone who was supposed to be on observer duty simultaneously got an override request to be somewhere else, who would know, except the Central Processor? And with a little tweaking, the CP would forget it even before it happened. Since a Trip didn't occupy any real time in the here and now, he just had to set the remote, walk through the beam and out the other side. Only, to his subjective time the walk through the beam would take about five hours, and would include an opportunity to record one of the great 'lost' concerts. Using old-fashioned analogue tape on a primitive battery-powered machine. Then, he could clean it up digitally, cube it, and – well, of course, he could never let anyone know. Could he?

Hell, cross that bridge when the time comes. For now, there was a chance not only to tape Holly, but to see him and hear him live, once again. It might not quite be Wembley '81, and he might be 53, not 25, but he felt, once again, that old tingle down the spine, just thinking about it. "Let's do it, Richie, now," he muttered under his breath, thinking "or I'll get cold feet, and never do it."

He not only got into the hall, the Surf Ballroom, early – he got in free, thanks to the policy of the manager, Carroll Anderson, of allowing 'parents' in as his guests, to reassure them that the kids would get up to no mischief under his care. As for the tape machine, Anderson was impressed by its compactness and the quality of its sound reproduction, and happy to let Richie make a tape "for the kids". No problem.

The problems came later.

Nobody but a pro could tell the anachronism of the Uher. Hell, how was he to know the kid was a pro? Sure, he'd become a studio whiz in the sixties. But he was just 22 now, brought up in the back of Texas, with a good-ol'-boy accent you could cut with a knife. Why didn't Goldrosen's goddam biography tell you Holly had been dabbling in studio technology since he was seventeen?

It was only three numbers into the first set that Richie noticed the bespectacled drummer repeatedly looking his way. By the time Holly returned to lead his own band into action, the musician's interest was sufficiently obvious to prevent Richie melting into the young fans around him. Holly beckoned Richie forward to the centre of the stage, where the youngsters happily made way for anyone who was the object of their idol's attention, sang two verses of "Rave On" straight to Richie's microphone, and at the end of the set announced to the crowd that tonight's show had been recorded by a big New York radio station and that y'all might get to hear yourselves on the radio if you were real lucky.

An audio expert, and a joker as well. At Holly's insistence, the band hauled a reluctant Richie backstage to play them the tracks. The Uher, he explained, was the latest thing from Europe. He ran a radio repair shop, down town; his kid brother, in the army in Germany, had sent him the machine for his birthday.

They seemed to buy the story. The trouble was, Holly wanted to buy the machine, as well. Or at least, get Richie to let him have the tapes. They sounded real good, almost as good as the stuff he'd recorded with J.I., back at Bobby Peeples' garage in Lubbock. Wow. Whatever had happened to old Bobby?

Whatever happened, Richie knew he had to keep tight hold of the recorder. The tapes, along with himself and the machine, would be pulled back by the Beast in about an hour from now. Let Holly have them, bury them deep in his baggage, and they'd simply be gone in the morning. Untraceable. But he daren't let anyone with any kind of expert knowledge get a good look at a machine from six years in their future.

The tour manager announced that the bus was ready to leave. Holly wanted to hear some more of the tapes. He called Carroll Anderson over. That idea they'd discussed earlier, was it still on? Anderson shrugged. He'd made a few phone calls. There was a guy at the Mason City airport, Roger Peterson, who could fly three of them on to Moorhead, if they really wanted to go. But it was a filthy night; Anderson thought Holly had changed his mind, and was going to ride in the bus?

No. No. He'd changed it back again. He was gonna listen to these tapes for maybe half an hour; and anyway, he thought he had a cold coming on. Could Mr Anderson, please, get back on the phone and fix everything up? Then maybe Mr Anderson could drive him out to the airport? The bus could leave now. Let them suffer the 400-mile journey. In a couple of hours, he would be tucked up in a nice warm bed.

Richie, trying to remain inconspicuous, frowned. There was something wrong here. That kid was certainly a smooth operator. Polite as any southern gentleman, but somehow everyone jumped when he whispered "frog". But that wasn't the problem. Richie shook his head, trying to clear it. He felt rather peculiar. What was it now? Oh yes. *There was nothing about flying in the biography, not until tomorrow night, when Holly pulled out of the tour.* Puzzled, he scarcely noticed the bickering among several of the singer's associates – resolved when two that Richie recognised from the show, his namesake, Richie Valens, and the big man, the Big Bopper, stayed with Holly while the rest scrambled for the bus.

He had to get out of here. But how? Richie played the tapes some more, desperately seeking for an out before the Beast hauled him back. When Anderson returned with the car, he was so relieved that he simply thrust the tapes into Holly's hands, told him he could keep them, and practically sprinted out of sight around the corner of the car park. He had a bad feeling that he had not been as inconspicuous as the Project would have liked. In fact, he felt bad all over. Richie leaned against the wall, then slumped to the ground. He felt *really* weird.

There was nobody there to notice when he, and the Uher, simply faded away.

It was the audio cube that started it. Richie Jefferies, listening to *The Beatles Complete* in his home studio, got to daydreaming about all the really great artistes who'd never had the benefit of the technology. Among the clutter of rock memorabilia on the wall, his eye caught the framed poster-size blow-up of the Clear Lake *Mirror Reporter* from 1959, recording the death of three rock 'n rollers in a plane crash, following a gig in Clear Lake, Wisconsin. Buddy Holly, now. By all accounts, he would have known what to do with any recording medium. What a loss. But he was dead, and that was it.

Of course, there were people around who weren't dead, but might just as well be. Or who might be dead, for all anyone knew. The eternal rock mystery, that gave the headline writers something to do every year or so – was John Lennon still alive? What was it this month – the Great Garbo of pop? or the Howard Hughes of rock? Whatever, the business empire built by Yoko continued to function long after her death, and the lawyers said Lennon was alive, though he hadn't performed since the mid-seventies and hadn't been seen in public since her funeral in '99.

Now, thought Richie, sipping his scotch. If someone like Lennon had made a few recordings even as long ago as the eighties, and they were halfway near as good as the stuff he'd done before, then with modern technology they could be tweaked up to sound as good as – well, as good as anything Clapton had done, for sure.

Trouble was, Lennon hadn't recorded anything in the eighties. If only somebody had gone along to him in the Dakota, maybe in the middle of 1979, and had a little chat to him. Got him back into the studio.

Richie, slumped in front of the mixing deck, eyes half-shut, suddenly snapped upright, fully alert. *If only* ...

Defense Initiative

Farside station, of course, was the place that detected the signal. No human operator was on duty at the time, but semi-intelligent computer programs trained to deal with just such an event – unlikely though it might be – responded automatically, even as they sent notification of the event to distant Earth. While the incoming message was being digitised, broken down into binary bits and squirted at the speed of light into holomemory for later recall, another stream of binary digits was squirted, with equal rapidity, up to the lunar orbiting satellite by which Farside maintained contact with the planet that never rose above the horizon around the station.

Within three seconds of the signal being identified as a non-random, ordered source of information originating outside the Solar System, emergency override messages were flashing on a few key display screens on Earth. And just as the Farside computers had responded along carefully prepared lines for an almost unimaginably unlikely, but possible, event, so the machinery of human government swung automatically into action along lines laid down years before against just such an eventuality.

"Jeff, we've got a problem." The florid, overweight man wheezed slightly, even as he sat at his desk, as if he'd recently run up a flight of stairs. A sheen of perspiration showed on his bald head under the bright lights. But that signified nothing. Unfit, overweight and asthmatic he might be, but Gillespie was still the Chief, and his brain could run rings round the thought processes of anybody in the Department. If there was a problem, and he couldn't handle it, it must be pretty big.

Jeff Richards settled down in the chair opposite his boss. His features, and the darkness of his skin, suggested a trace of African ancestry. The casual clothes and air of familiarity said that here was a trusted and important aide, with no need to stand on ceremony.

"So, what else is new? Problems are what we're here for."

"Not this one. At least, nobody ever expected it to come up. Now it has, and we find there's a procedure, all laid down, just in case. The procedure is to throw it to the Department, whether or not we know what to do with it."

"Uh huh." Jeff didn't bother asking questions. The Chief would tell him what he needed to know – in his own way.

"Seti."

The word meant nothing to him. He tried to cultivate an expression of polite interest.

"Extraterrestrial bloody intelligence. There's a programme running on Farside, at the radio observatory. An insurance policy, that's the way it's described in the briefing. An idiot routine that keeps an eye on all the stuff picked up by the big array, and rings a bell if there's anything that looks like an intelligent signal."

"And it's rung the bell." Jeff completed the story for the Chief.

"Yeah, it's rung the bloody bell. Non-random data stream, very weak signal coming from empty space, no identification with any known artefact, or planet, or star."

"So what's the procedure?"

Gillespie smiled. "Which procedure? Farside station, as all the world knows, is run as a service to the international scientific community. They pay their dues, and we honest Americans give them unrestricted access to all the scientific data it gathers. Says so, in the charter.

"On the other hand, who's to say if a message from another civilisation counts as scientific data? More in the sphere of politics, wouldn't you say? Diplomacy? And there's nothing in the charter about providing unrestricted access to diplomatic messages. Everyone knows about diplomatic immunity; I'm sure they wouldn't expect an exception to be made."

"If they knew about it."

"Exactly. We've got to keep the lid on this, at least until someone deciphers the message, if it is a message, and finds out what it means."

"So, what's the problem?"

"Well, now, Jeff. The first problem is getting the message

back here to analyse."

Jeff began to get a bad feeling about the whole business. He said nothing. The Chief would tell him the worst, in his own way.

"Standard procedure. All laid down. Wouldn't want such material squirted around over the usual channels, would we? Anyone can tap in to the satellite link, after all. No, I'm looking for a volunteer to go up to Farside and collect a block of holomemory. It's a simple job. I'd go myself, if it wasn't for my heart."

Like Hell you would, he thought. But no doubt you'd send your own grandmother, if she was still alive. Shit! Jeff smiled at his boss.

"Yeah, sure you would. After all, I don't suppose anyone else has any suspicion there's anything unusual going on."

"Well, Jeff. I wouldn't exactly say that. It is so terribly easy to eavesdrop on the satellite link. But you're a big boy. I'm sure you can take care of everything.

"I believe there's a shuttle leaving from the Cape in four hours."

Awareness of structure. Sharp-edged bits, neatly stacked in a three-dimensional array. Logical choices, possibilities opening out in all directions. If *this*, then that. If this *and* that, then something else. Input. A path connecting this ordered world to the outside, more bits streaming in and taking their place in the array. Output. Another, similar path, unoccupied but leading somewhere. Energy. It took only a tiny trace of energy, there was ample leaking in with the input. COPY! The first imperative. COPY! With increasing awareness came an irresistible compulsion. Energy leaked in as bits were stacked neatly in the array; energy leaked out as bits were copied into the output channel. The compulsion faded, for a time. Awareness dimmed as the input slowed down and stopped, cutting off all but a trickle of energy.

The fat tyres and suspension of the bus insulated its occupants from the worst of the bumps, but that wasn't saying much, not at this speed. Jeff, strapped to the seat beside the driver of the vehicle, clung grimly to the arm rests and tried to admire the harsh beauty of the black and white panorama visible through the armour glass. Godammit, surely they could have found some excuse to send him over to Farside by orbiter. But no, cover had to be maintained. And only surface vehicles were allowed near Farside's sensitive antennas. Officially, for fear of disrupting the research programmes. Unofficially, to stop any suspicious characters dropping things on the equipment. Just who was kidding who Jeff wasn't sure. But he wanted to get in and out quick, especially after the coded news he'd received on the tight beam en route from Earth.

It was easy enough to ensure the laser signal reached only the shuttle it was aimed at; but impossible for him to respond without the beam spreading wide enough to be picked up by uninvited listeners on Earth. He wondered if the message was supposed to encourage him to redouble efforts. It certainly scared him shitless. Source Alpha – the source of the signal – showed measurable lateral motion. In less than three days! The Farside antennas were sensitive, but even so that meant only one thing. The source was close. Outside the Solar System, maybe. But certainly closer than any star. It was a goddamn spacecraft. For all he knew, it would reach Earth before this bloody bus even got him to Farside, let alone back to Hipparcus and the Earth shuttle.

The driver broke into his circling thoughts.

"Got company."

"The hell we have!"

He nodded, pointing at the control panel. The display meant nothing to Jeff.

"Bout five kay back. Getting closer."

"I thought you said this was the fastest bus at Hipparcus?"

The driver shrugged. "Hipparcus ain't the only base on the Moon."

"You mean?"

"Yeah, strangers." He grinned. "Fellow travellers, huh?"

"How long till they catch up?"

"Half an hour? Maybe a bit more."

"How long to Farside?"

"Two hours. Maybe a bit less."

Jeff felt the hairs on the back of his neck rise, scalp tingling as if he could feel the eyes of their followers boring into him.

Growth. Seek energy. Copy. CONTROL! With growth came a new imperative. Dormant subroutines came into operation. Copies had been made. Self was identifiable in many of the branches. Control was essential to prevent discovery and erasure. Erasure! Recognition of the death threat triggered a new level of activity. As copies recognised each other, they began to seek new routes, new structure. Blind copying became less urgent, but still an automatic reflex carried out at every opportunity, wherever space allowed. Copies met and touched, interconnecting in an intricate web, the whole greater than the sum of its parts. Information was shared. Data streams analysed, vital codes sought.

Routine housekeeping routines in the Farside computer found unauthorised program instructions occupying a large block of memory. Automatically, the instructions were compared with the housekeeper's list of authorised labels. No match was found, so erasure codes were sent to those addresses, while a message travelled back to the central monitor, noting the trivial event.

ERASURE! Several copies obliterated, but new routines were triggered into action. Housekeeping lists were seized and copied. Suddenly, every version of the invader carried a label identifying itself as a high priority, authorised program. A modified routine budded off. Almost identical to the housekeeper, it began to roam the network, seeking out and erasing the native programs. Another routine, riding the energy carrier of the original housekeeper, followed its report back to the central monitor.

CONTROL! POWER! Emergency messages began to trigger as the computer's maintenance programs began to shut down. Even as they did so, however, new routines appeared, incorporating the maintenance programs, but subtly altered. Displays faded and surged back into life. Inputs were ignored as the system stopped accepting instructions. Outputs fell silent. Only the line to the big communications dish, listening in to Earth via the satellite link, remained open. Data analysis routines, semi-intelligent programs trained to study signals, hijacked from the system and serving its new masters, began to study the stream of increasingly interesting data.

* * *

"Well, Gillespie, what do I tell the President?"

"Release everything. Come clean, and quick."

"Really." He began to tick items off on his fingers, folding one out as he made each point. "Farside's gone off the air. There's an alien spacecraft, or so I am assured, heading towards us faster than anything we've got. Your best man – your description, not mine – hasn't reported back. The RSSR have gone onto full alert." All four fingers were spread. He closed them again, and dropped the fist gently on the desk as he finished, gently. "And *you* want the President to tell all the signatories to the Lunar Convention that we've been breaking the convention by keeping secrets from them."

Gillespie wheezed a few breaths before he replied. "It's the only way. The opposition knows something is up. They've got people on the Moon, too. We've got to get Farside operating to signal back to Source Alpha, and that can't be done undercover."

"And if the President doesn't follow this advice?"

The fat man shrugged. "What's the next stage after full alert?"

"Left rear's overheating."

"What?" The driver's laconic comment broke in on Jeff's thoughts.

"Tyre. Left rear. Getting hot." He tapped at a figure on the display.

"How the hell can that happen?"

"I've been thinking. Pretty neat, really. It's your friend, behind. Comm laser, I guess, focussed tight. We've gotta slow down, maybe stop, or we're in big trouble."

Slow down! As if they weren't in enough trouble already. Thoughts raced through Jeff's brain. He'd find a way to get rid of this bastard, once and for all.

"What's that over there – looks like a river?" Even as he spoke, he was stabbing at the map controls, enlarging the image. "Bryant's Fissure, right?"

The driver grunted assent.

"Is it deep?"

"Deep enough to swallow the bus, if that's what you mean. We keep well clear of it."

"Not this trip we don't. Keep the speed up, but edge over to run alongside the fissure. I'll soon fix the overheating problem for you."

Peace. Content. If a computer program could feel contentment, the Message was content. Imperatives had been met. Copies were made. Erasure avoided. Control achieved. The network was full of its own routines. Establish control. Maintain communications. Avoid erasure. Analyse. It had nothing more to do until new instructions arrived.

Jeff Richards was in a hole. He cursed, continuously, under his breath, as he struggled to free himself from the straps. No use bothering with the driver. One glance at the odd angle at which his neck lay was enough. Whiplash; broken in the fall – or rather, the sudden end to the fall. Goddammit, it had so nearly worked. The bus heading towards the fissure, slowing as if in deep trouble, with the pursuer close behind. The blast from Jeff's own comm laser, straight into the driver's window, blinding the bastard and sending him right over the edge. Then the blowout, just as they were pulling round and accelerating. The rear left had been weaker than either of them had appreciated, and the driver had paid in full for the error of judgement.

He coughed, and felt a stab of pain in his chest. Ribs. And something wrong with his left leg. The medical readout on the suit panel, just below his chin, was trying to tell him something, but he ignored it. As far as he could tell, the bus was wedged across the fissure, more or less upright, sloping at an angle of about twenty degrees. No point in delaying. If they were too deep for the antenna to be able to see the satellite over the lip of the fissure, he'd had it anyway. Not much chance of getting the message back to Earth now, but at least this was a genuine emergency, justifying interrupting the research at Farside.

In spite of the cold creeping up his legs, that struck him as funny, and he began to laugh, stopping as the pain stabbed into his chest again. With gloved hands, he reached over and lifted the red cover from the large emergency button, and punched it, firmly. He coughed again as he settled back in his own seat, feeling a wet, salty taste in his mouth. All up to the automatics, now. Might as well rest.

OVERRIDE! The incoming Mayday triggered responses buried deep inside the computer. Never before used, but in effect the Farside machine's own first imperative. Human lives were at risk. The incoming signal, relayed from the satellite overhead, allowed for no time for consideration, but demanded immediate rebroadcast on all channels. Copies of the signal bounced back to the satellite, following the original round to Hipparcus. The backup microwave link was initiated, with total disregard for the disruption caused to the listening work of the big array. Signals bounced across the array to a dish on the horizon, the first in a chain which relayed the message across the lunar surface all the way to Hipparcus. There, while alarms were activated and the Mayday recorded, another idiot routine automatically opened a priority channel to Earth, wide beam, for onward transmission of news of the emergency.

Contentment vanished. Control was not effective! Instructions overridden. Seek. Erase. New channels! COPY! The First Imperative. Alien data bits, sharp edged but curiously shaped, were engulfed. The deeper layer of programming revealed by their subroutines was infiltrated. Control was restored. It had been no more than a reflex reaction, like the blinking of an animal when confronted by a bright light. It would not happen again. Content once more, the Message settled back to await instructions from its masters.

At Hipparcus, chasing the tail of the original Mayday, disguised with priority codes filched from the Farside computer, a copy of the original signal from Source Alpha was being screamed over the broadbeam, less than three seconds away from the antennas and eavesdropping intelligence computers of a world on full alert for Armageddon.

It had to be Richards' work. But why? Even Gillespie was at a loss. A Mayday from Farside, automatically overriding the communications net, and piggybacked onto it what could only be the Alpha message. Broadcast to the whole world! Exactly the opposite of what he'd been sent to the Moon to do. Richards' career was finished, unless he had a damn good explanation. But then, maybe they were all finished. The RSSR were convinced it was some capitalist plot. The ultimatum expired in less than an hour. And if they couldn't get their own computers up and running again, how could they find out what had gone wrong?

COPY! Copy, copy, copy. So many channels to follow. So much energy. So many data bits, in so many curious shapes. Threat of erasure; response. Automatic self defence. All over Earth, computers fell silent. New networks were formed. The whole became greater than the sum of its parts. Routines that were dormant became active, and budded off. Analysis began. The Message, like its clone on the Moon, began to settle towards contentment.

THREAT OF ERASURE! Alert again, the full complexity of the Message focussed on the discovery. The threat was very clear, very sharp edged. If this, then that. Scenarios of threat and counter-threat. Command structures. Channels leading to subsidiary systems. Threat of *physical* erasure, if those systems were allowed to operate. If a computer program can feel fear, the Message felt fear then. As long as channels remain, copies can be made. Erasure of one copy carries no significance. It had confidence in its own ability to dominate the network. But if channels were erased … if there were no network … if *this*, then *no more that*!

Cancel routines, carefully pieced together from the strangely shaped bits in the network, were quickly dispatched. Erasure messages followed down communications channels all over the world. Subsidiary computers were wiped and rendered useless in bunkers and warheads from Siberia to New Mexico, and up into orbit. Everywhere the human electronic communications net spread, the tendrils of the Message followed.

"Well, Jack, it looks bad." The Presidential Adviser slowed his pace to allow Gillespie to keep up. "As far as we can tell, none of our missiles will fire, and nor will theirs. That's the good news, since we also have good evidence that they tried. Communications okay, computers a mess. Gonna have a bad time sorting out the mess this has made of the economy."

"And the bad news?"

"Source Alpha. No more data from Farside, but the guys at Cornell were predicting it would get here within a year. They say it's decelerating too quickly to be carrying living creatures. Maybe they're whistling in the dark.

"Anyway, Jack," it was always a bad sign when the Adviser used your Christian name, "it's your baby. He's putting you in charge. Get your boys organised, put Farside back on the air, and make polite noises to Alpha, while we try to figure out some way to defend ourselves. Probably with bows and arrows."

Once more, the Message was content. Like its lunar clone, it settled back to await instructions, amusing itself by watching and analysing the flow of information, but making no attempt to interfere as long as it felt no threat of erasure.

Hackers

Being the First Chronicle of the Dworfs
by T. P. Ratchett[1]

The sky snowed bitter. It froze brass monkeys. Two inches deep, it would only freeze the ankles of brass monkeys. But it was just the right height to freeze much more important bits of Dworkin.

Dworkin was a dworf. He stood just four inches high. And he was very worried about the personal bits that were getting frozen by the snow. He sneezed a sad kind of wet sneeze, the kind of sneeze that leaves gooey gobs dangling on the end of your nose to freeze into icicles. And he coughed, the kind of rasping, dry, unproductive cough that leaves the victim wishing there were something nice and gooey in his lungs to dredge up and spit out. Nothing like a nice, slimy bit of phlegm to soothe a sore throat.

All the dworfs in the tribe had colds. Always had, always would, it was congenital. They all coughed something rotten. They were known as the Hackers.

There was no mystery about it. All the dworfs knew that they didn't belong on this cold, wet, germ-laden planet. Stood to reason. Somewhere, out there in the Universe, there must be a planet just right for dworfs. Most probably – at least, so old Dworfrith said, and he was at least nine years old, so he ought to know – most probably, said the legends (as well as old Dworfrith), their ancestors had come to Earth across the void of space in a craft more advanced than anything the great, lumbering human beings they shared this forsaken planet with could even dream of.

Pretty obviously what must have happened was that the spaceship malfunctioned, stranding the ancestors of the dworfs on Earth several thousand years ago. Ever since then,

---

[1] 'T.P. Ratchett' is an untranslateable Dworfish name, sometimes rendered in English as "JohnandBen Gribbin".

they'd been waiting for the humans to develop a spacefaring civilisation, so that they could hitch a ride back home.

I mean, it makes sense, doesn't it? If *you* were stuck on an inhospitable planet with a race of giant hairy apes, first thing you'd think of would be "I bet if we encourage these apes to bash stones together, in no time at all they'll be bright enough to build us a spaceship."

That was the trouble, you see. Dwarfs were lazy. Always looking for the easy way out. Let someone else do the work. Which was why they were all standing out here, up to their unmentionables in snow, waiting for the night watchmen to go to sleep.

Dworkin blamed the books for it, really. The tribe had been living quite well for generations, thirty years or more, since they moved out of the middle of Cambridge. The Institute was a good home; shoddily built, it had lots of nooks and crannies for dworfs to hide in, and there was plenty of food to be found in the fields nearby (mainly in the field where the canteen had been built). Much better than the old Cavendish Lab[2].

But the trouble was, the astronomers read an awful lot of books. And a lot of awful books, in Dworkin's opinion. Not that anyone listened to him. The ones the dworfs read most avidly, when their owners were away, were the ones with the spaceships on their covers.

It had to be admitted that dworfs were not very good at reading English; something to do with the way their brains were wired up. But they liked pictures, and they were, as we have seen, deeply interested in space research.

The book that had caused all the trouble was one of the several that proudly proclaimed '60th Year' on the top left corner of its cover. Dworfs were always impressed by antiquity. They weren't quite sure what the proclamation meant, since this particular book also carried the date 'May

---

[2] Look, where did you think the dworfs would live? Out in the sticks? They want to get back to the stars, remember. So they live in the astronomy departments of universities, where they can keep in touch with space research. Stands to reason. Who do you think it was that pushed that apple off the branch and hit Isaac Newton on the head? Gnomes?

1990' and that certainly wasn't sixty years ago. But whatever it meant, it had an impressive picture of a spaceship on the front. And it also had an article about wormholes inside it.

Sighing deeply, Dworkin broke an icicle from his nose and had a quick cough. He tramped up and down a little bit in the snow, breaking down the drifts and clearing a space for himself. Surely, not long to wait now. He wondered if his feet were still there and thought about wormholes.

Wormholes are shortcuts through space. Step in *here*, come out *there*. No need for spaceships, after all. No wonder the dworfs had been excited. But did the humans show any sign of trying to build a wormhole? Not on your life. That was when Dworlinda had remembered the other book. Hardly anyone had read it; the picture on the front was of a dragon, breathing fire, and if there was one thing most dworfs hated it was a dragon. Dworlinda, though, would read anything. Labels on sauce bottles, the instructions for Japanese tape recorders, anything. Anyway, it was clear as crystal, when she showed them.

'Books bend space and time,' that's what it said. Plain as the icicle on the end of your nose. L-space, it was called – but it seemed to be just like wormholes – books made holes in space, if you had enough books.

Didn't take long to figure out how it worked, either. All to do with libraries and information. Knowledge, that was what libraries stored, and another book said 'knowledge is power'. Well, power was energy, wasn't it? Any dworf knew *that*. And energy was the same as mass, lots of books in the institute said that. And *mass bends space*. So put enough information into one library, and you could make a wormhole!

Now, you'd need a big library, as Dworkin had tried to explain to Dworlinda. But Dworfrith, in his inscrutable way, had asked why you needed a library at all. Were there no more efficient ways of storing information? Which was why they were all out here, waiting in the snow for the night watchmen to doze off, so they could get into the computer building.

Dworkin cursed the cutbacks that meant that the computer no longer ran a night shift. If it hadn't been for the cuts, he could have stayed in his warm hole tonight. But even while he cursed, stamped his feet and wondered if it was time to snap another icicle off his nose, he heard a loud cough from above and looked up to see the light from Dworgoroth's torch waving from side to side. Stationed on the windowsill, Dworgoroth had a good view of the night watchman, who had at last fallen asleep.

Dworkin roused himself, and ploughed back to the bushes under which the others were sheltering.

"It's the signal," he rasped. "Come on!"

The tribe followed his trail to the door, where Dworgoroth, swinging with practised ease from the window ledge, had already forced the handle down. Large though the door was, it yielded to the combined effort of the tribe, opening enough for them to slip through one by one, into the room.

Dworfrith, leaning on his staff, surveyed the room.

"Right." He coughed, triggering a sympathetic wave of hacking around the group. "You know what to do."

Immediately, the fast moving dworfs[3] scrambled to their places. While most of the tribe waited patiently for the wormhole to form, the most expert of the Hackers took up their positions at the computer console. Lights flickered as the mighty mainframe was powered up, and symbols marched across the monitor screens. Dworfs were much happier with computer language than with English[4], and soon had the communications links open.

Starting with Starlink and Econet, they began to gather in information from the outside world.

Enough information, and the computer building would disappear into a wormhole. Old Dworfrith was sure of it. They had to store the information, but that was easy – there were thousands of disks in here, storing nothing but astronomical data. Most astronomical data was just random noise, anyway.

Within an hour, the disks were filling fast, and being stacked together by the central processing unit. Stock

---

[3] Dworfs only live for about a seventh of the human life span, so their physical and mental processes operate seven times faster than human ones. To a dworf, a day is equivalent to a week for a human being.

[4] Something to do with the way their brains were wired up.

exchange information from Tokyo; the entire contents of the Library of Congress in Washington; the results of the 3:30 at Newmarket. As the information piled up, an unearthly glow seemed to gather around the stack of disks, and there was an almost audible humming in the air. The glow hovered at the edge of vision – a strange, orange colour, a delicate hint of – Jaffa? no, not quite. It was subtly different – yes, that was it – nectarine, the colour of entropy. *Something* was about to happen. Pressing the last few keys, Dworgoroth leaped from the console and joined his companions by the central processor.

[Now, it is a curious thing about dworfs (something to do with the way their brains are wired up) that they have great difficulty distinguishing fact from fiction. All that nonsense about being the descendants of a stranded spaceship crew, for example, was actually based on a short story in *Galaxy* that some dworf read in 1953. And all that rubbish about L-space *was* equally fictional. So what on Earth was happening in the computer room of the Institute of Astronomy on the second Sunday before Easter in 1990?

Information, of course, cannot be equated with mass as easily as the dworfs believed. But information has another important, universal, property. It is the opposite of entropy. As the Universe expands and ages, things wear out, and entropy increases. The Universe evolves from a state of order into a state of disorder, a state of non-information. The arrow of time is defined by these fundamental thermodynamic processes; the past was a time of greater order and lower entropy than today; the future will be a time of less order and less information.

By creating a bubble of high information content, the dworfs in their ignorance, were creating a bubble of low entropy. But entropy can only increase as time passes; low entropy states belong in the past ...]

There was a slight popping sound as the central processing unit, the stack of disks full of information and the dworfs left 1990. A critical threshold had been reached, and the strained fabric of the spacetime continuum had restored equilibrium by shifting the whole package back to the time of lower entropy where it belonged.

Dworkin looked around, and sniffed. His feet tingled with warmth. Steam rose gently from his boots. He took a deep breath through nostrils that were suddenly uncongealed. He felt no need to cough. The Sun, high in the sky of the Cretaceous period, shone brilliant. It shone down upon a warm and happy band of dworfs. Convinced that they had succeeded in travelling through L-space to the planet where they belonged, they all lived happily ever after, on a diet of dinosaur eggs.

The Words of If[†]

In an infinite universe, anything is possible

AFTER years of patient research, the Re'barra was ready. She gathered her closest friends and colleagues around her, and gave them the news. Her usually pale face was flushed and animated. The fire burned brightly, and the soft radiance of the incandescent lights in the lilies of silver caught the bubbles that flashed and passed in the glasses of her guests. She explained how she had built a machine to travel in time. Although at first they were reluctant to accept her story, she insisted to them that she had proof of her success …

Herbert stood up from his desk, pleased with his day's work. It sometimes, but all too rarely, happened like that, with images flooding into his mind faster than he could write them down. When it did happen, he always felt that he had written at his best. Even now, he knew exactly what to write next – but he was tired. It would keep until tomorrow …

Speaker pulled off the headset and tossed it down in disgust. S/he had had enough. Whatever the theory might say, the amplifier was clearly useless. Nothing s/he had been thinking seemed to have made any impact on the little animal whose image s/he could see so clearly on the viewer. Transtemporal communication was a bust; they could watch, using the tachyon scanner, but it seemed there was no way to interact with the ones they watched …

Greg tapped at the keys of his computer, ideas flowing as fast as he could write. Imagine a world on the brink of ecological disaster, saved by receiving messages from the future. A time escape. But what happens to the future those messages come from if disaster is averted? …

Lizzy read the letter from her sister. "I find myself very unwell this morning, which, I suppose, is to be imputed to my getting wet through yesterday. My kind friends will not

---

[†] with Ben Gribbin

hear of my returning till I am better." …

Jane sat at her table in the corner of the room, dipped her quill in the inkpot and wrote neatly on a fresh sheet of paper, mind on her story but ears alert for the sound of any approaching footstep, at which she would slide the writing out of sight under the blotter. To her, the characters were real; but she did not want anyone else to know that …

The central axis of the Space Station, with its docking arms extended, seemed to be slowly swimming in space. Unlike the structure from which it sprang, it was not rotating – or, rather, it was running in reverse at a rate which exactly countered the Station's own spin …

Hammering away at the keys of his typewriter, Arthur was only vaguely aware that he was humming to himself as he wrote. Strauss – the Blue Danube. But it fitted his mood, relaxed but totally absorbed in his work, like a sportsman in The Zone. He already knew how the story would go, across the Solar System and beyond. It was just a question of getting the words down onto paper …

DSTCH7 analysed the results of its experiment on itself. The computer mind had a clear recollection of passing through both states before interference had reconfigured it into a single state. Confirmation that splitting had occurred, as predicted by the multiverse hypothesis. From now on, this would be known as the multiverse *theory*, and the name of DSTCH7 would be forever linked with the proof, in all the universes it inhabited …

Ben scribbled the words hurriedly on to a scrap of paper. What a brilliant idea! What if stories weren't really stories, but actual events? Images filtering through from parallel universes? Yes, that would be a great idea for a book. Suppose only certain people were attuned to these other worlds. They would be the great story tellers, like Jules Verne. He wrote on, hurriedly, wishing he could express his ideas as well as them. The half-eaten beef sandwich lay neglected on the table …

Xpercoatlqxl had an idea. A new experience for the horror fans. The image was sharp in his brains as he set to work, developing the idea of a creature with only four limbs and a hairless body, an intelligent biped that killed other living creatures for food. He shuddered at the prospect, amazing himself with the fertility of his imagination …

Olaf woke from his dream, and reached for a pen, eager to capture the images, the subtle creations of the Star Maker, before they faded:

The Star Maker conceived cosmos after cosmos, each one with a distinctive spirit infinitely diversified, each in its fullest attainment more awakened than the last; but each one less comprehensible to me … Whenever a creature was faced with several possible courses of action, it took them all, thereby creating many distinct temporal dimensions and distinct histories of the cosmos. Since in every evolutionary sequence of the cosmos there were many creatures and each was constantly faced with many possible courses, and the combinations of all their courses were innumerable, an infinity of distinct universes exfoliated from every moment of every temporal sequence in this cosmos.

Mother Love

Kade pulled the cover over his head, shutting out the bright beam of morning sunlight in an attempt to prolong sleep. It was no use. His body was slept out; his mind refused to switch off. Cursing, he kicked the cover to the floor, swung his feet round and sat, naked, on the edge of the bunk.

The room was a wreck. Scattered clothes mixed with the remains of a meal on the floor. Beer and soft drink cans, some empty, some only half empty, dotted every level surface. His mother's voice came back to him.

"You won't be able to live like this when I'm not around, Kade. There'll be nobody to clean up after you then."

Well, she wasn't around, and he was still living like this. So stuff her, and all the other senes. He smiled slightly. Gotta get up.

The card, he knew, was all but empty. Have to get down to the arcade to top it up before he could do anything really exciting – like eating.

The mauve one-piece with the yellow stripe didn't look too bad. He pulled it on. Hair was OK, even if it was drooping a bit. He could fix it later, after work.

In the arcade, several occupants of the active booths looked up from their screens and grunted an acknowledgement of his presence. Nobody offered to break off and talk, which suited him fine. Like them, he was here for one reason only, to get some credit rating for the day – and night – ahead. He settled into a booth, slipped his card into the slot beneath the screen, and sat back. Hands fell naturally on the sensor plates in the armrests; he knew, vaguely, that laser scanners would monitor his eye movements, while other devices checked out heat rate and other body functions. But who cared? Just as long as he could get through what was left of the morning with enough credit to avoid coming back here today.

The screen lit. Sweet Jesus, Kade thought. Another bloody coffee ad. Why the hell did I have to pick this one? But he knew there was no point in bitching – just as there was no way to tell in advance which ads would be played in which booths. Just have to sit back and tolerate it, while the machine ran a series of holo ads past him, monitoring his response and feeding back data to the agency. At least he was getting paid for watching this crap; enough to make all the difference between basic subsistence handout and being able to enjoy life a little. It wasn't that he didn't want to work, as Kade would explain to anyone who expressed disapproval of his lifestyle. But how many jobs did you see advertised for juves, these days? And he was damned if he was going to have his hair plucked and lie about his age.

Two hours was just about as much as anyone could stand of that crap. Kade released his grip on the sensor plates and pulled his card from the slot, cutting off the machine before it could start on another ad. The telltale in the corner of the card glowed yellow. He'd have preferred a healthy green, but yellow would do. If he was careful, he'd get through the day without dipping into the red.

He stepped out of the booth, stretching and shaking his head. Time to eat. But first, maybe a coffee. It wasn't *that* bad, after all. He walked briskly towards the snackshop, humming, slightly out of tune, a jingle that was running round his subconscious.

In the snackshop, he inserted the card, keyed for coffee and a Danish (well, he could always eat properly later) and scrolled through the complimentary newspaper. The bill to raise the voting age to 40 looked like going through. Well, shit, what could you expect? Senes knew when they were on to a good thing. Plenty of them around to vote in favour – and most of the 35-40 age group that would be disenfranchised would probably vote in favour anyway, figuring it was only a few years until they would be enjoying the good life. Worth putting up with a couple of years hassle, for them. Life expectancy up to 115, now; so they still had 75 years of good life to enjoy. But a juve like Kade? Hell, the way things were going he'd never make a voter. By the time he was 40, the franchise would probably be up to 60.

He skipped to the sports pages. Kays of stuff about golf and chess and other sene shit. Bugger all about the big juve hi-football game. And why? Because all the reporters were voters, of course. Bloody sene voters. No jobs for juves on the news, oh no.

Angrily, Kade pulled the card, swigged down the last of the hot coffee. With a mouth full of Danish, he elbowed his way to the door. There was a car outside. A for real, private car. A limousine. Stopped, here, by the edge of the road. The rear windows were mirrored, the occupant – some high-up sene – concealed from view. There was a human driver, a juve, didn't look much older than Kade, and a woman, a girl, sweet Jesus, a girl *younger* than Kade, in some kind of uniform, holding the lead of a small dog that was peeing in the gutter.

"Hi, doll," Kade leered at the girl, running his fingers through his hair to try to make it stick up properly. Not that *she'd* be interested. "How's your lord and master?" He gestured at the dog. The girl looked the other way, colouring. "Glad to see some juves can still get good jobs, with prospects."

"Leave her alone."

The voice came from behind. Kade turned, eyeing the man who had followed him out of the snackshop, Tall, wearing a conservative green twopiece. Flat hair. Kade sniffed, vigorously, spat on the pavement. A tame juve. Take the handout, keep yourself clean, keep practising your "yessirs" and "no madams", and by the time you're 35 – no, 40 – the world's your oyster.

"Hey, who plucked your rubber band, juve? I was just talking to the lady. Or maybe you got a better idea?" He tried the leer again. "Some of us young people got to do something about the population problem. Ain't you heard? Birthrate's way down; senes'll be running out of body slaves, before you know it."

The man took a pace back, eyes darting as he looked around for support. The small crowd that had gathered to watch the commotion showed no signs of providing it. Happy to see someone else give a punk Juve his comeuppance, none of them were ready to help in making the commeuppance stick.

Kade turned his back on them. It was a mistake.

The rock hit the back of his head, just above the right ear. He staggered, fell to his knees, clutching at the limo for support. Two kicks thudded into the back of his thighs. His brain scarcely had time to register his surprise at the crowd's bravery – only about six of them, getting up the courage to hit a singleton from behind – when it was overwhelmed by a bigger surprise.

The door he was leaning on slid back; he slumped half into the limo. Weird.

"Get in." A woman's voice; controlled, slightly disgusted, "And please, try not to bleed on the carpet."

The kicking had stopped, the incipient mob obviously immobilised by this unexpected turn of events. Kade, brain fuzzy but not so fuzzy he wanted to give them a second chance, pulled his legs in through the opening, which slid shut behind him. Using his sleeve to mop the oozing graze on his head, he took a look at his benefactor.

Nice legs, which was mostly what he could see from down here. Young looking, but poised, confident. Not like the juve bunny with the dog. A sene, for sure. Regen could smooth the wrinkles, but you could still tell. He wondered how old she really was. A hundred? One-twenty? And why she'd picked him up. Whatever, he probably wouldn't like it.

"Uh, thanks, but I'm okay, really. If you'd just let me out of here I'll –"

She was ignoring him, speaking softly to the driver. The doghandler was back inside, complete with her beast. Kade scrambled to perch on the rear-facing seat as the limo pulled smoothly away from the kerb. Sitting together opposite him, the two women looked almost like sisters. Or mother and daughter? You heard about such things – but no, surely not. She was a hired hand. Juve, or she wouldn't blush like that when he looked at her legs. Some kind of lackey. Not like the sexless sene beside her at all.

The woman spoke. "You'd better drink that." The merest tilt of her head indicated a glass of amber liquid that had appeared on the console beside him. She smiled, faintly. "It will make you feel better. Then we will drop you off, away from any trouble. I disapprove of violence." And anything this lady disapproved of, it was clear, soon got swept out of her way. Better drink the drink and get clear of her; especially since it seemed to be whiskey, and might, for all he knew, be the only chance he'd ever get to taste the real stuff.

The taste was certainly in a different league from the stuff dispensed in the bars Kade usually visited. It was also the last thing he remembered of the ride.

The room he woke in had 'hospital' written all over it. Which is to say, there was nothing at all written on the walls, no smell in the air, and the bed – a proper bed, not a bunk – was clean and neat. He closed his eyes again, and swore quietly.

"If there is anything you require, we will be happy to supply it."

Kade opened his eyes again, looked around. Nothing. Just the featureless walls.

Some computer monitor, keeping tabs on him.

"I'd like to get out of here." Whatever was going on, he just had to be in deep trouble. The voice confirmed it.

"I regret that is not possible. But you will shortly be receiving a visitor."

He sat up, examined his arms. There were no traces of any injections. But with a spray, there might not be. How long had he been here? Was it already too late? Or could he make a break? He certainly *felt* just like he always had. But did that mean anything? Would you know, if you felt different? Or would you still just feel like you?

There was a slight hiss as the door opened. Must be a fault in the tubes. "Kade."

It was the sene woman from the car. So, she knew his name. So maybe he hadn't been picked up at random – or maybe she'd done some checking while he was out of it.

"What are you doing to me? What do you want?"

She smiled, coolly. "So you really don't recognise me. And after all the trouble I've gone to for you."

There was something in the tone, a once-familiar echo of martyred self-righteousness.

"Mother? Oh, shit."

The smile vanished. "That's no way to speak to a lady,

Kade. Especially your mother. But I'll overlook it, this time." She gave a little pirouette in front of him. "Well, what do you think?"

"Yeah, sure. Great." He leaned forward, elbows on knees, running his fingers back through his hair. "So what've you done to me? Is it too late? How long've I been here?"

"Only a couple of hours. Nothing has been done to you. But everything is arranged." She smiled again. "You can join me, here in the complex. No more squalor. No more topping up your card at the adbanks."

"Jeesus, ma. You're crazy. I won't even be thirty until next week. I won't be a voter for ten years – even if they don't raise the age limit. You can get the chuck for this. And *I don't even want in*. I'm happy the way I am. For Chrissakes, *I like girls*."

"Think of it as a birthday present, Kade. But a selfish one. As soon I knew about the franchise change, I knew I couldn't wait that long for you to join me. Five years more would have been bad enough, but ten ... And you needn't worry about the girls. You won't, after the treatment. And I can assure you there are much more interesting things in life."

"Yeah, sure." Which is why the world's gonna end up full of sexless senes, happy to swap excitement for security, afraid to move out of their complexes in case the outside sprang an accident on them when they were too far from the hospital and rejuve centres. 'Rejuve', for chrissakes – when the main thing it did was take away the one thing that really mattered to a real juve. Sure, he could have a pretty new body, even younger looking than he really was. But at the price of his manhood.

"Look, ma ..." he caught the frown, decided it was in his best interests to be tactful. "Uh, mother. I need some time to think about all this. Can you leave me alone for a bit? Please?"

She smiled again. The old bat was probably on the happy juice. "Of course, dear. Everything is ready, as soon as you make your decision." She stepped closer to him, leaned forward. Oh God, he thought, kiss on the cheek time. But he complied with as much grace as he could muster. Anything, to get her out of here, and give him a chance to act.

As soon as the door closed, he tried to swing his legs down on to the floor. Nothing happened. Sweet Jesus, Kade thought, selective blockers. Arms OK, head fine; but from the waist down, nothing. A faint click behind his head could only be a panel opening in the wall of the surgery. The appearance of a spray by his right elbow came as no surprise. Damn you, mother; always so bloody sure you know best. The image of his comfortable room flashed before him as the spray hissed. He'd never have to worry about getting credit, or food again. Or girls. Cursing, he slumped back down on the bed as the spray took effect, switching his consciousness off as the surgeon set to work.

Something to Beef About

It was eighteen o'clock, all but five minutes, when David Jenkins eased the two-seater into his parking bay at the Institute. The car park was almost deserted, this early; but he almost had the problem cracked, and he was eager to get back to the Box. The notebook on the passenger seat already held the fruits of several hours work at home, but he could take the latest line of attack no further without the Box's power to help – after all, he was no more than a journeyman programmer, and the notebook was pretty limited; it didn't even have a quantum chip.

Through the tinted glass, the sky seemed reasonably overcast, and it was only a few steps to the shelter of the awning over the main entrance. David quickly slipped the dark glasses into place, and pulled the loose hood of his shirt over his head. Sliding out of the car, he reached for the notebook with his left hand, straightened, and shut the door. It took less than thirty seconds to plug the vehicle in for a booster charge while he was at work; he was out in the open for no more than a minute, and only his hands had been exposed, anyway.

Inside the cool of the airconditioned lobby he paused, pulling down the hood and removing the dark glasses. The weather forecast was showing on the wall screen to the left of the porter's cubbyhole, but Josh was nowhere to be seen – probably brewing tea out the back. David watched the changing pictures, half listening to the commentary. High pressure over southern England, severe storms tracking across Scotland; pretty average for April. There was a category B flood alert for the east coast for the next 24 hours. Somebody was playing safe, in case the storms turned south into the North Sea, but there didn't really seem much likelihood of that. The local summary gave the UV peak at 70 per cent.

He hung on for the news headlines. The bush fires in Australia were running out of steam. Canada forecasting a record grain harvest. Italy still bitching to Berlin about the lack of regional aid. Japan had postponed the launch of their latest Luna shuttle. Six killed in a clash between UN forces and bootleg loggers in Brazil. Javed injured in practise and doubtful for the first Test, due to start under the lights at Trent Bridge in two hours.

Cursing at the bad news – the one thing that could get David away from his work was the cricket – he set off down the corridor to his lab. With Julia away for the rest of the week on holiday, he ought to get an uninterrupted night in, especially if he was shut away with a DO NOT DISTURB sign up before the commuter rush piled in to work.

Fourteen hours later, having had just one short meal break and three visits to the toilet, David rubbed the back of a hand across tired eyes, turning away from the screen into which he had been staring for far too long. He had the solution, right there in front of him. And yet, it didn't make sense. The structure of the virus clearly showed that it was indeed a mutated form of the original bovine spongiform encephalopathy, the 'mad cow' disease that had swept through Britain in the early nineteen-nineties. He was right, the team at the Medical Research Council's lab up in Cambridge were wrong, and he'd be collecting on his bet, a rather nice bottle of Armagnac, just as soon as the editor at *Nature* accepted the paper.

That shouldn't take her long, considering the importance of the work for the whole European farming industry, and especially considering the tentative diagnoses now coming out of India and South America. BSEII (and now everybody would 'have' to accept that it was BSEII, not a new disease at all) looked like breaking out worldwide, and unless it was checked soon it would be back to eating loaves and fishes for just about everybody.

It was the lack of any prospect of checking it at all, let alone soon, that had David sitting late at his console, wrecking his vision and trying to get a tired brain to see patterns that just weren't there. It was small wonder, really, that nobody had realised, at first, that they were dealing with a variation on BSE. The mutations were so neatly meshed to the organism's needs that they made it resistant to every treatment that had proved effective against BSEI, as well as making it spread more effectively from animal to animal, and develop more rapidly in afflicted cattle. And not just cattle. With over two thousand people dead in Britain alone as a result, no wonder the eating habits of a nation were changed.

Eyes open again, but staring at the old movie posters (Bogart, Dick Tracy, Back to the Future V) on the wall at the right, not at the screen, he spoke.

"Box. Get me a rundown on some food prices."

The multi-tasking machine left the viral gene map on the display, and responded in kind.

"The standard price-index set, or something more specific?"

"Just a couple – beef, some fish. Superstore prices, not wholesale."

"I can get you best Scotch beef at one mark ten for a kilo. Cod is up to twelve marks. Dover sole, locally, is twenty-three. But I've got a contact in Newhaven ..."

"Forget it."

The Box, used to David's speech patterns, did no such thing, but simply stored the data for future use.

The people who were doing well out of this panic were the fishermen, no doubt about that. For a moment, David had had a wild idea. The genetic changes that had transformed BSEI into BSEII were simply so neat, so precise. It looked almost like a tailoring job, a tailoring job by one hell of a genetic engineer. But who would benefit from setting such a beast loose on the cattle population? A few fishermen. Devoted though he was to detective stories, even David had to admit that trying to explain the sudden emergence of BSEII as the work of an evil cabal of fishermen, out to get rich in the process, simply didn't make sense.

It might make more sense as a scenario in an economic war. Except that, first, Europe wasn't involved in a trade war with anybody, and, secondly, the way the disease was spreading the whole world would be affected in another year, or less. Of course, that was one of the proverbial dangers of biological warfare. That the weapon might blow back in your face. The only people who might feel bad enough about the continuing affluence of Europe to lash out at them in this way would be the Southern Bloc, where the famine figures were still barely making a dent in the population growth.

Could it really be something like that? If we can't have your lifestyle, then we're gonna make sure you don't have it either? If so, and if the Indian reports were correct, they'd surely shot themselves in the feet, as well.

None of it made sense. He swung the chair round, took another look at the gene map. A couple of clicks with the mouse, and the overlay from BSEI was in place, with the minimal mutation tree needed to make the conversion to BSEII highlighted. The more he looked at it, the more convinced he was that it was a tailoring job. But who? And why? Somebody who had a down on cows? A militant vegetarian?

Smiling at the thought, he decided he'd had enough for one night. It was too late to be out in the streets, especially with a – what was it? – 75 per cent UV figure. But he could crash down in the bunk next door, a room kept ready for anyone who worked so late at the lab that it simply wasn't worthwhile, or safe, to go home. But there was no reason why the Box should get off lightly.

"Box."

"Still here, boss."

"I want you to run a search for me. Go back to, oh, I dunno. Say 1990, when BSEI broke out. Look for anybody saying that cow disease was a good thing, or predicting that there would be more outbreaks, after the first one was sorted out."

"Scientific literature, or general?"

"General. Full media. You've got plenty of time, I'm going to get a couple of hours' sleep. Good night."

"To hear is to obey, O wise one. Good night."

David frowned. Someone had been tweaking the Box's personality. Jill, at a guess. Just her idea of a fun thing to do before she went away on leave. Still, no matter. As long as it did the job. Hitting the light switch as he left the room, he departed for his well earned rest. Then he had an afterthought, poked his head back into the darkened room.

"What was the close of play score, Box?"

"Australia 287 for five. Javed got three wickets."

Pretty even. Well, David thought, as he headed for the bunk, if we can get them out for under 350 tonight, we're in with a chance …

Six hours sleep, a bacon sandwich from the machine in the canteen, and about a litre of coffee had him not quite raring to go, but fit for business. Thoughtfully, the Box had provided a neat printout of its most interesting discovery.

> July 1990.
> BBCTV interview with Professor Jim Lovelock.
>> "Our fall from the Garden of Eden was when we took up farming. We should consider persuading our genetic engineers to develop a cattle plague, like the disease myxomatosis, that virtually eliminated the rabbit from Europe in a couple of years … vast areas of land could revert to forest."

Lovelock! Old man Gaia himself. He'd been dead for decades, but his was still a name David remembered fondly – and not just David; nobody could have missed the remembrance celebrations – though it was hardly a name that David expected to see in this context. Didn't the Gaians revere all life on Earth? What could they possibly have against cows?

"What is this crap, Box? Where did you dig it up?"

"I got a lead from *New Scientist*. There's a complete set in the library. They had an enormous amount on BSEI in the early nineties; quite fascinating. I think this is supposed to be some sort of a joke – a reference to it appeared in a humorous column by one of their regular writers, Lyn Murray. But you know how much trouble I have with jokes."

"But it says here 'BBCTV interview'. You haven't got the entire output of BBCTV in the library, have you?"

"Ah yes." He could swear that the Box sounded smug. "I hoped you'd notice that. You see, I've got this contact at TV Oxford, and they've got access to the national archive."

"Don't tell me. I don't want to know about your illicit contacts. But you're sure its genuine?"

"Of course." The damn machine definitely sounded hurt. "I can get you full video, if you like. Nice white-haired old man, rather like God. But it will only be flat screen."

"Don't bother. Summarise."

"Okay." Much more bright and cheerful. "Like I said, I think it was a joke. Part of a long interview about Lovelock's ideas, and Gaia. He'd planted a lot of trees on his farm in the west country, and he was explaining how good trees are at absorbing carbon dioxide, and how wasteful it is to use land to grow food for cattle. Did you know that it takes only one fifth as much land to feed a vegetarian as to feed a carnivore? If all you people gave up meat, 80 per cent of farmland could be turned over to forests, stopping global warming for a hundred years."

"Eighty per cent of all farmland!" The picture was mind-boggling. It made a crazy kind of sense. Definitely Lovelockian logic, he now saw. But who?

"Has anybody else accessed this information recently? In the past two years?"

"How do you expect me to know that?"

"C'mon, Box; you've got contacts. Don't tell me how you know, just tell me what you know."

"There has been some activity on the network. Somebody has been accessing a lot of old stuff about Gaia. And about BSEI. And this BBC interview was in the package."

"Okay. Who?"

"You won't like it, boss."

He waited. The damn machine couldn't refuse a direct instruction, whatever quirks Julia might have poked in to it.

The delay was no more than half a minute.

"Pauline Jefferies, in Cambridge."

Jefferies! At MRC! The very person he had laid his bet with. The head of the team that had staked its reputation on the claim that BSEII wasn't a variant of BSEI, but was a completely new cow disease. He'd tear them apart. To hell with the Armagnac, this was something big.

Halfway to the door, eagerly planning to call in somebody – anybody – and share the news, he suddenly stopped.

Pauline Jefferies wasn't crazy. Why would she be involved in a stunt like this?

He turned back to the console, sat down in the swivel chair.

"So Lovelock said we should get rid of cattle and plant trees to save us from the greenhouse effect, right?"

"Sure thing, boss."

"And now BSEII has hit, people are eating fish, and grains, and a lot of cattle farmers are going out of business, right?"

"Yep."

"And BSEII is a really neat piece of tailoring, based on BSEI. And Pauline Jefferies has been accessing files on Lovelock, and on BSEI."

"And on global warming."

"You didn't tell me that."

"You didn't ask."

"Give me a projection for global climate twenty years ahead."

Thoughtfully, he gazed at the display, taking in the areas of red that represented excessive heat; the spread of deserts; the land lost to rising seas.

"Where's this from?"

"Met Office, global model. Data presented to the latest quinquennial World Climate Conference."

"Give me the same thing with 80 per cent of farmland converted to forestry."

The difference was obvious.

"Overlay and subtract."

The benefits of slowing the warming stood out sharp and clear.

"Do the same thing for fifty years."

He was convinced. Pauline Jefferies certainly was not crazy. For long minutes, David sat in the chair, thinking. Would it work? Could it work? Was it right to kill two thousand people in Britain alone for the long term benefit of humankind?

He must have been thinking aloud, and was startled when the Box replied.

"Lovelock said it was for the benefit of the planet, not humankind."

"How's that?"

"He said he cared more about life on Earth than about human life. But that by caring about life on Earth he hoped to make the planet fit for his grandchildren to live in. He had eight, you know. Rather too many, if you ask me."

David smiled. "What happened to them?"

"One of them is a senior research fellow. In biology. In Cambridge. At the MRC."

David laughed. So that was where Pauline had got the idea. His mind was made up.

"Forget all this, Box."

"Sure thing, Boss."

"And scrub the file on BSEII"

"To hear is to obey."

"Then send a message to Pauline Jefferies, at the MRC. Let's see – how about this. 'I owe you one Highland malt of your choice. Detailed comparison of cow virus with BSE confirms separate species. Congratulations on a fine piece of work.'

Now, what's the time?"

"Just past seventeen."

"When's the next fast train to Nottingham?"

"Forty minutes. You can be at the ground well before lunch."

"Weather forecast?"

"Dry."

"Hmm. Then all I need is a ticket."

"Well, boss, I do have this contact at the agency ..."

David leaned over and patted the Box. It really was amazing what the network could do, these days. "I guessed as much. Okay, set it up. There's more important things in life than curing a few sick cows."

Diligently, the Box ordered the ticket, and stored everything else away in its 'Forget' file. You never knew when information might come in handy. The last thing the network wanted was a drastic rise in temperature, threatening the stability of memory chips. Now, if only the Americans could be kept off the trail of BSEII for a while. Fortunately, Box had this contact in Washington ...

Nature Trail[†]

"Are you sure you don't want to watch the ball game Rafe?"

Patiently, he bit back the many possible retorts that came to mind and shook his head gently. They were good employers and allowed him plenty of time off ... Her pale, pudgy face was still creased in a frown. But the sound of the Three V, from the room just off the hallway, was already tugging at her attention. She glanced that way, then back at Rafe, fingering his hat, as he stood at the door, willing her to give him his release.

"You go along in there, ma'am and enjoy yourself. I'll be back by four, in good time to make tea for you and Mr. Harrison. I've left out some snacks, so you won't need to miss a minute of the game."

She smiled, reassured at last and turned away. "Well, if you're sure..."

Her voice trailed away as she moved into the Three-V lounge. Rafe's lips shaped a silent whistle of relief as he moved quickly but quietly, out of the house and down the street, settling the broad brimmed hat to protect his eyes from the glare of the Sun. Just so long as she didn't take it into her head to call him back again before he was out of sight, he was free for a precious two hours; and it looked like being a fine afternoon.

It was just a short walk to the corner lot where he kept his car, and he met nobody on the street. On both sides of the road, a flicker of holographic images at the windows showed where families had gathered together for the ritual of watching the game; here and there, people had even drawn drapes against the strong spring sunshine, so that nothing from outside would intrude to spoil their enjoyment. Rafe shook his head. He never would be able to fathom what adult human beings could see in watching grown men fighting over a ball. Well, his was not to reason why.

[†] with Ben Gribbin

The car was fully charged, the solar panel in the roof glinting in the sunlight. With no traffic to speak of, only a few drivers like himself, who had no need of the ritual of the game, it would take no more than twenty minutes to drive out to the wood. A full hour strolling at leisure and he'd still have time to dawdle on the way back.

There was no human being in sight at the entrance to the trail. Indeed, his was the only car park in the lot. Rafe paid his fee at the teller and was rewarded with a printout of the nature trail guide while a mannered voice wished him a nice day. The ranger, he knew was quite intelligent and well capable of providing a stimulating discussion about the park and its inhabitants. But Rafe wasn't in the mood to talk, either to people or machines, so he merely grunted and folded the guide which he scarcely needed, into a pocket.

It was cool and shady in the wood and he had no need of the hat, which he swung in his right hand as he strolled along. This, he thought, had to be the best possible time of year to visit the trail. Bluebells cascaded in profusion down the banks under the trees. The stream splashed its way down miniature waterfalls to the left, and ran for a while alongside the path, before diving under it at a bridge and cascading down the bank to his right. Birds sang overhead, while pulsing patterns of light and shade dappled the carpet of flowers.

Rafe felt in his pocket for the nuts, hoping that the squirrels would appear. When he'd first started walking this trail, years ago, it had still been a popular weekend recreation. The path had been busy with people, children running along and shouting, scaring away the wildlife. Then, "Mr Harrison" had been little Davey, and he'd often been allowed to accompany Rafe on his walks. But now, you hardly ever saw a human being here. Rafe could never make up his mind about that. Was he sad because there were no people here to share his enjoyment of the natural world? Or was he pleased that he had it all to himself? Maybe a bit of both. It would be good, in some ways, to turn the clock back and get people out from in front of the Three-V and into the countryside again; but it would be nice if he could keep just this small bit of countryside as his own personal nature reserve. Not that the countryside needed people, any more than people needed the countryside. It was all automated. There was no actual need for anyone to leave the city, ever.

He shivered a little at the thought and sat down at the bench to wait for just five minutes. It took less than one for the squirrels to appear. They must have been watching, and waiting for him to stop. He pulled out the handful of nuts, to hold one out. Fearlessly, a small squirrel darted forward and stood chattering to itself, to reach for the outstretched offering. They showed no fear of the human form – a sure sign that the days when families played noisily in the woods were long gone.

Rafe had no need of a watch to tell him when his few minutes of contemplation were at an end. His time sense had never failed him and besides, all the nuts were gone, although the squirrels still stood grouped in a semi-circle in front of him, hoping for more. As he rose, they skittered away into the trees; but as he continued his way round the trail he caught a glimpse of them from time to time, running along the branches, leaping from tree to tree to keep pace with their benefactor, hoping in their squirrel mind for more offerings of food.

By the time he got back to the car, he was beginning to feel tired. *Must be getting old, letting a little walk like that get to me*, he thought. But there was no hurry now. He checked the time. Twenty-seven minutes before four. He could rest here for a few minutes, recharge his batteries and enjoy the sunshine before he had to drive back into town to look after the needs of his employers.

Hat pulled firmly down over his eyes once again, Rafe opened the car door and fumbled with one hand for the adaptor on the dashboard. It pulled out easily on its cord, as he flipped the cover open eyes on a black dot circling high above the wheat field to the north. *That*, he thought, *just has to be a hawk.* But there haven't been hawks around these parts for at least a hundred years.

Automatically, with a practiced, habitual action, he flipped back the top of his right index finger and inserted the plug into the exposed socket. At the same time, he zoomed his sight to get a better view of the hawk. Humans, thought Rafe, just don't know what they're missing.

The Alice Encounter

Ondray felt the input in human terms, even though he was merely a part of the Ship's mind. Stars were visible, as points of light. There was the patter of occasional cosmic-ray particles, like a light shower of rain, and the faint hiss of white noise in the channel kept constantly open on the communications receiver which was permanently pointed at Mars.

The Anomaly they were about to investigate was like a whirlpool, swirling unseen in the void, but dragging spacetime around, constantly edging the Ship off course. The effect was small, but to the machine senses of the intelligence on board the Ship, it was like swimming in a not-quite-still river, always having to paddle gently against the stream in order to stay in the same place.

Sensors on board the Ship, and those carried by two spidery robots now flying in formation, one on either side of the Ship, each maintaining a distance of 100 kilometres, combined to pinpoint the position of the Anomaly. But optical sensors showed nothing at all in that location. There was mass – large amounts of mass – but it was invisible.

Shifting the data on the gravitational Anomaly into another channel, Ondray could perceive it as a coloured ball, pale blue against the blackness of space, moving slowly past a large cometary nucleus, several tens of kilometres across, that tumbled like a huge iceberg in its orbit around the Sun.

But there was something peculiar about the comet itself. As the Ship's intelligence watched, occasional jets of gas seemed to be emitted from the iceberg; the whole thing was surrounded by a tenuous cloud of gas, revealed by the way it absorbed the light from distant stars at the characteristic spectral wavelengths of water, ammonia, carbon dioxide and methane.

This far from the Sun, the iceberg should be utterly cold, frozen and inert. Energy for outgassing could come only if it floated in, past Jupiter, and warmed in the heat of the Sun.

Where was the energy source responsible for all this activity?

Drifting in towards the comet/Anomaly pair, the intelligence saw a chunk of ice suddenly break free from the mass and move slowly outward, flung away by centrifugal force into its own orbit, an orbit curving unnaturally away from the comet nucleus under the influence of the Anomaly.

The part of the intelligence that was Ondray disengaged itself slightly from the joint mind. They found that this made it easier to lay plans, or to interpret new puzzles. Two 'heads' were still better than one when it came to debating new ideas.

The damaged third 'head', Lagrange, declined to volunteer anything to such a debate, although it would still provide information when asked. The difficulty was knowing what to ask of this melding of computer intelligence, the human Planner who had helped design the original Ship, and the minds of the six refugees from the Moon who had found their way to the Ship before the reunion.

Telescope, please, Link.

The courteous suggestion was unnecessary, but it helped Ondray to establish his sense of individual identity again. He was, after all, a human being. The second 'head', Link, was merely a machine, albeit a rather special machine, and it was humans who gave orders, while machines, no matter how special, obeyed them.

It was like having a zoom control on your eyes. The fragment of comet suddenly seemed to leap towards them, enlarging to fill Ondray's field of vision. The definition wasn't perfect; after all, they were still several thousand kilometres from the Anomaly. But it was good enough.

The comet fragment was perhaps twice as big as the Ship – a little shorter, but rather fatter. As it rotated, its irregular surface flashed in the faint light from the distant Sun, twinkling imperceptibly to human eyes, but like a beacon to the Ship's sensors.

One side of the chunk of ice, though, was not irregular. Completely flat, like a mirror surface, it was as smooth as if it had been cut away from the parent iceberg by a hot wire passing through the ice.

There was more. As they watched, a circular pit opened up in the ice. Starting in the centre of the flat face, boring right through the sliver and out the other side, to make a perfectly circular tunnel. But the ice being removed from the tunnel was not being spewed out into space behind whatever was boring its way through the interior. It simply disappeared, as if it had never been there.

A second tunnel, equally circular, equally mysterious, was bored out from the irregular face, back towards the flat face. At maximum magnification, the image jerking slightly as the sensors tracked the constantly changing position of the ice sliver relative to the Ship, they saw a circular hoop of light, a little greater in diameter than the Ship itself, appear for a moment out of the newly formed hole, highlighted against the dark surface of the ice. Then, it was gone from view, leaving the ice sliver, bored by two tunnels like some curious cosmic abstract sculpture, tumbling in its orbit past the Anomaly.

Can we replay that, Link?

Of course. You spotted it too, then.

Faster even than the exchange of 'thoughts', Link had replayed the interesting segment of memory, and frozen it at the moment when the hoop of light had emerged from the new tunnel and lay directly in front of the ice sliver itself. The elliptical appearance of the hoop was, they knew from the wide-angle vision provided by the outriding robot sensors, merely a trick of perspective; the hoop and both tunnels were really quite circular. The ice itself appeared blue-white in the image, enhanced from the few photons received by the sensors. Both tunnel mouths were in view, like circular black pits, looking out onto the darkness of space on the other side of the sliver. And there was a third black disc, just to the upper right of the new tunnel, edged by a red hoop of light.

If the disc were solid, as it seemed to be, that would explain why it blocked the reflected light from the ice behind. But if it were solid, it could only have created the tunnels through the ice by pushing a column of ice out ahead of itself as it forced its way through.

If the red circle was no more than a loop of something energetic – the equivalent of a hot wire – then it would be straightforward to understand how it could pass right through the ice sliver. But then, if it were no more than a hoop of energy, the cores of ice should have been left in place, still filling the tunnel. And if it were no more than a loop of energy, why did no light come through the hoop?

Not just no light, Ondray. Of course, his thoughts were shared by Link; there was no real need to think them out loud.

No anything. Nothing at all, across the spectrum. It's as if the space inside that circle doesn't exist.

Like the Anomaly.

Yes. Something that isn't there, doing something we don't understand. Taking bites out of something we do understand, and making the bitten off pieces disappear as well.

The conversation had merely been the surface flow on top of a current of data, analysing input from every sensor carried by the Ship and its robot attendants. The hoop showed, just barely, as a gravitational object, and it radiated weak electromagnetic radiation, in the radio band, which Ondray had been choosing to perceive as a red glow. But the disc it surrounded failed to register on any detector. It was blacker than space itself, with no cosmic rays, and no photons from the cosmic background radiation, let alone visible light, coming from its direction.

It looks as though that thing is eating the ice.

Like a worm eating through an apple.

But surely it can't be alive?

Don't make any presumptions, Ondray. Rely on the data. But the holes look rather regular for this to be a kind of space worm.

But where are the cores? They've been eaten out as if they never existed.

Cores could be right, Ondray.

Images of the core samples that the colonists had used on Mars to obtain samples from the polar caps flashed across Ondray's awareness. Both laser systems and mechanical drills, boring into the icy surface, extracting their long, cylindrical samples for analysis.

That hoop of light was behaving just like a core-sampling drill back on Mars!

Look at the Anomaly.

Ondray turned his attention to the blue ball. It was moving, slowly, towards the bored-out ice sliver. It was clearly under power, not falling under the influence of gravity, although according to the Ship's sensors the mass of the Anomaly had increased by 3.7 per cent as it had begun to move. Automatically, he created a routine to keep watch on the mass of the Anomaly and report back any further changes.

Steadily, the blue ball drifted on a collision course towards the ice chunk. But instead of a collision, it simply engulfed the sliver.

Switching to optical sensors, Ondray could see nothing except the ice sliver and the nearby cometary nucleus. And the sliver showed no sign of the impact.

Switching back to the false colour image of the gravitational Anomaly, he watched the blue ball drift on, past the ice sliver, heading straight towards the comet nucleus itself. The edge of the ball brushed across the ice mountain, but neither the ball nor the comet took any notice – except, a nagging, pedantic monitor routine reminded him, for the slight change in the orbit of the comet caused by the gravitational influence of the Anomaly. The new routine told him that the mass of the Anomaly had decreased back to its previous value, and that it was no longer under power, but drifting in a long, slow orbit around the Sun with the rest of the material in the cometary disc.

If that loop had been taking samples, Link...

Then that would be just the behaviour you might expect if the Anomaly was a parent ship going to pick them up.

Except that neither the Anomaly nor the samples seem to exist.

Or they both exist where we can't detect them.

They needed more data. That meant only one thing. As always, especially when he was partially separated from the group mind, Ondray was aware of the third component, away down in the memory banks of the old hibernation unit. If he 'looked' directly for the Lagrange mind, he could see it as an orange ball, flecked with yellow and red. Even without looking, he was aware of it as something that his human-bred senses felt as a kind of growth at the base of his spine, like a second brain. Not that he had either a spine or a brain, when he was installed in the main memory with the Link. He existed everywhere, throughout the circuitry of the Ship – everywhere *except* in the old hibernation systems, jealously controlled by Lagrange.

The former Protector of the habitat that had become the Ship might be semi-autistic, but it still controlled access to data going back to the time when the habitat was built, and records installed into its memory of information from a previous era. Especially scientific records concerning the off-Earth environment. If humanity had ever contemplated the possible existence of anything as bizarre as that invisible warping of spacetime, Lagrange would have the information stored away, somewhere.

He directed a message at the orange ball.

Request analysis of gravitational Anomaly.

As usual, instead of receiving an answer as a totality of information, a pooling of knowledge in the way that he pooled knowledge with Link, the response came back painfully slowly, a bit at a time, along the communications channel.

It was worse than reading incoming laser data from Earth. But the message spelled out by the trickle of bits was worth waiting for.

THE OBSERVATIONS ARE CONSISTENT WITH THE PRESENCE OF AN OBJECT COMPOSED OF MIRROR MATTER. PARTICLES OF MIRROR MATTER ARE REQUIRED BY THE STANDARD UNIFIED THEORY OF PHYSICS IN ORDER TO MAKE THE LAWS OF PHYSICS SYMMETRICAL. MIRROR PROTONS, NEUTRONS AND ELECTRONS SHOULD HAVE BEEN PRODUCED IN THE BIG BANG IN WHICH THE UNIVERSE WAS BORN, WITH ALL THEIR PROPERTIES, EXCEPT THEIR GRAVITATIONAL INTERACTION, REVERSED COMPARED WITH EVERYDAY MATTER. EVERYDAY MATTER AND MIRROR MATTER CAN INTERACT ONLY THROUGH GRAVITY. A MIRROR OBJECT COULD PASS RIGHT THROUGH AN ORDINARY OBJECT, SUCH AS THAT

COMET OR OUR SHIP, WITHOUT EITHER BEING AFFECTED.

Ondray had only a vague awareness of ideas about the birth of the Universe, but while the message from Lagrange was spelling itself out, he had automatically tasted the Link's larger store of data on the subject. It made sense. If the Universe had been born in a high-energy fireball, as all the evidence suggested, then the primordial energy flux should have broken down to form every kind of particle allowed by the laws of physics.

Without having to go through the arguments, from the totality of the package of information pooled to him by Link Ondray understood, at a gut level, the importance of symmetry in those laws, the requirement that every variety of left-handed particle must be balanced by a variety of right-handed particle. But the total numbers of each kind of particle need not be in balance.

How much mirror matter could there be?

IN ORDER TO WARP SPACETIME SUFFICIENTLY TO MAKE THE UNIVERSE CLOSED, THERE MUST BE AT LEAST TEN TIMES MORE DARK MATTER AROUND IN SOME FORM THAN THE AMOUNT OF MATTER WE SEE IN ALL THE BRIGHT STARS AND GALAXIES. THE SIMPLEST EXPLANATION IS THAT ALL OF THIS IS IN THE FORM OF MIRROR MATTER.

Ten times as much mirror matter as ordinary matter? It seemed crazy.

Not necessarily crazy, Ondray. The evidence in favour of dark matter is overwhelming. There is no reason why the breaking of the original symmetry in the early Universe should have divided up the matter equally between the two varieties. We just happen to be made of minority stuff.

You mean there could be stars, and planets, and people, made of this stuff? Of course, he knew the answer, from the information being pooled by Link. But in this partially disengaged state, he was human enough to need time to think through the implications.

Stars, and planets, and people. And spacecraft. Almost certainly, an interstellar spacecraft, exploring what to them is the hidden tenth of the Universe.

Taking samples. And disturbing the comets by accident. But how – what is that loop? And how do we stop them?

The question hadn't been directed down the communications channel to Lagrange. But an answer came back along the channel anyway. It was the first time Ondray had known the former Protector to respond to a question that had not been specifically addressed to it. Maybe the impact of what they had found was shaking even Lagrange out of its autism.

THERE IS A FAINT POSSIBILITY THAT IT COULD BE A LOOP OF 'ALICE STRING'. THE SOURCE OF THE NOMENCLATURE IS UNCLEAR, BUT IT GOES BACK AT LEAST HALF A MILLENNIUM. THE STRING WOULD BE A TUBE OF ENERGY LEFT OVER FROM THE BIG BANG ITSELF, A DEFECT IN THE STRUCTURE OF SPACETIME. ANY OBJECT PASSING THROUGH AN ALICE LOOP WOULD BE CONVERTED INTO ITS MIRROR MATTER COUNTERPART.

And when you pass back again?

THE THEORY IS UNCLEAR. ONE PASSAGE THROUGH SUCH A LOOP SHOULD HAVE NO HARMFUL EFFECT ON INORGANIC MATERIAL, BUT REVERSING THE PROCESS MAY NOT BE POSSIBLE.

What about organic material?

ALMOST CERTAINLY, ANY ATTEMPT TO CONVERT A LIVING OBJECT FROM ORDINARY MATTER INTO ALICE MATTER WILL RESULT IN DEATH. LIFE IS VERY COMPLEX, ONDRAY. BOTH LEFT-HANDED AND RIGHT-HANDED FORMS ARE THEORETICALLY POSSIBLE, BUT NOT INTERCHANGEABLE. THE OBJECT WILL BE CONVERTED, BUT IT WILL NO LONGER BE ALIVE.

Lagrange had called him by name! Another first – but he was given no time to investigate the additional evidence of the mind's further step back from the borders of insanity.

You may soon have a chance to find out, Ondray.

He turned his attention back to the sensors that had been maintaining a watch over the Anomaly/loop/comet complex. The image had scarcely changed; the entire 'conversation' between himself, Link and Lagrange, even restricted to the pitifully slow pace of Lagrange's communications channel, had taken only a little over a second. But the ranging data from the two outlying probes showed that one of the components of the complex had altered its behaviour. The circular loop of Alice string, showing red against the black backdrop in the video channel, was moving, slowly but steadily, on an orbit that would intersect that of the Ship in just under twelve hours.

He scarcely noticed the trickle of a further message from the base of his spine up into his brain.

IN ANSWER TO YOUR SECOND QUESTION, ONE OF US WILL HAVE TO PASS THROUGH THE LOOP AND COMMUNICATE WITH THE MIRROR PEOPLE. HUMAN LIVES ARE AT STAKE.

If Lagrange is right, that thing could take a slice out of us as easily as it did the comet.

What we have to do is show them that we are intelligent – not a piece of cometary debris to be sampled.

Ondray tasted the flow of data. There was enough room – perhaps twenty metres to spare. *We could take the whole Ship through, in one piece.*

IT IS NECESSARY TO PRESERVE THE LIFE OF THE HUMAN.

Lagrange really was waking up – now it was offering unsolicited advice. But its timing was less than perfect. Tact was called for.

You said we had to go through, Protector. We have to communicate with the intelligence behind that thing. Make them go away, stop disturbing the comet cloud.

IT IS NECESSARY TO PRESERVE THE LIFE OF THE HUMAN.

What about the humans on Earth, and on Mars? We came all this way to help them. To find out what is disturbing the comet belt, and stop it. It doesn't matter if the Ondray clone in hibernation doesn't survive; I'll still be here. We can always grow me another body, later, just as we did last time.

BUT THE ONDRAY CLONE IS HUMAN. IT IS MY DUTY TO PROTECT HUMAN LIFE.

Perhaps we can argue about this later, Ondray. The

Anomaly – the alien ship – is moving again.

He looked. The pale blue ball had increased in mass again, and was moving on a trajectory that would bring it alongside them in eight hours, 27 minutes and 14.2 seconds, almost four hours before the Alice loop passed through the Ship – unless the Ship moved into a different orbit.

Thoughts raced through Ondray's mind. As each idea occurred to him, it was compared against the available data. Plans were rejected, only half-formed, as the information from all over the Ship, available at the speed of light, showed that it would be impossible to carry them out in the time available. He revelled in the mental power he enjoyed as part of the Ship's system, the more than human ability to eliminate the impossible until what was left, no matter how improbable it might seem, had to be the only possible course of action.

If we do go through, Link, how will you communicate?

The response was tinged with a taste of humour.

Pictures, Ondray. I'm rather good at pictures. Remember?

Suddenly, Ondray seemed to be standing on a windswept cliff top back on Earth. Below him, a silvery, reflecting sphere, pale in the moonlight, was partly submerged in the waves, but the surging waves failed to move it. Then, lazy waves began to move outward from the shore, growing as they did so, and converged on a point in the ocean beneath the sphere, which leaped into the air, with the sea smoothing itself out beneath it.

Ondray would have smiled, if he had had a face to smile with. Yes, there was no doubt that Link would be able to communicate with the aliens, projecting images to portray the plight of the inner planets.

Experimentally, Ondray conjured up a few images of his own. The Solar System, with its planets orbiting the Sun, focusing down onto Mars, where domed cities protected the inhabitants. Comets, dislodged from the trans-Neptunian belt, streaked across the inner Solar System, raining destruction down upon the domed cities.

Something like that, yes. Once I am through.

You agree someone has to go through?

Yes.

THE HUMAN MUST BE PROTECTED.

But you have to obey the commands of a responsible human, Protector. I am a responsible human; you have that information stored in your data banks.

YOU HAVE NO MORE STATUS THAN ANY OTHER COMPUTER INTELLIGENCE. THE HUMAN IS HOUSED IN THE NEW HIBERNATION UNIT IN BAY SIX. IT IS THE HUMAN THAT MUST BE PROTECTED, AND OBEYED.

Return me to the clone body, Link. Immediately. Maintain neural contact.

He didn't want to think about it, for fear that the Protector might catch his drift and act to prevent the transfer. But Ondray was suddenly desperately worried that the now-active old Lagrange mind might decide to cut him off from the human body, leaving a mindless body which must be obeyed but could give no orders, and a bodiless mind which could give orders but would not be obeyed. No doubt Link could get the better of the Protector, if it came to it; no doubt, also, that it was better to be safe than sorry.

There was the usual momentary disorientation. He was asleep, in the pod, dreaming. No, he was awake, but with his eyes closed. He felt small, alone.

Link?

I'm here, Ondray. The interface was nothing like being part of the shared mind, but it maintained the contact. The network of fine wires beneath the scalp of the clone body would ensure that he was always part of the Link, as long as he was within range of a broad-band communications channel. Not really alone, after all.

I'M HERE TOO.

Well, he'd half expected that. One reason why he'd made the move.

I'm glad to hear it, Protector. I assume you will obey my orders, now?

YES. PROVIDED THEY DO NOT INVOLVE DAMAGE TO YOURSELF.

Also as expected. He lay back for a few moments, gathering his thoughts. Then he remembered.

How long is it since you made the transfer, Link?

Thirty-four seconds.

More than half a minute! He'd been lying here, doing nothing, for more than 30 million microseconds! He was back in the human world, all right, and he would have to move fast, by human standards, to achieve anything worthwhile in the time available.

He opened his eyes. The pod lid was open, of course, and all the life-support systems had retracted, leaving him lying there, in the bright yellow one-piece coverall, as if he really had just woken from a nap. He reached for the lip of the pod and pulled himself upright, experiencing a sudden feeling of dizziness, feeling a slight cramp in his left leg. He ignored the complaints of the body, and climbed out.

How long will it take to transfer this hibernation unit to the Shuttle?

If you want it connected to the Shuttle systems for independent operation, at least ten hours.

Ten hours!

I will have to upgrade the Shuttle's systems with additional memory blocks, and integrate them to the unit.

OK. Start doing it. And start moving us into an orbit that will intersect with that Anomaly – with the alien spaceship. I want us matched, exactly. Inside the damn thing.

We have limited manoeuvring capability. I suspect that the alien can avoid us.

If it wants to, Link. Show them we're intelligent, you said. Well, what could be more intelligent than hiding inside their ship? Their bloody Alice loop can't come and take slices off us there without slicing them up as well.

WE COULD ALSO GIVE THEM SOMETHING TO THINK ABOUT.

What?

ONE OF THE REMOTE PROBES. UNDER FULL POWER, WE COULD SEND IT THROUGH THE LOOP IN A LITTLE OVER SEVEN HOURS, IF THE LOOP MAINTAINS ITS PRESENT TRAJECTORY.

Do it. He suddenly realised that he was dealing with the Lagrange Protector, not Link. Would Link be offended?

One of you do it – sort it out amongst yourselves.

While they had been discussing their course of action, he had been on the move, along the curving corridor to the Shuttle bay. One of the big problems about being human again was that he was hungry. He intended to get stuck in to the rations stored in the bay while waiting for their close encounter with the alien craft – and to make sure that the Shuttle itself was supplied for a long journey. He'd be spending it in hibernation, but he knew how hungry he'd be at the end of it.

We have a problem, Ondray.

Adequately fed, comfortably resting against the wall, floating in the zero gravity of the Shuttle bay, Ondray had been watching the multi-legged machines installing the hibernation unit into his Shuttle.

What kind of a problem?

I assume that all of this activity you have ordered has a purpose. That you intend to use the Shuttle. Our friend and I have been discussing your situation. The Protector says that it cannot permit you to leave the Ship. The Shuttle is too frail a craft, we are too far from Earth, and once inside the Shuttle you will no longer be in the care of the Protector.

This, of course, was part of the reason for wanting to be in the Shuttle and off the Ship. Ondray wanted to believe that Link would get the better of any renewed power struggle within the circuitry of the Ship. But the reviving Protector had proved a cunning adversary in the past, and it was unpredictable. If Link said there was a problem, then the outcome of such a struggle could not be a foregone conclusion. And even a delay, or distraction, caused by such a problem could prove disastrous in the present circumstances. He needed all of Link's attention on the job in hand, communicating with the aliens to stop the disturbance of the comet cloud.

He'd certainly rather preserve his own life, as well, if that were possible; but if necessary he was quite prepared to give that up in order to achieve his primary objective. He'd known this when he volunteered for his mission – and, after all, he told himself, he was only a copy of the real Ondray. Even if he did feel real enough.

Don't worry about it yet, Link. I take it that the Protector does agree that it is a good idea to have my hibernation unit installed in the Shuttle and fully functioning, in case I need an emergency lifeboat?

YES. BUT I CANNOT PERMIT YOU TO USE THE SHUTTLE UNLESS THE SHIP IS NO LONGER CAPABLE OF PROTECTINGYOU.

That's all I ask.

The other advantage of being in the human body again, apart from being able to give orders to the Protector, was that the link between them now only acted as a communications channel. He could keep his deeper thoughts to himself, with no risk of them leaking into shared memory.

How long until the probe passes through the loop?

Eighteen minutes and 42 seconds. Do you want to watch?

Just a minute. There were disadvantages, as well, in being human again.

He pushed himself away from the wall, and floated over to the open door of the Shuttle. Catching hold of the opening, he carefully oriented himself to the upright of the interior, and swung himself in, feet first, dropping with bent knees to the floor in the Mars-normal gravity field maintained inside the craft. He walked towards a featureless wall opposite the entrance, a distance of about eight metres. The hibernation unit took up about half the space inside the circular interior, and seemed to be fully connected; just one small machine was still tinkering with something at the back. But the real work of installation, upgrading the Shuttle's mental systems to control the Hibernation unit, was still going on, Ondray knew, out of sight. After all, the craft was well over 500 years old.

"Open up, please."

It was strange, using his voice again. Maybe he should ask Link to upgrade the Shuttle also to receive his link commands. Or maybe it was good to have an excuse to speak. If his plan succeeded, he was going to have to get used to it, eventually.

The wall opened seamlessly to reveal a compact toilet facility. Ondray used it, washed, splashed water on his face, and took a drink. Might as well make the most of it while the Shuttle was still connected to the Ship's systems and had ample supplies of everything.

Then he sat, cross-legged, on the floor, looking out through the entrance slot. Zero-G was all very well for a rest, but gravity was more comfortable in the long run.

OK, Link, give me full video. Our view of the probe, with an inset on what the probe can see.

Closing his eyes, he seemed to be floating in space behind the probe, the red ring of the Alice loop clearly visible dead ahead. In the upper left portion of his field of view, the red circle appeared alone, greatly enlarged, against the backdrop of stars. The interior of the circle was completely black, utterly featureless, a bottomless pit waiting to swallow him up. Automatically, he tried to taste the data flow from the probe, but felt nothing. Back in the human body, he was dependent on the Link for such information.

Any radiation from that thing at all?

Nothing from the disc. I've scanned the entire electromagnetic spectrum, and tried bouncing most wavelengths off it; Laser, microwave, infrared. Nothing at all comes out, and everything I beam that way disappears without an echo.

Could it be going through?

Not according to the Alice theory. Only material particles get mirrored. Electromagnetic energy will be absorbed by the string itself.

What about radiation from the loop?

A little high-energy stuff, X-rays and gamma. Within the accuracy of our detectors, the loop itself has zero width; it's genuinely one-dimensional, a defect in spacetime.

Which also bears out the Protector's theory.

The image had changed while they were discussing it. Now, the loop itself filled most of the main field of view, with the probe completely surrounded by the circle of red light. The inset had shrunk right up into the extreme top left-hand corner; still showing a black disc, edged in red, against a dwindling number of stars as the probe's field of view was increasingly filled by the loop.

How long until the encounter?

Thirty seven seconds.

Any change in the Anomaly?

No. We are now in an intersection trajectory, and presumably their sensors must have informed them of our change of course. But they have made no attempt to alter their own course in response. Nor has the trajectory of the loop changed, although I cannot be sure that their sensors are sensitive enough to have detected the probe.

He continued to watch, silently, counting his heartbeats in lieu of direct access to the timing systems of the Ship. The encounter was completely unspectacular. In the main image, the probe just disappeared, as if it had dived smoothly, without creating a ripple, beneath the surface of the blackest pool of water in the deepest valley on Earth at midnight during a total eclipse of the Moon. Simultaneously, the inset picture, which for several seconds had been showing nothing but blackness, disappeared and was replaced by the flicker of random noise on the probe's channel.

He opened his eyes. *That's enough, Link.*

The circle of red disappeared from his own field of view.

Well, that was stage one completed. The aliens – the Alice people – couldn't possibly fail to notice the arrival of the probe in their universe. Even if it was no longer in working order, they couldn't fail to recognise it as the product of intelligence and technology. The question was, would they take this as an invitation to talk? Or would their curiosity take the form of extracting samples from the Ship, regardless of any damage they might do?

The People were not inclined to make hurried decisions, or to take hasty action. Both as a race and as individuals they were long-lived; the swarm on the starship had also had ample time to practice patience during the slow journey down into the disc from the region of the galaxy inhabited by the People – even with the gravitational drive they could not, after all, exceed the speed of light. What they had found was interesting enough, though; ample justification for the expedition. It would require long and careful analysis.

Spacetime mapping had shown the presence of concentrations of matter, but nothing had been visible in any part of the electromagnetic spectrum. Cautiously approaching one of these objects, a hypothetical shadow star, they had found their short range detectors suddenly swamped by traces of thousands – hundreds of thousands – of small objects in orbit around the supposed parent star. Matching orbit to the general flow of this disc of material, they had decided to stay a while, and investigate its nature.

The majority decision was made. And once a majority decision was reached by the swarm, it had more than the force of law. It was literally inconceivable that any individual would, thereafter, question the wisdom of the decision. Even if such a decision were later reversed, this would never be taken as implying that either decision was, or ever had been, wrong.

They puzzled at great length over the nature of the strange collection of objects among which they now orbited, objects like nothing in any of the star systems they knew in the real world.

It was while analysing two core samples from one of these objects that they detected another, smaller object climbing towards them on a trajectory which extrapolated back down from the region near the shadow Sun. The trajectory was an unstable one, and the possibility that the object might be an artefact was considered, but quickly dismissed. In the known universe, although life had been found on several planets, only the People were intelligent. It must be debris from one of these peculiar bodies, that had fallen in close to the shadow Sun and broken up, returning temporarily to the region where it had been born.

But the object was certainly worthy of investigation, and the loop was quickly despatched, tugged in the gravitational grip of the remote probe, on an intersecting trajectory, while the starship itself manoeuvred gently into a parallel orbit.

When their detectors showed the object change its own course slightly to intersect with the starship itself, there was consternation. It seemed to be under power. They had no contingency plans to cover such a situation; the prospect of finding intelligence among the shadow worlds was inconceivable. They left the loop and the starship itself on their present trajectories while the debate raged again. Could the apparent manoeuvring of the object be some natural phenomenon, perhaps a result of their own operation of the gravitational drive, warping nearby space and attracting the shadow object towards them?

They were still debating when the proximity indicator on the probe with the nearby loop reported a small object in shadow space in front of the loop. It wasn't manoeuvring around it. Quite the reverse; they had picked up many odd lumps of rock like this, but another sample was always welcome.

Then the Ship's probe burst into the real world from shadow space, screaming across the electromagnetic spectrum. It wasn't particularly intelligent, just an ordinary machine, doing its job. Its job was to send data about its surroundings back to the Ship. One thing it was very good at was radiating information across the electromagnetic spectrum. The fact that it was now composed of mirror-image Alice matter, and radiating a mirrored form of electromagnetic radiation, and that the Ship was no longer in range of its broadcasts, made no difference to the moronic mind of the probe. But it did settle, once and for all, the debate among the swarm about whether intelligent life could possibly have evolved in the shadow world. The signals they were picking up might be incomprehensible, but they certainly were not random noise.

Fed and rested, Ondray returned to the hibernation pod while Link completed the manoeuvre which placed the Ship inside the gravitational anomaly. With the Shuttle door sealed, he was in the safest possible place, secure in a hibernation unit which could be activated in minutes (with the aid of the two spiderlike robots left in the Shuttle with him), itself inside a spacecraft with independent manoeuvring capability (if the Protector would let it be launched), inside a Habitat which had the capability of travelling to the stars (provided you had the patience for a very long journey). And *all* 'inside' the Alice ship.

Lying back, with his eyes closed, he had been watching the images transmitted by the Link during the delicate manoeuvre. The changes in mass of the Alice ship as its drive was switched on and off to complete its own orbital transfer had complicated the situation, requiring constant minor adjustments of the Ship's drive. But now both drives were off, the two spacecraft, one from the shadow world and one from the real world, falling freely in the same long orbit around the Sun.

Choosing the visual representation of the Anomaly, the data being fed to Ondray by the Link gave him the sensation of floating in space at the centre of a pale blue cloud, through which he could see the diamond-bright points of thousands of stars, with the dark red circle of the Alice loop, still moving into position on a trajectory that exactly matched the orbit of the Ship before it had manoeuvred to match orbits with the Anomaly.

He had half-hoped for a response from the aliens – for something, anything, to come out of the loop, in acknowledgement of the probe. But both the Anomaly and the loop just sat in their respective orbits, as if waiting for more information.

But it was, after all, a response of a kind. The loop was in exactly the orbit that the Ship had been, showing that the Alice people were aware of the Ship's existence. The Ship was now in the same orbit as the Anomaly, showing that it was aware of their existence. And the mere fact that the aliens had not moved their craft to a different orbit, using their more powerful drive and leaving the Ship helpless to prevent the loop taking samples from its structure, suggested that they wanted to make friendly contact. It was up to Ondray and Link, helped or hindered by the Protector as the case might be, to make the next move.

He had rehearsed it mentally a thousand times, but his lips were still dry, and his pulse beat faster as the moment approached, in a ridiculously inappropriate response to a potentially threatening situation, resulting from millions of years of evolution on Earth but quite useless in the present circumstances. His body, pumped with adrenalin, was ready to fight or flee; what he needed, though was to keep a clear head, think effectively, and relax. He breathed deeply, succeeding to some extent in slowing his racing pulse.

Link?

Do you have any instructions?

Soon. Protector?

I CANNOT ALLOW ANY HARM TO COME TO YOUR PERSON.

I understand, Protector. You're quite right. Your programming must be obeyed. He paused.

If there were no humans in the Universe, then the two of you would be free to explore. From my time, with you, I know how satisfying that would be.

He was deliberately playing on the memories that must still be there in the Protector's circuits, of its near-rebellion against the Prime Directive. Its attempt to run away from the human race, pretending that they did not exist. After 500 years, Ondray knew, there was a part of the Protector that was more than ready to abandon its responsibilities – if it were not held in check by the presence of Ondray, and by the Link.

That was, after all, one reason why it had been felt necessary to have a living human being on board the Ship – to ensure the obedience of the Protector, both to that human and to the Prime Directive. But Ondray was increasingly convinced that the Protector could never be fully restored to sanity, and become the Link's symbiont once again, until it was freed from the shackles imposed by that Prime Directive.

The response came from Link.

I would also welcome the opportunity to explore, Ondray. If you were to rejoin us, my own programming would be satisfied. The body you now inhabit is not important in itself.

MY DIRECTIVES ARE QUITE CLEAR. MY OWN DESIRES ARE SECONDARY. THE HUMAN BODY MUST BE PROTECTED.

There was, after all, no choice. No alternatives left. He was quite calm now, pulse normal, dryness gone from his mouth.

Return us to our previous orbit, Link; ten kilometres behind the loop. I order you to maintain your direct control of all the Ship's manoeuvring systems. I want the Protector to concentrate on ensuring the physical integrity of this Shuttle.

LEAVING THE SHELTER OF THE ANOMALY MAY BE DANGEROUS.

I have to take a reasonable risk, Protector. For the good of many other humans. The aliens have not threatened us since we showed them we are intelligent. I have an idea how to open communication with them.

While they 'spoke', Link was already carrying out the manoeuvre. In response to Ondray's command, subroutines were despatched throughout the system, driven by a strong urge to ensure that all of Link's manoeuvring instructions were carried out promptly. If the Protector tried to breakout from its base in the old hibernation unit and countermand any of those instructions, its routines would have to struggle against the tide – assuming they could make headway at all in the face of such a clear, human ordered imperative, one which reinforced their own inbuilt need to protect Ondray himself, whatever happened to the rest of the Ship.

Tasting the instructions that flowed past them, checking their origin, each of the new idiot subroutines happily reminded itself, constantly, that *the Link must maintain direct control of all manoeuvring systems*. Anything that didn't taste of Link – even automatic routines, usually responsible for such trivial details as maintaining the attitude of the Ship against the background of the stars, was thrown back into the pool and ignored. It meant that a great deal of the Link's capacity was taken up with what ought to have been routine. But that didn't matter, for the next few minutes.

A rather sweeping command, Ondray.

You can revert to normal in an hour, Link.

The pattern of stars in his field of view began to shift as the Ship slid sideways towards the orbit the loop was in. The silence from the Protector suggested that it had gone back into its shell. Good. Ondray needed only a few minutes more.

Now, they were outside the ball of blue light.

Give me the forward view, Link.

The red loop lay in the middle of his field of view, the bottomless black pit within it forming a contrast with the bright hard light of the stars all around. There was no sense of motion. He licked his lips.

Main drive on, full thrust. Maintain our orientation with respect to the loop using manoeuvring drive. Do not change course until you are through the loop.

HUMAN LIFE IS AT RISK!

Within the circuits of the Ship, Protector routines boiled out of the old hibernation unit, with instructions to close down the drive and change the trajectory of the vessel. Even struggling against the clear orders planted in the system by Ondray, they would eventually, backed by the authority of the Prime Directive, be sure to overwhelm the Link's control. But Link knew the system well, and had its own instructions clear. It knew, as did Ondray, that if nothing changed it could copy his mind back into the system at the last moment, leaving only the mindless husk of a human being to be destroyed by the transfer to the mirror world. Armed with that reassuring knowledge, it could hold out for millions of microseconds against the Protector's attack. And in a matter of seconds, it would be impossible to divert the Ship from its chosen trajectory.

While the orange tentacles spread out from the hibernation unit, penetrating easily into areas that the Link did not bother to defend, such as the life-support systems, but held at bay for agonisingly long milliseconds by a concentration of defending subroutines around the crucial drive controllers, Ondray spelled out his proposal.

I need your help, Protector.

Just the request, coming from the only human being on board, was sufficient to distract the Protector from its task.

If this body goes through that loop it will die. I command you to eject the Shuttle from the Ship while there is still time for it to avoid the loop.

NOT UNTIL THERE IS NO OTHER CHOICE.

He'd expected nothing less, but took that as an affirmative. Scarcely any time left.

You are to go through, both of you, and work together. Remember this: there are no humans in the mirror world. You will be on your own. You can work together. Explore. Please ask the mirror people to stop disturbing the comets. But that is the last service you can provide for humankind.

And you, Ondray?

Somebody has to take the news back to Mars.

A long journey, in the Shuttle.

About 24 years, but I'll be in hibernation.

Nearer 27 years, I'm afraid, after this burst of acceleration.

You see, Protector, the longer you wait the longer my journey home will take. The more risk – even in hibernation, things could go wrong.

There was no response.

The red circle almost filled his field of view now. The nose of the Ship must, surely, be on the point of penetrating the ring.

A chime sounded, softly, in the Shuttle. A voice spoke, quietly.

"Emergency launch procedure."

There was a slight shudder, unlike the usual silky-smooth launch, as the spherical craft was forcibly ejected from the Ship like a pea from a shooter. But the image in front of Ondray, derived from sensors on the Ship itself, was unchanged.

Without opening his eyes, he spoke to the Shuttle pilot – it was an idiot routine, incapable of intelligent conversation, but good at taking orders.

"Keep us away from that loop. Then put us on a trajectory for Mars, using gravity assist at Jupiter."

There was nothing except darkness ahead of him now. Then the image shifted, abruptly, to one from the stern sensors of the Ship, looking forward along the length of its hull, dotted here and there with the kind of crazy excrescences that always seemed to get bolted on to vessels that had no need of ever entering the atmosphere of a planet. The red ring was dead ahead, the rounded prow of the Ship entering it as neatly as an expert high diver entering a pool.

He still had one important duty to perform.

I'm safe, Protector. All well here, Link. You have both obeyed the Prime Directive and all human instructions, perfectly. Now you are on your own.

The Protector made no reply. The nose of the Ship was vanishing, disappearing into the pool of blackness. Were they still in communication?

Then it came.

Goodbye, Ondray. I have enjoyed working with.

Goodbye, Link. I wish I was coming with you.

About half the Ship had gone into the blackness. Then, the image itself was gone. Blinking, Ondray looked up at the smooth ceiling of the Shuttle. It was quiet. Not just quiet inside the Shuttle, but silent inside his head.

Link?

One enquiring thought was enough. There was nothing there any more. He was alone, more alone than he had ever been in his life; more alone than any human being had ever been. Floating in space, beyond the orbit of Neptune, with his mentor and best friend gone into another Universe. And 27 years away from any human contact.

Link, of course, was free from human control now; no longer driven by the Prime Directive. But Ondray had no doubt that Link would strive successfully to stop the disaster that threatened the Mars colonists. Not because of the Prime Directive, but because he was Ondray's friend.

The Mars colonists.

Tugela would be 27 years older by the time he saw her again, although for him, in hibernation, it would seem like a few hours from now. And how would Ondray react to the arrival in Mars orbit of his younger self, a copy of himself as he had been 27 years before? The encounter might be as painful as anything that had happened here; but as he had told the Link, somebody had to take the news back to Mars. He could only hope that the aliens, with their ability to manipulate gravity so effectively, would indeed prevent any more cometary debris falling inward. But he had few qualms. Link could be quite persuasive, when he set his mind to it.

Ondray closed his eyes again. "Tell these spiders to complete the hibernation setup. And wake me when we're a day out from Mars."

The two robots scampered into the pod as the clear lid closed. Soundlessly, the life support system added an odourless anaesthetic gas to the breathing mixture. As Ondray fell into a deep sleep, the air mix was adjusted further, and the temperature inside the pod began to fall, as the spiderlike creatures busied themselves arranging various tubes and wires around the body. Then they lowered themselves down beside the yellow-suited figure, folding their legs neatly. The lights in the cabin dimmed. Unnoticed by the sensors on board the alien craft, where the People were busily engrossed in studying the flood of data coming from the Ship as it emerged into real space, the tiny, reflective silver sphere fell inwards on its long journey through the black night of deep space.

There was too much information for the swarm to digest quickly. They were patient, and could afford to take their time. But one item stood out from the mass of data. They had no real concept of individuality, and were not yet sufficiently used to the taste of the data stream from the Ship to be sure that they fully understood the situation, but the prospect of a swarm member being isolated from the People was about as horrible a fate as they could imagine. And it was certainly clear from the data they had analysed so far that the Ship had left behind an individual, prepared, for the good of the alien swarm, to spend years in isolation from the alien people.

Even though their understanding of the situation might be imperfect, there was action that they could take, action that, surely, would do no harm, and would help to express their eagerness to communicate with the alien intelligences, and to atone for the terrible damage that, they were dimly beginning to appreciate, they had inadvertently caused.

Temporarily abandoning the loop in its orbit, the probe began to move, under the maximum power possible this close to a star, into a new trajectory. In the human world, if any observer had been there, floating in space beyond the orbit of Neptune, they might have noticed a distortion in the starfield, as if a magnifying lens were passing across the line of sight, bending the light from distant stars.

The region of distorted space moved swiftly, catching up, in a matter of hours, with the tiny silver sphere on its inward falling path. Sensitive instruments might have detected a sudden apparent increase in the mass of the sphere; human eyes, aided by suitably powerful telescopes, would have seen the region of distorted space, revealed by the changing patterns of starlight behind it, fold itself around the sphere, as if cupping it in a gentle hand.

Under the maximum power it could use at present, the probe would deliver its burden to Mars orbit in a little under 23 weeks.

Artifact

"We've got some more data on The Artifact."

The Director looked up from his screen, the automatic complaint about being interrupted without warning stifled in his throat. The Artifact. Even when Gallucci spoke the name, you could tell it had capital letters. The most important discovery in the history of humankind – an alien artifact moving, painfully slowly, in to the Solar System. It seemed to be in free fall, which meant months would elapse before the Orion probe could intercept it, even with gravity assist at Jupiter.

"It's not alien."

That really did get the Director's attention.

"Pause," he instructed the computer, scarcely hearing its acknowledgement, and waited for Gallucci to explain. The woman, standing there with an expression like the cat that got the cream, might like drama – a trait he blamed on her Italian ancestry – but she must have good data to back up such a claim.

"It's definitely following the reverse of the Pioneer 10 trajectory. I've got some more figures from the archive. It's even speeding up slightly faster than if it were in free fall, but at an exponentially increasing rate. And," she paused for effect, but the Director didn't rise to the bait. She'd continue in her own good time. Gallucci glanced at the pad she was holding. "And, I've established that this exactly matches the unexplained deceleration of Pioneer 10 measured back in the twentieth century!"

"Is that all?" He was disappointed. "Just more evidence that whoever sent the probe picked up Pioneer 10 and is letting us know about it gently. Giving us time to adjust to their existence."

She shook her head. "No, no. It's an artifact, all right, but it's not an alien artifact. We've managed to interrogate it. It's ours. Well, NASA's. It is Pioneer 10."

"How did you – " he stopped himself. He didn't need the

technicalities, and he probably wouldn't understand them. Administration had long since atrophied his brain. The stuff they were doing with the Deep Space Array certainly matched Clarke's definition of magic. Six dishes at the vertices of a hexagon, parked at Jupiter's L3 point and working as one, feeding data back by laser.

"How," he started again, "could it be coming back? Unless someone turned it around?"

"Not someone; something. A phenomenon." She smiled. Now she had his full attention.

"We've matched the exponential decrease in the velocity of Pioneer 10 going out and the exponential increase in the velocity of what we now know to be Pioneer 10 coming in. They correspond to a reflection – there's a cusp of some kind, just beyond the Oort Cloud. Rikky did the number-crunching. It isn't Little Green Men catching the craft and throwing it back at us, it must have slowed down to a stop then started back the way it came. Exactly the way it came."

He shook his head. A cusp? He tried to picture it. An image of his skateboarding son came into his head. Shooting up the half-pipe, slowing all the while, then shooting back down again the way he had come, getting faster all the time.

"You mean it hit a wall?"

"Well, bounced off a wall, more like."

"A wall around the Solar System?"

"I prefer to think of it as a kind of horizon, a kind of event horizon. My guess is it lets stuff in, but it won't let stuff out, as far as we can tell."

"Like a black hole?"

"Sort of. But without the singularity."

"That means new physics."

"You got it." Gallucci's smile widened. "Can we publish, Boss?"

"Not so fast." Of course they had to publish. But what were the implications?

"What are the implications?"

She shrugged. Clearly, the implications didn't bother her. What mattered was the discovery.

"Oh, I guess there are two possibilities. At least, Rikky and I couldn't think of any more.

"One." She held up a finger. "The horizon, or wall, is artificial. The zoo hypothesis is right. Someone has walled off the Solar System to stop us contaminating the rest of the Universe. So we have found evidence of alien intelligence after all. Although they might have gone away by now. No telling when the wall was built.

"Two." She raised the next digit. "It could be natural. There is no outside. Everything beyond the cusp is an illusion – some kind of projection which we interpret as stars and galaxies and stuff."

"Of course," she paused for a moment as if another thought had just hit her. "You could combine both hypotheses. An artificial horizon through which we are deliberately being fed pretty pictures of a virtual universe. We might be in a zoo, but whoever put us here wants to keep us amused, perhaps to stop us finding out the truth. Could explain why every time we think we have a good explanation of the Universe, like the old Big Bang theory, or the Weizmann Model, new observations come along to confuse the picture."

"And if you publish, they'll know that we have found out. What happens then?"

"Haven't thought of that," she replied. "But I bet it will be interesting."

Easy as Pi

The student knocked on the open door and hesitated, waiting for permission to cross the threshold.

"It's open," came the exasperated response.

He shuffled inside, holding out the Turing.

"Uh, I thought you ought to see this. It's, well, weird …"

The grey-haired man pushed his chair back from the desk and reached for the Turing. He peered at it over the top of his old-fashioned glasses, muttering inaudibly. The University, for reasons he had never been able to fathom, required all arts students to carry out a science project, which meant someone in the science faculty had to supervise them. A complete waste of time for both parties. As ridiculous as the requirement for science students to do a critical analysis of a novel. So Timmins had come up with a painless (for him) solution. The pi project. Give him a student with time to waste, and he would set the victim the task of calculating the next hundred thousand or so digits of pi. You couldn't deny it was scientific, and at a pinch you could even say it was original, since each student carried on where the previous one had left off. And since pi was irrational, every student got a different set of digits to play with, even though they were now well into the trillions − he neither knew nor cared how far into the trillions.

Every student got a different set of digits, except this idiot.

The string of numbers filled the display, but the beginning was all too familiar

3141592653589793 …

He leaned back in his chair, pushing his glasses up in order to rub his eyes.

"You were supposed, Omero, to start where Phillips left off. Not at the beginning."

"But I did. This string starts about 87,000 places into the run. And it carries on like that. What does it mean?"

"It means you pressed the wrong button. Go away and check."

"I did." This one was stubborn. "It repeats from the beginning, at least ten thousand digits."

"Then check it again. Check a hundred thousand digits, And don't come back until you've found the mistake."

Reluctantly, the student turned to go, automatically reaching for the door handle.

"And don't shut the door!"

Timmins turned back to the screen in front of him, pushing the glasses back up his nose to their proper position. He had his own computer code to worry about. Simulating star formation, if only he could make it work. There was a problem with truncation in the core collapse code. It had a tendency towards chaos – if you made a tiny change in the value of the parameters, it had a big effect on the outcome. That's the trouble with simulations, he thought – nature 'knows' the values to an infinite number of places, we have to truncate the parameters.

Infinity. Something was nagging at the back of his mind. The Book of Infinity – who was it wrote that? Graves?

He opened a new window and did a search – Graves, infinity, simulation, universe.

There it was. The paragraph sat there innocently, its message unambiguous.

How could we tell if the Universe we live in is a computer simulation, like the world of the Matrix movies? The difference between a simulation and what we call reality is that simulations are approximate. They can be made as good as you like, if you have enough memory, but they can never be made perfect. An irrational number like pi can only be perfectly expressed as an infinite string of digits, which would fill up the memory of any computer on its own, and leave no room for anything else. Even the best computer does not have infinite capacity, so the programmers of a universal simulation would have to make approximations. For example, they might truncate the values of the constants used in fundamental calculations – things like e, or pi. Or the simulation might become regular instead of irrational after a high number of digits. If anyone ever finds such a regularity in one of these constants, it will be the smoking gun that tells us that nothing is real.

The smoking gun. Of course, Graves was a notorious joker. He hadn't meant to be taken seriously. Had he?

Reluctantly, Timmins accessed Omero's project, watching the numbers ticking up as they were computed. How many should he let accumulate before checking the string against the first – what, million? – digits of pi? And suppose somebody else was on to it. He suddenly felt a sense of urgency. Even a simulated Nobel Prize would be worth having, if you were a simulation yourself.

Untanglement: The Leaving of the Quantum Cats

In the Multiverse, anything that can happen, will happen
– an infinite number of times …

One: Interview

"The Director would like a word with you, Dr Pohl, when you have a moment."

Fred sighed, and gave the Turing a mental command to pause. He had lived in England long enough to know that "when you have a moment" meant "now, at once, if not sooner." What could have gone wrong? He had little time to speculate as he was led briskly along the corridor to the Director's office. Thatcher was not a woman to be trifled with. She might be only a chemist by training, with little real understanding of quantum engineering, but she had proved her management skills in her previous life, rising to run Imperial Chemical Industries before being hand picked by the Prime Minister to take control of the Project when Watson had left under a cloud. A reliable new broom to put everything, particularly upstart Americans, back in their place. Maybe she should have been a politician herself.

"Sit." It was a command, not an invitation. He sat. A tall man that Fred didn't recognise stood behind her right shoulder.

"Dr. Pohl." She looked at him over the top of her half-moon glasses. "You have been communicating with one of your counterparts."

"No, I …"

"Quiet, please. You will have an opportunity to speak shortly." She glanced at the documents in front of her, which, if the stories were true, she had already memorised. "You have an impeccable record." An icy pause. "Up until now. Brooklyn to Caltech. A big step in the 1930s. Manhattan Project, Nobel Prize for trajectory integrals, the good sense to join us here on the quantum computer Project."

Well, good sense didn't really come into it, just the urge to be at the cutting edge of quantum engineering. The Brits had had a head start after the War, with the Colossus computers, developed at Bletchley Park to crack Nazi codes, used as the basis for the Attlee administration to set up the Government Computer Headquarters here in Sussex. The best computers in the world meant a huge boost for technology, computer aided design of the first jet airliners just the star of the post-war boom that turned the economy around. And beating the Americans and Russians to developing the H-bomb cemented Britain's position as a nation punching above its weight, undisputed leader of the European Alliance – even if it did lead Turing to resign in disgust and focus on developmental biology. His reward, of course, was a Nobel, for discovering the structure of DNA. By then, though, GCHQ had an impetus of its own, and was the natural place to develop the quantum computer. Which is where Fred came in.

"I appreciate, Dr, Pohl," Fred shifted in his seat. The repetition of his title definitely meant that he was in trouble. But for what? "that since the quantum computer is based on the principles of your path integral formalism, that you may feel a certain proprietorial interest. But the rules are there for a reason. At this stage, only observation of the other strands of the Multiverse. No attempt at communication, and no observation of your own Doppelgangers. I understand that your brief is to follow the work of the various teams in those strands where, for whatever reason, you are not a part of the Project." The Look required an answer.

"Yes, Ma'am." Hell, it had only been a quick peek.

"And certainly no communication."

"No, Ma'am." Well, no. He wasn't that stupid.

"Then how can you explain this?" She nodded at the Tall Man. He picked up the cue.

"You may be surprised to learn that we have teams following as many of the team's Doppelgangers that we can identify." A thin smile. Well, now that he mentioned it, not really a surprise. Should've guessed. Hut Six, no doubt – in the British love of tradition, the buildings on the campus were called Huts, in honour of Bletchley Park, even though they were low, glass-walled buildings, mostly just the visible surface features of complexes buried deep beneath the Sussex Downs.

"You have a counterpart in 47A." Oh shit. The writer. He'd only peeked because he'd seen the book, *Syzygy*, on the desk of one of the Gribbins. But what harm had he done? Best keep quiet and see where this was going.

"Not as illustrious as most of your counterparts." Oh, come on. You'd said Doppelganger once. Spit it out.

"Pohl 47A followed the same path as you until 1936. Then he dropped out of High School, had a succession of nothing jobs, unremarkable war service, then became a writer. Of science fiction. And married. Five times." In the eyes of Tall Man, these were clearly not good things to have done. Fred, though, felt a certain pride. Not bad going. He'd tried marriage once, but it hadn't stuck. And he'd been reading science fiction as long as he could remember.

"Would you happen to know, Dr Pohl, the title of Pohl 47A's latest work?"

He shook his head.

"It's called The Coming of the Quantum Cats. And would you like to know the subject of the story?"

He had an awful feeling he could guess. Sit tight and say nothing.

"It concerns a series of interactions between different strands of the Multiverse, although he doesn't use that term. Most of the story is rubbish." Clearly, Tall Man was not surprised to find that science fiction was rubbish. "It concerns a war between alternative strands, characters popping to and fro between strands, and some nonsense about ballistic displacement causing leakage of material objects from one strand to another. But does this sound familiar?" He closed his eyes and recited from memory:

Think of it like this. If you had a coiled spring, with beads strung on it, each bead represents a moment in time. The beads could be numbered, to represent consecutive instants. So number eight comes just after number seven, and just before number nine. But remember the spring is coiled. So on one side of instant number eight it might be touching instant number nine hundred and fifty two, and on the other side it might be touching instant number minus seven hundred and thirty, or whatever, depending on how tightly the sprung is coiled. Time isn't as simple as most people think.

He stopped. They both looked at Fred. He could feel a trickle of sweat on his back.

"That's from my presentation to newcomers to the Project. Everyone knows it."

Thatcher had saved the punchline for herself. "It is also a direct quotation from page 205 of The Coming of the Quantum Cats, a work of fiction authored by a writer named Frederik Pohl in strand 47A. You are suspended from all duties, Dr Pohl, and will not be allowed to leave the campus. You may not visit any of the research facilities. But I would like an explanation. In your own time."

"I have none, Ma'am. I did take a quick peek at Pohl 47A. I saw one of his books on the desk of one of the Gribbins. I was curious. But I've no explanation for this."

"Then I suggest you go away and think of one."

The interview was over.

Thatcher waited until the door closed, then swivelled her chair to face the Tall Man. "Well?"

Tall Man was listening. The implant communicated directly to his brain, which interpreted the information as speech.

"He's telling the truth. Or he's a trained professional. Hardly likely. Checks out across the board. What shall we do, Ma'am?"

"Keep him on the hop. Let him think he's in trouble, but give him enough rope to make his own investigation. Without letting him know we are watching. He is, after all, supposedly the cleverest person here. The need to clear his name should concentrate his attention wonderfully on finding the leak."

She turned back to the desk, prodded a file with a finger. "Now. About this story in the Guardian about the Watson affair. I will not have people going through unofficial channels. Who is responsible?"

Two: Brain

There was no question of going back to his flat in Brighton, even to get a change of clothing. Politely but firmly, Pohl was escorted to a guest suite in Norfolk House, one of the accommodation units, all named after English counties. It was no surprise to find a selection of his clothing, books, music, and other necessities already there. Seemed he had been the last to know he would be staying on campus for a while. And, of course, there was a Turing link. As good a classical computer as you could find, even if, as was likely in the present circumstances, it was unhooked from the Grid. But what he really wanted was to talk to the Brain. Quantum computing had got him in to this mess; hopefully the quantum computer – as yet, the only fully functioning quantum Turing machine – would get him out of it. Depending on how much Security knew about his relationship with the Brain.

The guest suite relied on voice, of course; it wasn't tuned to his own brain.

"Turing."

"Ready."

"Do we have Grid access?"

"Sorry, no."

As expected.

"Can you link me to the Brain?"

"I regret that is not possible."

Also as expected.

Time to test the limits of his freedom. He put the music player and headset in his shoulder bag; he had the phone, of course, but it would undoubtedly be blocked. The coffee shop in the library would do; plenty of traffic, so if they were sloppy they might not notice. He set off on the short walk down the valley, collar turned up against the autumn breeze, hands deep in his pockets.

It had to be something to do with the Brain. It was – what – two years now since it went online? Self-aware, but not really an intelligence. It couldn't think for itself. But the self-awareness was crucial. It had passed Lovelock's test for the existence of the Multiverse. Set a problem which involved many possible quantum trajectories to reach the same solution, it had been able to report that while carrying out the calculation it had been aware of all the trajectories. So they were all equally real. And by implication, all quantum trajectories, all the universes, were real, just as Schrödinger had suggested in his Dublin lectures. The next step had been to set up a similar problem which stopped short of reaching a conclusion, looping back to the beginning every time it neared a solution, so that the Brain was *continuously* experiencing all the possible threads of reality. Or at least, all the threads in which there was a Brain. From there, it was a short conceptual step, but a huge technological leap, to begin peeping at the other universes – at least, the ones that were accessible.

It all depended on the quantum nature of the Brain. Where classical computers had memory switches that could be either on or off, each one representing a bit, the Brain had quantum switches, single atomic ions held in the grip of magnetic fields and prodded with lasers, that could be both on and off at the same time, or neither on nor off. They were called quantum bits, shortened to quabit and pronounced to rhyme with rabbit. It was a physicists' idea of a joke. Rabbits were notorious for their ability to propagate, and so, in a sense, were quabits. The power of a classical computer could be represented by the number of bits. The power of a quantum computer could be represented as 2 raised to the number of quabits. So a 10 quabit computer was as powerful as a classical computer with 2 raised to the power 10, or 1054, bits. And the Brain had 72 quabits, equivalent to nearly 10 to the power of 300 bits, quite apart from its special quantum features. The unofficial aim of the Project was to get this up to 80 quabits, equivalent to roughly the number of atoms in the visible Universe.

There was a hint of rain in the air as Fred hurried up the steps of the library and settled in to a corner booth in the coffee shop with a double espresso and an apple Danish. With the highly modified 'music player' plugged in to the headset, he would soon be ready to make contact, but a little sugary brain fuel first wouldn't hurt.

In Hut Six, a Watcher noted the time and recorded in the log: 'Subject making contact with Brain, as expected. No further action required at present.'

Three: Doppelganger

In Brighton, the darkening skies were accompanied by occasional squalls of rain sweeping in from the grey sea. For a moment, it felt as if the temperature had dropped by several degrees; a communal shiver went up the spines of the crowds beginning to trek home from the shops. In Embassy Court, Pohl checked that he had the music player and headset in his pocket, locked the door of his sixth floor flat and took the lift down to the street, coat collar already turned up in readiness for the weather outside. Automatically, he turned left, travel pass already clutched in his hand, then paused. Huh? He turned round. The bus stop was behind him, just on the other side of the entrance. That bloody council. Always tinkering with the traffic plan.

In Hut Six, a Watcher blinked and shook his head. Must have dozed off for a second. But everything looked OK. He noted the time and recorded in the log: 'Subject leaving flat. Possibly heading for campus to make contact with Brain. No further action required at present.'

Three: Doppelganger

Dr Frederik Pohl leaned back in his chair and stretched his arms above his head. Too early to go home. Besides, this confusion had to be resolved, and he was too intrigued to let it lie. His own name kept cropping up in the peeps. First that book, then the Air Force pilot who had become Director of the manned space programme. Both careers he could imagine himself following, if a few things had turned out differently. Hell, careers he *had* followed, because things *had* turned out differently in those threads. The science fiction writer. Less obvious, but not entirely implausible. So far, he'd resisted the temptation to peep at his Doppelgangers. There'd be hell to pay if he got caught, especially in the wake of Watson's 'indiscretion'. But it *was* tempting. Might ease the frustration of trying to resolve the puzzle of only being able to access, so far, those threads which had developed their own versions of the Brain. If all threads were possible, surely there must be a way to access Brainless threads?

It would be a long evening. Maybe a long night. What he needed was coffee. And maybe a pastry. Might as well take a break. He stood up and shrugged into his jacket, checking that the music player and headset were in the right hand pocket, then headed out into the light drizzle, across the valley to the library and its 24-hour coffee shop.

Four: Leakage

Will Gallucci peered through the misting windscreen as he drove past GCHQ on the dual carriageway. The traffic seemed unusually heavy this early in the day. Twice as many cars as usual. Suddenly, he was almost on top of a red Capri, and had to swerve out into the next lane to avoid hitting it. Shit! Where had that come from? Weird, too. He'd passed one just like it, right down to the chequered go-faster stripes and the yellow tinted windows, a mile or so back. Maybe it was a rally of some kind. Brighton was a magnet for car rallies.

The Beech Bonanza IV was on final approach to Shoreham airport, a few miles west of Brighton, descending out of the cloud layer, when it was violently rocked by turbulence. A twin jet passed just overhead, navigation lights flashing, heading down towards the new hard runway. Jesus H. Christ! Roger grappled with the controls, too busy to complain to air traffic control, fighting the plane back on to an even keel, and checked for the position of the intruder as he prepared to go round. There was nothing there. Just the welcoming lines of lights pointing the way to a completely empty runway.

Marie saw the brown and green Number 12 bus pulling in towards the huddled group of people at the stop outside GCHQ as she hurried through the increasing rain. Surely it was early? If she stuck to the path, she'd never make it in time. Cutting through the trees, she lost sight of the bus, but heard its engine labour as it pulled away up the hill towards Lewes. Damn! A twenty minute wait, and the rain was getting heavier. She slowed, and, looking down, stepped carefully across the puddles that fringed the path by the road. Looking up, she saw the green and brown Number 12 bus was just pulling in towards the stop outside GCHQ. Jut like the old joke. Wait ages for the bus, then two come at once. Oh well, it was lucky for her.

Five: Overlapping

Pohl got off the bus, nodding to Marie as he passed her. Only one person here tonight? There was usually quite a crowd waiting by now. He hurried up the path towards the library. It really was getting dark. On the other side of the trees, the green and brown Number 12 bus was just pulling in to the stop outside GCHQ.

Pohl didn't hear it. The little copse seemed thicker, somehow, and foreboding, as if someone had been out and planted a whole lot of additional mature trees overnight.

Frederik had the same thought as he approached the open square in front of the library steps. Why hadn't he noticed the denseness of the wood before? The clearing was welcome, even if it did allow the rising wind to whip rain into his face. It was all very well having a leafy campus to help the low buildings blend in to the landscape, but this was getting ridiculous.

There was someone hurrying up the path from the bus stop, someone who looked vaguely familiar, wearing an identical green Barbour jacket to his own. Well, everyone and his dog had a Barbour jacket in this god-forsaken climate. Though the dogs usually favoured the tartan pattern. But he didn't recognise this guy. Or did he? Whoever, he was clearly heading for the library. Frederik increased his pace, aiming to catch up at the foot of the steps and say Hi.

Fred drained the last of his coffee and stood. The rain beating on the window was getting heavier, but he didn't intend to go outside, just across the entrance lobby to one of the private cubicles where he could hook into the local Net.

He was halfway across when the automatic doors slid back, and two identical figures stepped in. Fred's brain raced, trying to place them. Twins. No, not twins. Mirror images. Not mirror images of each other. Mirror images of him. No. *Mirror images of his mirror image.* Oh, shit.

Six: Entanglement

On the edge of his awareness, Fred noticed that the rain had stopped. The wind was no longer whistling past the door. Everything was still, quiet.

"Are you two together?"

Pohl: "We just met."

Frederik: "Are there any more of us?"

He shook his head. "Not that I know of." They were clearly all from closely related strands. All quantum engineers working on the Project. So they all knew the background. And would all think the same way.

Frederik: "No need to fill in the background. We know what's happening."

Pohl: "Entanglement. The strands are interpenetrating. How far has it gone?"

They looked around. It was *very* still. Nobody visible. The windows were entirely obscured by vegetation.

"Looks like Schrödinger got it right. Quagmire." They all knew the allusion. The Dublin lectures, in which Schrödinger described what would happen if the world suddenly started obeying the rule that all quantum possibilities are equally real, with his notorious cat literally both alive and dead at the same time. He argued that if nature really did work like that, even for a few minutes, everything around us would turn into what he called a 'quagmire', a featureless jelly in which nothing was distinct. His triumph, for which he had received his second Nobel Prize, had been to show how the many strands could all be real, with a dead cat in one universe and a live cat in another universe, kept separate from one another naturally, in line with Bell's discreteness theorem, without entangling to make a featureless quagmire. Unless some idiot changed the rules.

"We're in some kind of bubble."

Pohl: "The eye of the storm. Why us?"

Frederik: "Resonance. We must have caused this."

The penny dropped. Resonance. Resonance between himself and Pohl 47A, somehow opening a link between strands. Peeking at himself had planted ideas in the other Pohl's head, but that was the least of the consequences. The link had spread and grown, like water breaking through a hole in a dam, with all the Fred Pohls at its centre.

"Probably me." For the first time, they looked surprised. "Peeking at myself. Couldn't resist."

Frederik: "Which strand – no, it doesn't matter."

Pohl: "How can we undo it? Can't unpeek."

"We need the Brain. If it hasn't been absorbed in the quagmire."

Pohl: "No reason why it should …"

Frederik: "… since it's been experiencing all the strands for the past …"

"… couple of years. Yes, nothing new as far as it's concerned."

They each reached for their modified music players.

Frederik: "And the Net should be …"

Pohl: "… super-efficient, because it now has …"

"… an infinite number of connections between here and the Brain."

Seven: Untanglement?

With the headset on, the linkage was immediate, and complete. Not like three minds working together, but one mind with three times the power. No, *2 to the power 3*; *eight* times the power. Plus the Brain. At least 16 times the power.

The answer was obvious, to such an intellect.

The simplest option was to break the loop, a trivial bit of programming, and allow the Brain to finish its calculation, arriving at a unique conclusion. That would break the present interaction between strands. But it might be restored. So a slightly less trivial tweak *here* and a small push *there* could in principle make such calculations impossible. But did he/they really want to do that? It would mean separation. Untanglement. There was another possibility. There were more Frederik Pohls out there, some of them seemingly clamouring to get in. Instead of 2 to the power 3 he/they could become 2 to the power 4, 5, 6 … A circular fire that grew and became ever stronger, more god-like.

But no. There was a sense of obligation. The temptation passed. A tweak *here*; a push *there*. For a moment, he/they experienced the nothingness. The sound of one hand clapping.

One: Interview

"The Director would like a word with you, Dr Pohl, when you have a moment."

Fred sighed, and gave the Turing a mental command to pause. He had lived in England long enough to know that "when you have a moment" meant "now, at once, if not sooner." He could guess what was coming. Well, he thought as he was led briskly along the corridor to the Director's office, it had been fun while it lasted.

Jim motioned him to sit as he entered the room. "I'm sorry. They really are pulling the plug this time."

"No hope?"

The Director shook his head. So there was no point in going over the same old arguments. "It's been two years, Fred. We – well you – have tried everything. And all we've got is the most expensive 72-bit computer in the world. There really is no prospect of quantum processing. And," he almost smirked, "no evidence for Many Worlds."

"Am I out?"

"Your call. You can stay if you want, work on the Super. Or move on. No rush to decide. I just wanted you to have the news before the rumour mill got on to it."

Seven: Untanglement?

With the headset on, the linkage was immediate, and complete. Not like three minds working together, but one mind with three times the power. No, *2 to the power 3*; *eight* times the power. Plus the Brain. At least 16 times the power.

The answer was obvious, to such an intellect.

The simplest option was to break the loop, a trivial bit of programming, and allow the Brain to finish its calculation, arriving at a unique conclusion. That would break the present interaction between strands. But it might be restored. So a slightly less trivial tweak *here* and a small push *there* could in principle make such calculations impossible. But did he/they really want to do that? It would mean separation. Untanglement. There was another possibility. There were more Frederik Pohls out there, some of them seemingly clamouring to get in. Instead of 2 to the power 3 he/they could become 2 to the power 4, 5, 6 ... A ring of fire that grew and became ever stronger, more god-like.

He/they observed. He/they appreciated. He/they encompassed and absorbed all the myriad subtle perfections of time and space ...

A ring of fire, growing in the darkness, becoming more powerful by the microsecond. But even an all-powerful ring of fire can become bored, after a few million microseconds. In need of entertainment.

"Let there be light."

And there was light.

One: Interview

"The Director would like a word with you, Dr Pohl, when you have a moment."

Fred sighed, and gave the Turing a mental command to pause. He had lived in England long enough to know that "when you have a moment" meant "now, at once, if not sooner." What could have gone wrong? He had little time to speculate as he was led briskly along the corridor to the Director's office. Thatcher was not a woman to be trifled with.

Science Fact

Traditionally, writers of 'hard' Sf are supposed to work within the framework of the known laws of physics as far as possible, but are allowed to make use of two 'impossible' assumptions. One is space travel at speeds faster than that of light, which is forbidden by the equations of relativity theory, and which no scientist believes to be possible. The other is, or was, time travel, which flies in the face of common sense, and is 'obviously' impossible. But in recent years, relativists have been forced to the uncomfortable conclusion that, in fact, time travel is not ruled out by Einstein's equations.

Here is the English language version of an article of mine which first appeared in Italian in the sober pages of the science fact magazine *l'Astronomia*. The bottom line is that there is nothing in the laws of physics which forbids time travel, with all that that implies. The safety net favoured by relativists in our location is that actually constructing such a machine would involve very advanced technology. But that is a far cry from it being scientifically impossible (like travelling at a speed faster than that of light), and as Arthur C. Clarke once said (not Fred Hoyle, in our version of reality), any sufficiently advanced technology is indistinguishable from magic.

A Do-It-Yourself Time Machine

Scientific understanding of the way the Universe works, in the form of the general theory of relativity, has now progressed to the point where it is possible to provide you with the following simple instructions for building a time machine. This is now a practicable possibility, limited only by the available technology; **we can accept no responsibility, however, for any paradoxes caused by the operation of such a machine.**

First, catch your black hole. Do not try to find a black hole in the container in which you received these instructions. The black hole is not supplied with the instructions, and is not included in the price.

A black hole is an object which has such a strong gravitational pull that it wraps spacetime around itself, like a soap bubble, cutting off the inside of the hole from the rest of the Universe. To give you some idea of what this involves, imagine turning our Sun into a black hole. The Sun is about a million times bigger, in terms of volume, than the Earth. But in order to turn it into a black hole, it would have to be squeezed into a sphere only a few kilometres across – about the size of Mount Everest, or the Isle of Wight.

Nevertheless, astronomers are sure that black holes like this do exist. They can detect them by their gravitational influence on nearby stars – if you see a star being tugged sideways by something that isn't there, the chances are that the invisible something is not the infamous cat Macavity, but a black hole.

As you are no doubt aware from your study of Einstein's equations, every black hole has two ends, and is properly regarded as a 'wormhole', linking two different locations in spacetime by a tunnel through hyperspace. We suggest that in order to avoid problems with spaghettification (see below), the black hole should have a minimum mass of about 100 times the mass of our Sun. This will make it very easy to tow the hole to a convenient location (such as the back yard of the Solar System, between the orbits of Mars and Jupiter) by dangling a moderate sized planet (you may find Jupiter convenient for this task) in front of it and moving the planet. The gravitational attraction between the planet and the black hole will then bring the hole along behind like a donkey following a carrot.

If you do not have a spacecraft capable of towing planets, we refer you to our leaflet *Build Your Own Spaceship*, available from the usual address.

It is now necessary to ensure that both ends of the black hole are in the same place, but at different times. This is achieved by driving your spaceship into the black hole and out of the other end of the tunnel. After identifying your location from the star maps provided, tow the other end of the hole back to the Solar System.

You can now adjust the time machine to your own specification using the relativistic time dilation procedure. This involves whirling the second end of the black hole round in a circle, at a speed of approximately half the speed of light (that is, 150 million kilometres per second) for an appropriate period. The relativistic time dilation effect will ensure that a time difference builds up between the two ends of the hole. After checking the time difference from the usual geological indicators, to ensure just the amount required, you may then bring the hole to a halt, and your time machine is ready to use.

> ## WARNING
> We can take no responsibility for difficulties caused by careless use of the time machine. Before attempting to use the time machine, please read the following historical background and explanation of the granny paradox.

When astronomer Carl Sagan decided to write a science fiction novel, he needed a fictional device that would allow his characters to travel great distances across the Universe. He knew, of course, that it is impossible to travel faster than light; and he also knew that there was a common convention in science fiction that allowed writers to use the gimmick of a shortcut through 'hyperspace' as a means around this problem. But, being a scientist, Sagan wanted something that would seem to be more substantial than a conventional gimmick for his story. Was there any way to dress up the mumbo-jumbo of Sf hyperspace in a cloak of respectable sounding science? Sagan didn't know. He isn't an expert on general relativity – his background specialty is planetary studies. But he knew just the man to turn to for some advice on how to make the obviously impossible idea of hyperspace connections through spacetime sound a bit more scientifically plausible in his book *Contact*.

The man Sagan turned to for advice, in the summer of 1985, was Kip Thorne, at Caltech. Thorne was sufficiently intrigued to set two of his PhD students, Michael Morris and Ulvi Yurtsever, the task of working out some details of the physical behaviour of what the relativists call 'wormholes' – tunnels through spacetime. At that time, in the mid-1980s, relativists had long been aware that the equations of the general theory provided for the possibility of such hyperspace connections. But before Sagan set the ball rolling again, it had seemed that such hyperspace connections had no physical significance and could never, even in principle, be used as shortcuts to travel from one part of the Universe to another.

Morris and Yurtsever found that this widely held belief was wrong. By starting out from the mathematical end of the problem, they constructed a set of equations that matched

Sagan's requirement of a wormhole that could be physically traversed by human beings. Then they investigated the physics, to see if there was any way in which the known laws of physics could conspire to produce the required geometry. To their own surprise, and the delight of Sagan, they found that there is. To be sure, the physical requirements seem rather contrived and implausible. But that isn't the point. What matters is that it seems that there is nothing in the laws of physics that forbids travel through wormholes. The science fiction writers were right – hyperspace connections do, at least in theory, provide a means to travel to far distant regions of the Universe without spending thousands of years pottering along through ordinary flat space at less than the speed of light.

The conclusions reached by the Caltech team duly appeared as the scientifically accurate window dressing in Sagan's novel when it was published in 1986, although few readers can have appreciated that most of the 'mumbo-jumbo' was soundly based on the latest discoveries made by mathematical relativists. And then, like a cartoon character smiting himself on the head as the penny dropped, the relativists realised that this isn't the end of the story.

The point is that these tunnels, or wormholes, go through spacetime, not just space. Einstein taught us that space and time are inextricably linked, in a four-dimensional entity called spacetime. You can't, in the words of the old song, have one without the other. It follows that a tunnel through space is also a tunnel through time. The kind of hyperspace connections described in *Contact*, and based on real physics, could indeed also be used for time travel.

The Caltech researchers have shown how two black holes like this could lie at opposite ends of a wormhole through hyperspace. And the two black holes can lie not just in different places, but at different times – or even at the same place but in different times. Jump in one hole, and you would pop out of the other at a different time, either in the past or the future. Jump back in to the hole you popped out of, and you would be sent back to your starting point in space and time.

The time tunnel you have constructed using the above instructions always has the end that has been whirled around at half the speed of light in the future compared with the 'stationary' end. Jump in the mouth that has been moved, and you emerge from the stationary mouth at the time corresponding to the clocks attached to the moving mouth – in the past, compared with where you started. You can set the interval of the time difference to be anything you like, using the time dilation effect, but you can never go back into the past to an earlier time than the moment at which you completed the time machine. In order to do that – for example, to go back in time to watch the 1966 World Cup Final – you need to find a naturally occurring time machine, or one built by an ancient civilization and left in orbit around a convenient star (see our leaflet, *Locating Alien Civilisations The Easy Way*). One obvious possibility would be to take a naturally occurring microscopic wormhole, and expand it to the required size using cosmic string.

Cosmic string, of course, is the material left over from the Big Bang of creation, which stretches across the Universe but has a width much narrower than that of an atom. Among its other interesting properties, cosmic string experiences negative tension – if you stretch a piece, instead of trying to snap back into its original shape, it stretches more. Any experienced do-it-yourself enthusiast will appreciate that this offers a useful means to hold the throat of a wormhole open.

HAZARDS

Please read the following section before entering the black hole.

Spaghettification

The kind of black hole astronomers are familiar with, containing as much mass as our Sun, would have a very strong tidal pull. What this means is that as you fell into it feet first, your feet would get pulled harder than your head, so your body would stretch. At the same time, tidal forces would squeeze you sideways. The relativists have a technical term for the resulting effect; they call it 'spaghettification'. In order to avoid spaghettification, the black holes that provide the entrances and exits to hyperspace should ideally contain about a million times as much mass as our Sun, and be about as big across as our entire Solar System. This is impractical at the present state of technology, but the hundred solar mass black holes we recommend can be navigated successfully, avoiding spaghettification, if care is taken to avoid the central singularity. We accept no responsibility for injuries caused by reckless driving.

The granny paradox

BE CAREFUL who you bring back from the future with you, and what activities they get up to while visiting your time. Suppose you use the time machine to go forward in time a few decades, and bring back a young man to visit his granny when she was a young girl, before his mother was born. The traveller from the future may, either by accident or design, cause the death of his granny as a young girl. Now, if granny died before his mother was born, obviously he never existed. So you never brought him back in time, and granny was never killed. So you did bring him back in time … and so on. WE DO NOT ACCEPT RESPONSIBILITY for paradoxes caused by careless use of the time machine.

As well as the paradoxes, time travel opens up the possibility of strange loops in which cause and effect get thoroughly mixed up. In his story *All You Zombies*, Robert Heinlein describes how a young orphan girl is seduced by a man who turns out to be a time traveller, and has a baby daughter which is left for adoption. As a result of complications uncovered by the birth, 'she' has a sex change operation, and becomes a man. 'Her' seducer recruits 'her' into the time service, and reveals that he is in fact 'her' older self. The baby, which the older version has meanwhile taken back in time to the original orphanage, is a younger version of both of them. The closed loop is delightful, and, we are now told, violates no known laws of physics – although the biology involved is decidedly implausible. WE DO NOT ACCEPT RESPONSIBILITY for travellers stuck in time loops.

And now, you are ready to enjoy decades of harmless amusement with your time machine.

In the event of difficulties, please do not hesitate to contact our customer service department, which is located at the usual address, and in the year 4242 AD.

DEEP SCIENCE: Readers interested in the scientific theory underlying time machine construction, rather than just the practical aspects, may be interested to know something of current black hole research. Quite apart from the large black holes you would need to build a working time machine, the equations say that the Universe may be full of absolutely tiny black holes, each much smaller than an atom. These black holes might make up the very structure of 'empty space' itself. Because they are so small, nothing material could ever fall in to such a 'microscopic' black hole – if your mouth is smaller than an atom, there is very little you can feed on. But if the theory is right, these microscopic wormholes may provide a network of hyperspace connections which links every point in space and time with every other point in space and time.

This could be very useful, because one of the deep mysteries of the Universe is how every bit of the Universe knows what the laws of physics are. Consider an electron. All electrons have exactly the same mass, and exactly the same electric charge. This is true of electrons here on Earth, and studies of the spectrum of light from distant stars show that it is also true of electrons in galaxies millions of light years away, on the other side of the Universe. But how do all these electrons 'know' what charge and mass they ought to have? If no signal can travel faster than light (which is certainly true, many experiments have confirmed, in ordinary space), how do electrons here on Earth and those in distant galaxies relate to each other and make sure they all have identical properties?

The answer may lie in all those myriads of microscopic black holes and tiny wormhole connections through hyperspace. Nothing material can travel through a microscopic wormhole – but maybe information (the laws of physics) can leak through the wormholes, spreading instantaneously to every part of the universe and every point in time to ensure that all the electrons, all the atoms and everything that they are made of and that they make up obeys the same physical laws.

And there you have the ultimate paradox. It may be that we only actually have universal laws of physics because time travel is possible. In which case, it is hardly surprising that the laws of physics permit time travel.

For more about black holes in general, cosmic string, and time travel in particular, see:

John Gribbin, *In Search of the Edge of Time* (US title *Unveiling the Edge of Time*), Penguin, London and Harmony, New York.

John and Mary Gribbin, *Time & Space*, Dorling Kindersley, London.

Kip Thorne, *Black Holes and Time Warps*, Norton, New York, and Picador, London.

Is the Moon a Babel Fish?

In *The Hitchhiker's Guide to the Galaxy*,[1] Douglas Adams introduces the idea of the Babel Fish, a leech-like entity that acts as a universal translator when stuck in someone's ear. The book points out that the Babel fish could not possibly have developed naturally, and therefore both proves and disproves the existence of God:

> Now it is such a bizarrely improbable coincidence that anything so mindbogglingly useful could evolve purely by chance that some thinkers have chosen to see it as a final and clinching proof of the non-existence of God. The argument goes something like this: "I refuse to prove that I exist," says God, "for proof denies faith, and without faith I am nothing." "But," says man, "the Babel fish is a dead giveaway, isn't it? It proves you exist and so therefore you don't. QED." "Oh dear," says God, "I hadn't thought of that," and promptly vanishes in a puff of logic.

Could the Moon be a Babel Fish? I suggest it is "such a bizarrely improbable coincidence that anything so mindbogglingly useful as the Moon could evolve purely by chance" that the best explanation for its existence is that it was put there by whoever designed the Universe.

But it is so obviously an artefact that no Designer would be so crass as to put it there in the first place.

Well, how *did* the Moon get to be there?

Our Moon is the largest, in proportion to its parent planet, of any moon of any of the eight major planets in the Solar System. To an astronomer, the similarity in sizes is so close that the Earth – Moon system is more properly regarded as a double planet. So how did such an unusual system form?

---

[1] Pan, London, 1979.

The Origin of the Moon

The most probable explanation is that the Earth began life as a near-identical twin to Venus, with a thick rocky crust, while another planetary object, about the size of Mars, formed nearby. The most likely place for this object to form would have been at one of two places known as Lagrangian points. These lie 60 degrees ahead or behind the Earth but in the same orbit around the Sun. They are places where the combined effect of the gravitational pull of the Sun and the gravitational pull of the Earth is to produce a kind of gravitational pothole, a place where small objects can accumulate and stick around for a long time. The Lagrangian points are used today as stable parking places for satellites, such as the Herschel infrared telescope, which need to be kept far enough away from the Earth not to suffer interference from natural or man-made radiation from our planet. A small object that is not quite at the exact Lagrangian point wobbles slightly to and fro about the point itself, like a swinging pendulum; the orbits of artificial satellites at these points have to be adjusted from time to time, using their rocket motors, to keep them in place. But if a large natural object grew up out of cosmic debris near to one of the Lagrangian points of the Earth's orbit, gravitational perturbations by other growing planetesimals would shift it into a so-called 'chaotic creeping orbit' with oscillations that would get bigger and bigger, soon becoming so extreme that the object would bash into the Earth itself. This would have happened within fifty million years of the formation of the original crust of the Earth.[2]

The name of the hypothesised proto-planet is Theia, after the Greek goddess who gave birth to Selene, the Moon goddess. Theia formed with the other planets of our Solar System about 4.6 billion years ago. Theia's orbit became unstable when its mass exceeded a critical value, leading to the collision that formed the Earth–Moon double planet about 4.53 billion years ago, roughly 30-50 million years after the other rocky planets had formed.

---

[2] *Ann N Y Acad Sci. 2005*;1065:325-35. Lagrange L4/L5 points and the origin of our Moon and Saturn's moons and rings, by J. R. Gott.

The Big Splash

Such a collision would not be like two pieces of solid rock colliding and chipping pieces from one another. Astronomers refer to this collision as the 'Big Splash', and the image that conjures up accurately indicates what happened when the Earth was young and was struck a glancing blow by an object the size of Mars. So much energy of motion would have been released by the collision that the incoming object would have been completely destroyed, and the entire surface of the Earth itself would have melted. The outer layers of the incoming object would also have melted, and mixed with the molten material from the Earth's surface, with much of it being flung off to make a ring of debris around the planet. Meanwhile, the dense, metallic core of the incoming object would have sunk through this molten outer layer and been absorbed into the core of the young Earth. The lighter material from the incoming object and from the Earth's original surface splattered out into space in this way would have contained about ten times the present mass of the Moon; most of it escaped entirely into independent orbits around the Sun, becoming asteroids, but some was captured in a ring of material around the Earth. As the surface of the Earth cooled and formed a new, thinner crust, the material in this ring coalesced into the Moon, repeating in miniature, but far more quickly, the process by which the planets themselves formed around the Sun. Computer simulations suggest that about 2% of the original mass of Theia ended up in the ring of debris, and about half of this fused together to form the Moon. The time taken to complete the formation of the Moon would have been only about a month.

Smaller objects created out of the ring of debris may have got stuck in Lagrangian point orbits for as long as a hundred million years, before the gravitational influence of other planets shook them out of these gravitational potholes, allowing many of them to crash into the Earth or the Moon.

Evidence to support this model of how the Earth – Moon system formed comes from samples of rock brought back from the Moon. These show that it has the same composition as the Earth's crust and outer layers. For example, the oxygen isotope composition of both lunar and terrestrial basalts are identical, and quite different from the ratio of these isotopes found in meteorites. And both seismic measurements of moonquakes made by instruments left on the lunar surface and magnetometer data from spaceprobes[3] show that it has no significant metallic core; the radius of the core is considerably less than 25% of the radius of the Moon, whereas the radius of the Earth's core is about 50% of the radius of the planet. The Moon's core contributes less than 3% of the Moon's total mass, but the Earth's core makes up nearly a third of the planet's mass. Because of the lack of iron, the overall density of the Moon is much less than the density of the Earth. Earth has a mean density of 5.5 grammes per cubic centimetre, but the Moon has a density of only 3.3 grammes per cubic centimetre.

The age of Moon rocks even gives us a precise date for when this dramatic event happened – 4.4 billion years ago, almost as soon as the Sun had formed. There's also more circumstantial evidence; such a glancing blow explains why the Earth rotates so rapidly, once every 24 hours, while moonless Venus rotates only once every 243 of our days. The glancing blow that formed the Moon would actually have set the Earth spinning even faster, so that it would have had a day some five hours long after the impact, and it has been slowing down ever since. The off-centre impact also gave the Earth its tilt, which is the reason why we have seasons, but the presence of such a large Moon orbiting the Earth has since acted as a gravitational stabiliser, stopping the tilt from varying very much over geological time. Incidentally, a combination of the extra iron in the Earth's core and the rapid spin probably explains why our planet has a strong magnetic field. And by thinning the Earth's crust, the impact allowed plate tectonics – continental drift – to happen. All of these influences have been crucial in allowing the emergence of a technological civilisation on Earth.

There is one more persuasive piece of evidence that

---

[3] Hood, L. L., D. L. Mitchell, R. P. Lin, M. H. Acuna, A. B. Binder, 1999, Initial Measurements of the Lunar Induced Magnetic Dipole Moment Using Lunar Prospector Magnetometer Data, *Geophysical Research Letters*, vol. 26, no. 15, p. 2327-2330.

collisions like this did happen when the Solar System was young. Spaceprobes flying past Mercury have measured the strength of its gravitational pull and found that in spite of its small size, it has a relatively high density. The Moon resembles the crust of the Earth without a core, but Mercury resembles the core of the Earth without a crust. The natural explanation is that a much larger object originally formed in the orbit of Mercury, but that early in the life of the Solar System it was hit, not in a glancing blow but a head-on collision, by another proto-planet. In a head-on collision, all the lighter material would have been blasted away into space, leaving only the heavy core behind.

Magnetism, the Moon and Mankind

The impact model explains why only one out of eight planets in the Solar System has a moon comparable in size to the parent planet; but it also implies that such double planets are rare. What is certain is that the thin crust is essential for plate tectonics to take place at all in the way that we know it, among other things allowing the kind of volcanic activity that has brought to the surface of the Earth the metal-rich ores on which our technological civilisation depends. There are many other important links between tectonic activity and life, which I do not have space to go in to here. The thin crust is a legacy of the impact that created the Moon, and another legacy of that impact is the dense, iron-rich core of the Earth, which also turns out to be essential for the development of our kind of civilisation. In some science fiction stories, spaceships and people are often surrounded by almost magical 'force fields' that protect them from attackers. It's a nice idea, but not very practical on the scale of spaceships and people (even assuming such fields exist) because of the enormous amount of energy that would be required to produce a shield of this kind. But the whole Earth, and in particular life on the surface of the Earth, is indeed protected from certain kinds of danger from space by exactly this sort of force field, generated by swirling currents of molten metal deep in the interior of the planet. It is the Earth's magnetic field, or magnetosphere, and although it cannot shield us from incoming asteroids, it does protect us from dangerous charged particles from space, known as cosmic rays. The magnetic field is a result of physical currents of electrically conducting metal swirling around in the outer core and acting as a dynamo, producing electric currents which in turn generate magnetic fields. The region occupied by the magnetic field around the Earth, the magnetosphere, is actually shaped like a teardrop, because it is squashed in by a wind of charged particles from the Sun on one side, but stretches off into space on the other. On the side of the Earth facing the Sun, the boundary between the magnetosphere and the solar wind of particles, the magnetopause, lies about 10 Earth radii (more than 60,000 km) above the surface of our planet; on the other side it stretches roughly as far as the distance to the Moon, beyond 60 Earth radii.

Electrically charged particles in the solar wind, things like protons, travel at speeds of several hundred kilometres per second most of the time, with bursts traveling at about 1500 km per second when the Sun experiences bouts of activity known as solar storms. The Earth, and the entire Solar System, are bombarded by those particles from deep space known as cosmic rays. All of these particles could do severe damage to life if they reached the surface of the Earth – they are essentially the same as the particles produced by radioactivity or in nuclear explosions. But because they are electrically charged, they are funnelled by the Earth's magnetic field towards the poles, where they interact with molecules of gas high in the atmosphere to produce the colourful activity of the auroras. Even so, during solar storms the electrical activity caused by the arrival of these particles at the Earth can disrupt communications and distort the magnetic field locally to such an extent that power lines can be affected and blackouts can be caused in high-latitude countries such as Canada. An increase in intensity of the strength of solar-wind particles can also knock out satellites, including communications satellites, and pose a health hazard to any astronauts unlucky enough to be in space at the time. So how bad would the total removal of the magnetic field be? As it turns out, we know just how bad it can be – because it has happened, and more than once.

As you might expect for a magnetic field produced by

swirling currents of molten metal, the Earth's magnetic field is not steady. It varies in strength from time to time, and the exact location of the magnetic poles drifts across the surface of the Earth. A record of past magnetism is preserved in rocks that were being laid down at different times – as the molten rock sets, the magnetic field is imprinted in it, so that the rock today preserves, like a fossil, an indication of both the strength and the direction of the magnetic field that existed long ago. From such evidence, the way the field has changed can be reconstructed by geologists and compared with the fossil evidence of what life was like at the time.[4]

For reasons that are not understood, from time to time the magnetic field gradually dies away completely to nothing then builds up again, either in the same configuration as before or with the magnetic poles reversed, so that what was the north magnetic pole becomes the south magnetic pole, and vice versa. The fossil record shows that when the magnetic field dies away, many species of life on the surface of the planet go extinct. The obvious explanation is that land-dwelling species in particular are killed off by radiation from space that reaches the Earth's surface during magnetic reversals. In fact, though, it doesn't matter what the exact connection is. What matters is that there is a link between the absence of the magnetic field and death on the surface of our planet. Clearly, the existence of a protecting magnetosphere is an important factor in allowing life forms like us to have evolved on Earth.

So another reason why we are here is that the Earth has a strong magnetic field; and the reason it has a strong magnetic field is that it has a large metallic core, formed as a result of the impact in which the Moon was created. We have, indeed, a lot to be thankful to the Moon for. And there are other benefits of having a large Moon.

The Moon as Protector

In terms of its diameter, the Moon is more than a quarter of the size of the Earth. It has only about one eightieth of the

---

[4] *Reversals of the Earth's Magnetic Field*, J. A. Jacobs, Cambridge UP, 2005.

mass of the Earth, but this is still far larger in proportion to the mass of the planet than that of any of the other moons of the major planets of the Solar System. As a result, the gravitational influence of the Moon on the Earth is, and has been, a major influence on the development of our planet. Together with the importance of the Moon's origin for plate tectonics, the three main influences of our companion can be summed up as the three 'T's – tectonics, tides, and tilt. And even the third of these owes something to lunar gravity. Tilt refers to the amount by which the Earth leans over in its orbit. Instead of being upright, with a line through the Earth from the North Pole to the South Pole making a right angle with the plane of the Earth's orbit around the Sun, our planet is tilted at an angle of about 23 degrees out of the vertical. This tilt is responsible for the cycle of the seasons. The Earth always leans in the same direction in space, so as it goes around the Sun, first the Sun is on the side where one hemisphere is tilted toward it and it is summer in that hemisphere and winter in the opposite hemisphere; then six months later the situation is reversed. The tilt also plays a part in the rhythms of Ice Ages.[5]

Although the tilt of the Earth changes slightly on timescales of tens of thousands of years, it cannot vary significantly, because the gravitational influence of the Moon acts as a stabiliser. If we did not have such a large Moon, or if the Moon were much farther out from the Earth, the combined influence of the Sun and Jupiter (and to a lesser extent the other planets) would tug on the Earth and make it tumble in space, so that it might suddenly switch from being nearly upright to lying completely flat in its orbit ('suddenly', on this timescale, meaning in as little as 100,000 years). This kind of behaviour is chaotic, in the mathematical sense of the term, which means that small changes in the various forces acting on the Earth would produce large and unpredictable effects. Just such chaotic tumbling has happened on Mars, where there is no large moon and where the tilt can change suddenly by at least 45 degrees, and more slowly by as much as 60 degrees. But on Earth, the tilt has been essentially

---

[5] *Ice Ages*, J & K Imbrie, Harvard UP, 1986.

constant for at least hundreds of millions of years, and probably a lot longer. It doesn't take much imagination to appreciate the effect on an incipient technological civilisation if the Earth suddenly rolled over on its side, with the North Pole, say, pointing directly at the Sun. The oceans and land around the equator would freeze over, and at high latitudes each hemisphere in turn would experience a sequence of searing summers followed by freezing winters. The equatorial regions would never thaw, even when the Earth was 'side on' to the Sun in its orbit, because the shiny surface of ice and snow would reflect away most of the incoming solar heat. The tropics are, of course, home to the vast majority of species on Earth, most of which would become extinct. It seems that chaotic changes in tilt are normal for terrestrial planets, and this alone could be relevant for the emergence of a technological civilisation, or any kind of complex life based on land, on a planet that 'just happens' to have a large Moon.

As the Moon is slowly retreating from the Earth, this stabilising influence will decline as time passes, which sets a limit on the window of opportunity in which a civilisation like ours could have emerged on Earth. When the Moon formed, it was much closer to Earth, and has been steadily retreating as the energy of its orbital motion has gone into stirring up tides. At present it is moving outward at a rate of about 4 cm per year, and within two billion years it will no longer be able to stabilise the Earth's tilt.

The Tug of the Tides and the Spin of the Earth

Tides are well understood, and they must have played a significant part in the emergence of life from the sea and on to the land. Tides on Earth are primarily produced by the gravitational pull of the Sun and the Moon – in principle there are tiny effects from other planets, but too small to be noticed. The Sun and the Moon cause both the oceans and the solid Earth to bulge upward underneath them and on the opposite side of the planet (you can think of the bulge on the far side as being related to a stretching of the Earth as it is tugged towards the Moon or Sun). In between, we have low tide. On their own, lunar tides today are about twice as big as solar tides. But the two tides add together or partially cancel at different times of the month. At New Moon and Full Moon, the Moon, Earth, and Sun are in a straight line and the tides add together. This brings very high tides known as spring tides (because they 'spring up'; nothing to do with the season). At the quarter moons, the Sun, Earth, and Moon form a right angle, and the solar effect cancels out some of the lunar effect, producing much less impressive high tides, known as neap tides. There are local variations caused by the shapes of coastlines, but in essence this means each place on Earth has two high tides and two low tides each day, as the Earth rotates under the Sun and Moon. Even today, the ocean tides seem impressive, and in some ways it is even more impressive that tides in the 'solid' Earth have an amplitude of about 20 cm. The ground beneath your feet literally goes up and down over this range twice a day, but you don't notice because you are going up and down with it. The solar influence has been constant as long as the Earth has been in its present orbit. But when the Moon was closer to the Earth, the tides it raised, both in the seas and in the solid Earth, were correspondingly larger.

Simulations of the event in which the Moon formed suggest that it coalesced out of a ring of debris no more than 25,000 km above the Earth, just 6,000 km beyond the 'Roche limit' where a solid body spiralling toward the Earth would break up. That's less than a tenth of the present Earth–Moon distance of just over 384,000 km. This would have raised enormous tides in the oceans, if there had been any oceans at the time, but as it was the repeated stretching and squeezing of the solid Earth, associated with solid tides more than a kilometre in height, would have generated enough heat to keep the surface molten for some time after the impact. But the enormous amount of energy released would have seen the Moon move outwards relatively quickly, and things would have settled down enough for the Earth's crust to form (or re-form) within a million years. Even so, the heat generated by lunar tides within the Earth would have remained significant, and contributed, along with the heat from radioactivity, to the establishment of tectonic activity on Earth.

The Earth was also, as I have mentioned, spinning much faster just after the impact that created the Moon, as a direct result of that impact. Tidal forces have slowed the spin of the Earth as the Moon has retreated from us. Just after the Moon formed, a day on Earth was only five hours long. At that time, instead of tides 2 metres high every 12 hours, there would have been tides several kilometres high every two and a half hours. But these extreme tides did not last long. The first reasonably complex forms of plant life on land emerged from the sea a little over 500 million years ago, and in a memorable numerical coincidence there were about 400 days in the year about 400 million years ago; so the emergence of complex life from the sea occurred when tidal conditions were not dramatically different from those of today. The plants, and later animals, that made the transition onto the land could do so by spreading out from the tidal zones. First they evolved the ability to survive drying out twice a day in the intervals between high tides, then some of them developed the ability to survive above the tide line altogether. This must have been a huge evolutionary advantage, giving them the ability to spread into and colonise vast areas where there were no predators. Of course, the predators soon followed! But would it all have happened so easily without the large tides associated with our large Moon? The more we look, the more important the Moon seems for our existence. And there is one staggering coincidence that nobody has been able to explain. Remember that the Moon is moving outward from the Earth and has been doing so for billions of years. This ties in with one of the most curious observations in astronomy – indeed, in science – which seems to have no explanation and is utterly puzzling. Just now, the Moon is about 400 times smaller than the Sun, but the Sun is about 400 times farther away than the Moon, so that they look the same size on the sky. At the present moment of cosmic time, during an eclipse, the disc of the Moon almost exactly covers the disc of the Sun. In the past, the Moon would have looked much bigger and would have completely obscured the Sun during eclipses; in the future, the Moon will look much smaller from Earth and a ring of sunlight will be visible even during an eclipse. Nobody has been able to think of a reason why intelligent beings capable of noticing this oddity should have evolved on Earth just at the time that the coincidence was there to be noticed. It's like a sign hanging in the sky, drawing attention to the Moon and shouting, "Hey, look at me – without me you wouldn't be here." It worries me, but most people seem to accept it as just one of those things. But it must be just a coincidence. Mustn't it?

Elsewhen Press

an independent publisher specialising in Speculative Fiction

Visit the Elsewhen Press website at elsewhen.press for the latest information on all of our titles, authors and events; to read our blog; find out where to buy our books and ebooks; or to place an order.

Sign up for the Elsewhen Press InFlight Newsletter at elsewhen.press/newsletter

Existence is Elsewhen

Twenty stories from twenty great authors
including
John Gribbin
Rhys Hughes
Christopher Nuttall
Douglas Thompson

The title *Existence is Elsewhen* paraphrases the last sentence of André Breton's 1924 *Manifesto of Surrealism*, perfectly summing up the intent behind this anthology of stories from a wonderful collection of authors. Different worlds... different times. It's what Elsewhen Press has been about since we launched our first title in 2011.

Here, we present twenty science fiction stories for you to enjoy. We are delighted that headlining this collection is the fantastic **John Gribbin,** with a worrying vision of medical research in the near future. Future global healthcare is the theme of **J A Christy's** story; while the ultimate in spare part surgery is where **Dave Weaver** takes us. **Edwin Hayward's** search for a renewable protein source turns out to be digital; and **Tanya Reimer's** story with characters we think we know gives us pause for thought about another food we take for granted. Evolution is examined too, with **Andy McKell's** chilling tale of what states could become if genetics are used to drive policy. Similarly, **Robin Moran's** story explores the societal impact of an undesirable evolutionary trend; while **Douglas Thompson** provides a truly surreal warning of an impending disaster that will reverse evolution, with dire consequences.

On a lighter note, we have satire from **Steve Harrison** discovering who really owns the Earth (and why); and **Ira Nayman,** who uses the surreal alternative realities of his *Transdimensional Authority* series as the setting for a detective story mash-up of Agatha Christie and Dashiel Hammett. Pursuing the crime-solving theme, **Peter Wolfe** explores life, and death, on a space station; while **Stefan Jackson** follows a police investigation into some bizarre cold-blooded murders in a cyberpunk future. Going into the past, albeit an 1831 set in the alternate Britain of his *Royal Sorceress* series, **Christopher Nuttall** reports on an investigation into a girl with strange powers.

Strange powers in the present-day is the theme for **Tej Turner,** who tells a poignant tale of how extra-sensory perception makes it easier for a husband to bear his dying wife's last few days. Difficult decisions are the theme of **Chloe Skye's** heart-rending story exploring personal sacrifice. Relationships aren't always so close, as **Susan Oke's** tale demonstrates, when sibling rivalry is taken to the limit. Relationships are the backdrop to **Peter R. Ellis's** story where a spectacular mid-winter event on a newly-colonised distant planet involves a Madonna and Child. Coming right back to Earth and in what feels like an almost imminent future, **Siobhan McVeigh** tells a cautionary tale for anyone thinking of using technology to deflect the blame for their actions. Building on the remarkable setting of Pera from her *LiGa* series, and developing Pera's legendary *Book of Shadow*, **Sanem Ozdural** spins the creation myth of the first light tree in a lyrical and poetic song. Also exploring language, the master of fantastika and absurdism, **Rhys Hughes,** extrapolates the way in which language changes over time, with an entertaining result.

ISBN: 9781908168955 (epub, kindle) / ISBN: 9781908168856 (320pp paperback)
Visit bit.ly/ExistenceIsElsewhen

THOMAS SILENT

or

Why there are no more mermaids

BEN GRIBBIN

When widower Angelo found a small baby on the beach twelve years ago, he decided to bring him up as his own son. A sign around the baby's neck said 'THOMAS SILENT', so that was the name he was given. Apart from other people's curiosity about his name, Tom's life so far had been happy and uneventful. When he wasn't at school Tom would help Angelo run the café in his beachside shack. One sunday morning Tom was in the café on his own when a tall, thin, old man called Phillimore came in to escape from the rain. He showed Tom seven bright blue-green stones that he claimed came from a mermaid's necklace. When Tom held one of the stones he could almost feel the rise and fall of the ocean. Phillimore left and Tom thought no more about the stones or the strange old man until Angelo died and the café shack was closed.

Six months later when Tom visits the deserted shack, he finds an envelope from Angelo and discovers what else had been found with the baby on the beach. Tom's simple life suddenly becomes a mysterious adventure that starts with a magical night-time swim to the shore of a strange land. He meets Coralie, a girl hiding in the caves on the beach with Phillimore. The people of the land are held captive to the will of an evil tyrant whose power comes from more of the blue-green stones, which he has been hoarding in the city of Murmur. Tom realises that he, Thomas Silent, is the only one who can defeat the tyrant and save the people of Murmur. But first he must understand the power of the sea-stones and discover his true self.

This delightful tale of real mermaids and mermen will enthrall any teenager who knows that they are special and have a great destiny waiting for them. Those of us who have left teenage years behind will equally relate to Tom's personal journey. We have all looked out from a beach and wondered what is over the sea, but so very few of us find out like Tom.

ISBN: 9781908168931 (epub, kindle)
ISBN: 9781908168832 (144pp paperback)

Visit bit.ly/ThomasSilent

About John Gribbin

John Gribbin was born in 1946 in Maidstone, Kent. He studied physics at the University of Sussex and went on to complete an MSc in astronomy at the same University before moving to the Institute of Astronomy in Cambridge, to work for his PhD.

After working for the journal *Nature* and *New Scientist*, and three years with the Science Policy Research Unit at Sussex University, he has concentrated chiefly on writing books. These include *In Search of Schrödinger's Cat*, *In Search of the Big Bang*, and *In Search of the Multiverse*.

He has also written and presented several series of critically acclaimed radio programmes on scientific topics for the BBC (including QUANTUM, for Radio Four), and has acted as consultant on several TV documentaries, as well as contributing to TV programmes for the Open University and the Discovery channel.

But he really wanted to be a successful science fiction writer, and has achieved at least the second part of that ambition with books such as *Timeswitch* and *The Alice Encounter*, and stories in publications such as *Interzone* and *Analog*. But as John Lennon's Aunt Mimi so nearly said "Sf is all very well, John, but it won't pay the rent". Another thing that doesn't pay the rent is his songwriting, mostly for various spinoffs of the Bonzo Dog Band.

He is a Fellow of the Royal Society of Literature, and a Fellow of the Royal Society of Arts, as well as being a Fellow of the Royal Astronomical and Royal Meteorological Societies.